ONE

Leigh Ann Kopans

Praise for *One*

One balances a fully imagined, *super* world with deep, well-crafted characters and took me on a heart pounding, heartbreakingly authentic journey I hated to see end.

~Trisha Leigh, author of *The Last Year* series

"Exciting, edgy, romantic and beautifully written, ONE is a book from an incredible new writing talent that will leave you longing for more!"

~Emma Pass, author of *Acid* (Random House 2013) and the upcoming *The Fearless* (Random House 2014)

"I opened *One* and didn't put it down. On the surface it's a fast-paced superhero story combined with all the wonderful and terrible aspects of teenage life, but beneath that is the story of a girl who only wants to be more than she is. It's a fun adventure cloaking a simple but powerful truth of the human condition."

~Francesca Zappia, author of the upcoming *Ask Again Later* (Greenwillow/HarperCollins 2014)

For anyone who's ever felt like only half
of what they are supposed to be.

Two things of opposite natures seem to depend
On one another, as a man depends
On a woman, day on night, the imagined

On the real. This is the origin of change.
Winter and spring, cold copulars, embrace
And forth the particulars of rapture come.

Wallace Stevens, Notes Toward a Supreme Fiction IV

ONE

Most nights, and some mornings before sunrise, I sneak to the back of the shed, and I practice. I push myself off the ground, telling my body to go weightless, and hover. An inch, two, six, a foot. I stay there for seconds, then minutes.

I can't generate enough tension between my body and the air to take a step — can't even make myself drift. I'd give anything just to be able to float along like a freaking ghost.

I'm a One — a half-superpowered freak. It's the same sad story for all of us. Every superpower is made up of at least two distinct abilities. A kid can only fly if she can make her body light and then somehow propel herself forward.

Two powers. Not one.

Every One puts up with getting teased at Superior High, waiting for their second ability to show up. While they do, that One power starts to fade. There are still shimmers of it, but after a while, the kid quits trying and the One fizzles into nothingness. Then their disappointed Super parents ship them off to Nelson "Normal" High, like mine did.

Here's my secret — I never quit trying.

This morning, standing in our weedy backyard surrounded by a chorus of crickets, behind the ancient shed with chipping red paint, I go weightless. It happens so fast that I feel like I'm being pushed upward. My heart jumps.

Maybe...

I try to move, try to resist the air or push it away from me, and...nothing. I've been practicing so much that I've gotten fast at going light. So I'm a speedy floater. Great.

I could hover here forever, until my muscles strain, then burn, then ache, then tremble, weeping and getting eaten alive by mosquitoes. I'd just end up collapsing on the grass.

Nevertheless, I smile when I have to will some weight into my body to keep from floating above the shed. I definitely cleared three feet this time. Four years of hard work, and I can float an extra two feet.

Maybe by the time I'm eighty, I can say "hi" to the folks taking hot air balloon rides at the Nebraska State Fair.

I've watched all the old-school cartoons about misfit superhero kids that just need to work on developing their powers in order to totally rule. But I'm not a freaking X-Man. I know I can't work on my One power hard enough for it to become something better, something more. And it's not like I can magically give myself a Second.

I know. I know.

But my body whispers to me. It tells me I can fly, if only I'm brave enough, strong enough, determined enough.

I sigh and trudge back to the house, being careful to dry the dew from my shoes before heading in to get ready for my first day at Normal.

Dad slows the car as Nelson High comes into view. It's about a third of the size of Superior High, and the building's face is shot through with mossy cracks, dull with years of dirt the groundskeepers didn't bother to power wash before the first day. It's a strange contrast to the slick solar panels that blanket the roof, glinting silver-blue and reflecting the sky full of white, fluffy clouds. Most people think these older-model panels are hideous, but I always love it when a building's roof looks like an extension of the sky.

I can't take my eyes off the school, but I can feel Dad looking at me from the driver's seat.

"Dad." I pat his knee, a little awkwardly. "I'm just going to school. A different one, but still just school. I'll be fine. Maybe better. You know…than I was."

Dad eyes me. He doesn't believe me, but he's going to pretend he does.

I clear my throat. "You could have let me drive

myself."

"What if you didn't get a pass? Or couldn't find a spot? Best to figure out the lay of the land…"

"The lay of the land" is one of the phrases Dad uses when he's worried. To be honest, I'm worried myself.

It's been ten years since my One power — going weightless — showed up. Seven years since Mom and Dad started to worry in whispered voices that I'd never get a Second, like the other kids. Only one year since I'd pretty masterfully failed at Superior High. One year since we all knew I would always float instead of fly — knew I would only ever be a One.

I was worried sophomore year at Superior would suck anyway, what with the fliers and the speeders and the teleporters rubbing their superpowers in my face just by being there. This way, maybe it doesn't have to.

"Did your hair for the first day, Merry Berry?" Dad flips an end of my hair with his finger. He's lucky I'm feeling slightly optimistic this morning, or I might mess his up right back. It looks flawless for work at the Hub, as usual.

I don't answer.

"Well," he says, "you look beautiful."

I humor him with a shake of my head and a smile.

All my features are slight, like my stature: a pixie

nose, near-translucent skin with not even a freckle to decorate my cheeks, sparse eyebrows.

But my hair is the worst. The longer I let it grow, the more it tapers from thick brunette into dull, baby-fine ends, so I keep it short, at my shoulders. At least it waves instead of lying stick-straight. It's as wispy as the clouds on a clear day.

"I know Mom gave you a new lock. Did you clear out your smartcuff from last year?"

I roll my eyes and push up my sleeve to show him that, yes, the three-inch-wide, flexible tablet that holds all the information I need to get through the day (besides acting as a phone, GPS, and universal ID) has been wiped clean of all the stuff I needed at Superior. I don't tell him that I spent days hacking it to change the ID status from "Merrin Grey: One" to "Merrin Grey: Normal."

I pop the handle open and crack the door before we're even fully stopped. The football field, which peeks out from behind the school, has a fresh frame of bright white lines and a state-of-the-art looking scoreboard. I imagine the classrooms and locker rooms feature an according disparity. Great.

"Three-thirty, Dad. Okay?" I scoot myself out of the seat and onto the sidewalk. I let the door fall shut before he can answer. Not because I'm trying to be rude, but because I think if I hear Dad's voice now, I might cry and mess up the first mascara I've worn for about 10 months.

I'm not really upset about transferring from Superior High to Nelson.

I'm not. I'm not.

No one really says it out loud, but everyone knows Supers and Normals hate each other — too much decades-old bad blood. Supers say the Normals were jealous of them, and that's what caused tensions in the first place. Normals say they didn't know anything about Supers or whether they could be trusted.

I can see that. The way the Supers treated me — a sad, powerless kid — at SHS, I figure maybe the Supers scared the crap out of Normals sixty years ago. Super-strength or teleporting or being able to shoot fire could be terrifying if it was used as a threat.

Being a One is the worst — we're caught exactly in between Super and Normal, between stuck-up and terrified. Supers assume we're jealous, and Normals assume we're full of ourselves.

But here, I'm the new kid. No one knows anything about me. And no one has to. I take a deep breath through my nose, trying to ease the pit in my stomach.

I'm feeling a little too light this morning.

The wind feels like it might blow me away today. My loose, tissue-thin shirt hangs off my bony shoulders, blows against the curve of my back, and I know that everyone can tell how thin I am in the tank top underneath. My cuffed denim shorts go down to my knees, and because Mom picked them up in the girl's department, they fit snugly to my legs. That's fine since I learned that baggy pants only made me look ridiculous and even tinier.

I look down at the ground and take a deep breath. *Heavy. Be heavy.* My eye catches the one thing that can make me smile: my blue plaid Chucks. My brothers, Michael and Max, gave them to me for my sixteenth birthday last month. They thought I would like them, and they were absolutely right. Awesome kids, no matter how jealous I am of their insanely rare water-walking skills.

With any luck, this year will just be the boring prelude to where I really belong: occupying one of the spots in the Biotech Hub's summer internship program. I can do anything if it leads to that. I breathe deeply, hoping the air pressure in my lungs will make me heavier, and take my first steps toward a normal year at Nelson High.

I'm guessing there are 300 students in the whole school, which means everyone here knows everyone else. I let out a slow sigh of relief when I realize none of the students milling through the halls look at me. Either no one notices me, or no one cares. Or, since it's the first day and I'm new, I'll pass for a freshman.

I find the administrative office easily enough. I have to pound on the ancient touchscreen installed there to get my schedule, and when I finally manage to download it onto my cuff, it takes another torturous several minutes of waiting for the map of the school to appear. Through the thick, translucent office wall, something catches my eye. A tall, middle-aged man with glasses and black hair slicked back from his forehead pushes out the door. I swear the faint scent of licorice wafts out after him. He looks just like my organic chemistry professor from Superior High.

Maybe not everything about Normal High will be awful and unfamiliar after all.

I wave my wrist under the ID scanner in a variety of positions, but it just won't register. It's all I can do not to growl at it. Finally, it beeps its recognition, and I push out through the door as the stilted robotic voice croaks, "Good morning, sophomore Merrin Grey."

The hallway teems with students, but I think I see him. Yes. The black hair and those thick-rimmed glasses. That's got to be him. He's talking to a petite woman in a navy suit at the end of the hallway, leaning close to her ear, his eyes darting around at the students. They both nod at each other and start to walk down the hall, away from me. She motions toward a door.

As I get closer, I see the placard next to it reads "Principal Lee." I push through the crowd, but just as they reach the door, some clumsy kid rams into my shoulder, spinning me around. I don't even care enough to be embarrassed or yell at the jerk because, when I look up, the door's closing behind them.

I pinch my lips together, cursing under my breath. Mr. Hoffman is the one who came and dragged me out of the first horrific day of freshman biology, gave me a test, checked it over in about three minutes, and walked me to his class full of AP organic chemistry seniors without another word. While the other freshmen were trying to impress each other with their superpowers, I was staying behind in his classroom while he graded assignments, building models and generally kicking Orgo's ass. By the end of the year, I was working from a college textbook.

Mr. Hoffman's the one who made me think I could score a spot in the Biotech Hub's summer internship. Only five kids get to go every year, and I don't think a One has ever landed a chance.

I slump against one of the walls and check my schedule on my cuff. Nothing with Hoffman. I'm sure that, whatever he's teaching, it's so high level I'll have to get notes from Mom and Dad and a meeting with the principal just to get me a seat in the class. That is, if I actually did see him. I can't imagine why he would actually leave the state-of-the-art Superior classrooms to come teach at this dump.

I pass my locker, number 5637, noting its location. I have nothing to put in it yet and don't feel like programming the new print-scanning lock Mom slipped in my bag, so I don't even stop.

My first class is History: Modern American. I sigh with relief. At Superior High, freshmen take this class, so I should've already learned all this stuff. When I click through my reader to find the textbook, though, it's not *AMERICA: PATHWAYS TO PROGRESS*, the one we used last year. Instead, it's *AMERICAN HERITAGE AND YOU*.

There's no teacher's desk at the front of this classroom. When one of the few adults I've seen walks into the classroom, plugs a cartridge into a port on the back wall, and a 3-D projector displays a life-sized image of a teacher at the front of the room, I almost cry with disappointment.

This year, the weird projected holo-teacher says, we'll be focusing on American history post-Uranium Wars, but that she wants to go through a brief summary of that thirty-year period before we begin.

"Seventy-five years ago, foreign missiles suddenly and deliberately attacked a transport of uranium cores being transported to safe storage in the American desert, triggering the Uranium World Wars. The leakage into Lake Michigan made thousands sick, killing some and fundamentally altering the genetic structures of thousands of others.

"Many of these individuals developed extraordinary powers: for example, super-speed or -strength, control of natural forces, teleportation, or telekinesis. Twenty years later, a diabolical group of five of these mutants, all leaders in their communities, formed a plan to assassinate the President of the United States and overthrow the government. Thankfully, it was stopped before damage was done.

"Never had our nation experienced such a threat from within our own borders.

"Most of the mutant population, some 30,000 strong, was concentrated around the Great Lakes. Even after the investigations and trials in the aftermath of said threat, we knew that some among them were potentially dangerous. Though most were loyal Americans, no one knew what would happen among this concentrated population if the new leaders' efforts congealed into a full-fledged revolution.

"Military authorities therefore determined that all of them would have to move. Tens of thousands of men, women, and children, all affected by supernatural abilities caused by the *uranium contamination decades earlier, were removed from their homes to communities in established, out-of-the-way places. Of course, the government helped in any cases of financial hardship and — once the families had reached their destinations — provided housing and plenty of healthful nourishment for all.*

"The mutated citizens wanted to go to work developing their abilities for the betterment of society. Many were allowed to do so in areas away from our main government and weapons stores and under appropriate safeguards, with the condition that they would work together with the existing United States government for the welfare of all United States citizens."

After every sentence this non-teacher speaks, my mouth drops open just a little farther. This is not the history they taught us at Superior.

Of course, they taught us about the Uranium Wars and the attempted government takeover. But the story of the camps sounded totally different at Superior.

Notices were posted. All mutated persons and their families were required to register. The evacuation was not cheerful. Stones were thrown, and jeers were screamed. It was out of fear, they taught us at Superior. Of course the Normals feared the Supers. But this twisting of history was inexcusable.

The lecture doesn't include video footage of the internment camps' shoddy housing or the mothers clutching their crying babies while they waited for the food trucks. It doesn't show the Supers waiting in long lines to see doctors they didn't trust or the makeshift schoolrooms full of dirty-looking kids in clothes that didn't fit quite right.

The holo-teacher directs us to the touchscreens in our desktops to answer some multiple choice questions about the lecture. I force my brain to go numb as I answer them the way I know the textbook wants us to.

I don't know exactly what this means for the next three years I'm supposed to spend here at Nelson High, but after hearing this lecture, I know I can't spend my life among Normals. No way.

I've got to get that internship.

By the time I've sat through calculus, bio, and English, I'm feeling grateful for the remote-lecturing holo-teachers — it means there's no one to ask me to stand at the front of the classroom and introduce myself. That is, until I realize that people are going to start asking me who I am to my face.

I have no idea what to expect from these Normal kids. Will they suspect that I'm not like them? Can they see that I can float if I want to?

I manage to keep my head down all the way to my

locker. All I want is to get there to ditch my sweatshirt, retreat to the girl's room — if I can figure out where it is — lock myself in a stall for a few minutes, and take a deep breath for the first time since I got here.

And maybe eat my lunch in there. Just for today.

I wiggle the handle of my locker, but it won't open. I bend down to take a look at it. No jerk's poured superglue in there or anything.

Before I know it, I'm shaking the stupid locker handle so hard that it's making a racket, and a few people standing near me look over and cock their heads. When I almost whack my own face with my struggling hand, I give up, resting my head against the cool, solid metal for a second, breathing in through my nose.

I am seriously losing it. Over a locker.

Half a second later, a shoulder taller than my head pushes into the metal door, and a large hand with long, thin fingers jiggles the handle side-to-side a couple of times and wrenches it up, letting the locker pop open.

I feel the warmth of his nearness against my cheek, countering the chill of the locker, like a shock on my skin.

The guy clears his throat, and says quietly, "They're tricky."

I barely glance at him before I look down at the floor, but I do catch that he has blond hair and glasses.

"You new here?"

Before I can answer, some guy halfway down the hall hollers, "E! Coming?"

The guy at my locker — "E" — gives his head half a shake, smiles a little, then turns to walk away.

And now everyone's staring at me. Great.

As soon as I find my way to the bathroom, I place both hands on the rim of one of the sinks, steadying myself there. After a few seconds, I splash my face with water and reach over to the soap dispenser. Everything about this place feels dirty.

As I'm lathering my hands, I notice the logo on the soap dispenser. Hub Technology — it appears on every product they make. It's four arcs, one for each Hub, intersecting in the shape of a circle. Someone has crossed out the "Hub" in "Hub Technology" and written "Freak" next to it.

Suddenly I can't get enough air into my lungs. I duck into a stall, sit on the toilet, bury my face in my hands, and take one, two deep breaths.

I hope with everything in me that all the other kids actually eat in the cafeteria.

TWO

I loathe the idea of art class. Something about the idea of ripping out part of my soul, translating it into colors and materials, and putting it on paper or canvas for everyone to gawk at and misinterpret is completely horrific to me. For self-expression, I've always loved my drums. Drumbeats dissolve on the air — they're out in the world for a moment before they go away. No one knows whether there was anger or frustration or passion or excitement behind them. They don't give anyone else the time to mess with them. Drumbeats are all mine — the only things I've ever had that are.

There are ten of us in the class: three jocks, a couple of girls in tight jeans and new shoes who reek of hairspray, a handful of others. There's no orange-shirted adult coming in, though. When the bell rings, everyone scoots their seats to a place at one of the wide, black tables.

The sound of metal legs scraping against the floor makes me cringe. I whip my head around, and that blond boy from the hallway scoots his stool a little closer to my desk.

Well, "boy" isn't an accurate term. It's even clearer now — with him sitting right next to me outside of the hustle and confusion of the hallway — that he's a giant.

He's easily six foot two, with a shadow of stubble running across his jaw. My feet barely reach the bottom rung of the art stool, while his slide comfortably on the floor.

"You're a freshman?" he asks, and looks right into my eyes. For a second, I can't look away.

He is 100 percent generic looking. He could be anyone. Except for those eyes. I see his irises right through the thick lenses of his glasses — light brown sparked with streaks of green and flecks of blue. I have never seen so many colors in someone's eyes before.

Then I feel like an idiot because I have spent exactly two seconds too long thinking about the color of some guy's eyes. I cast my gaze downward, trying to focus on anything but his face.

His jeans don't have a single rip or fray, but they're not pristine, either. His gray t-shirt hugs his waist, letting me see how thin he is. Even though he's two heads taller than me at least, he probably doesn't break 160 pounds.

"No. Sophomore. I transferred from Superior." The words come out of my mouth almost before I can think them. "My parents — uh...*I* thought I'd try something new. They bought a house on the border when I was nine," I explain, like he should care. Like he needs to know.

For an instant, he looks surprised, and then his eyes sparkle at me when he gives a little smile. "Well. For the electives — music, art, architecture, film, whatever — we just scan our cuffs into the tabletop and pick an assignment. Then it records whatever we do." I raise an eyebrow. "It probably doesn't teach us much, I know, but at least no one hassles us."

"Yeah, okay." I press my cuff into the input section of the tabletop and choose *Option 1: Draw a picture of what you did this summer.* Lame, but at least it'll be over with soon. The blond guy chooses the same option on his half of the table.

"I didn't get to introduce myself. I'm Elias — I'm a junior." He sticks out his hand, and I stare at it. It's so huge — strong but thin, tendons showing in the back of it. If I put my hand against his, palm to palm, my fingertips probably wouldn't reach his first knuckle.

"I started out at Superior Public," he says. "Parents took me out after first grade."

My heart jumps. Is he another One? No, he can't be. He wouldn't have transferred away that early unless his parents were absolutely sure he wasn't going to go Super, and six or seven years old is too young. He must be a Normal.

It would make sense for me to mumble some comment or even get up and walk away, but the space between us suddenly feels weird — charged or something.

The fine hairs on my arm stand on end, and I can swear I feel my skin prick. It's like a magnet, keeping me there, even though I know it's probably not the best idea to keep talking to this guy because I will waste even more time thinking about his eyes.

I can't speak to him, but I can't make myself move away either.

He drops his hand, smiles that slight smile again, and looks down at the blank tabletop in front of him. He pulls a stylus out of his bag. In bold handwriting, all caps, he writes at the top of the screen: "What I Did Over Summer Vacation." He draws a stick figure lying on a hill in the sunshine, staring up. Then he draws an arrow pointing at it and writes, "Bored," beside it.

He draws a vertical line to make a new frame and then swipes the old one out of view. Next, he draws a stick figure with a backpack on and a massive building in the distance with a huge sign that says, "Normal High." A dotted line with an arrow at the end shows him walking in. He motions for me to move my arms off the surface in front of me, and I lean back without thinking. In front of me, he draws a room with long rectangles for chairs and circles for stools and a handful of bodies filling them. He writes "Art Class" at the top, the quotation marks greatly exaggerated. I hold a giggle back in my throat.

I never giggle.

He sketches two stick figures sitting closer to each other than any of the other ones, one much smaller than the other. He labels one "Elias" and the other "Girl Who Won't Tell Me Her Name." Then he writes, "(Pretty blue eyes.)"

Well, that does it. This doesn't feel like the only attention I got from a boy last year — the kind I definitely didn't want — but I still can't tell whether it's good or bad. My stomach does flips, and I have to get out of there. Have to. I hoist my body off my perch on the stool with my left hand, hop down and grab my backpack with my right, and walk toward the door.

I scan my cuff at the door, mumbling, "Bathroom." The door registers my exit, and I get the hell out of there as fast as I can, not even looking back at his — *Elias's* — stupid lanky frame and ridiculous sparkling eyes.

THREE

I pace the hall. I tremble from my core and all the way out to my limbs.

In one short year there, I'd seen a few new girls come to Superior High, girls who got shipped in from across the country for the "community" and hadn't been around those asshole boys for their whole lives, so they didn't know any better. I heard the jeers of, "Hey, sweetie, you know I've got X-ray vision, right? Might as well take it all off right now." I saw superhuman strength used in threats against girls, veiled or not-so-veiled.

In junior high, Patrick Ryan, who could make people do anything he wanted by talking to them, convinced a girl to drive away with him in his car. The next day, she came to school dressed in the same clothes as the day before, and everyone knew what had happened with her. Her brother kicked the shit out of Patrick, but still.

I was relatively normal when I got to Superior High. Even tried to dress cute for my first day. Sean Cooper, the quarterback, started watching me, and a few days later, he was talking to me kind of a lot. Everything was fine until I realized his Super was strength.

One afternoon in an emptying hallway, he stood so close he forced me back against my locker and put his hand on my shoulder, and I realized everyone else was gone. He leaned down to kiss me, and everything closed in on me, and I told him to stop, but…

His thumb pressed on my cheek, and his breath steamed in my face, suffocating me. I tried to struggle away from him, but I guess he was angry that I didn't want to kiss him because rage flooded his face, and he glared straight into my eyes as he dug his thumbs into my shoulders. The only way I stood a chance against his iron grip was a swift knobby knee to the balls.

Sometimes I still feel the bruises he left there, like they've been pressed into my bones.

Michael and Max were only in the third grade and too young to kick his ass, though they would have loved the chance. I never told them about it. Never told Mom and Dad either. They only thought I was having some pretty serious popularity problems, which, if they noticed how I started dressing after that day, made perfect sense.

Ever since then, I've hated to look right into a guy's eyes. No matter how beautiful they are.

When I hop back in the car with Dad after last bell, I finally feel like I can take a deep breath. Even though I've always hated having to remember to plug in the damn electric car, I do love that it lets us ride home in silence. I park myself at the kitchen counter while Dad starts dinner.

My eyes flash to the vintage Public Super Service poster on the kitchen wall. A little girl flies up to a tree branch to rescue a kitten. Below the pigtailed heroine and the unbearably cute kitten, the poster reads, "Supers: Making the World a Better Place." I know that Mom and Dad bought that poster 10 years ago, when I first went light, and had it framed for our kitchen. Probably hung it with tears in their eyes. That girl was supposed to be me.

"Do you want to talk about it? Your first day?" Mom calls as she enters the house, carefully setting her briefcase on the big bench in the hall. The boys' shouts fill the back of the house. Mom sighs and walks over the kitchen counter, looking as exhausted as I feel.

"There's nothing to talk about," I say, shoving a piece of licorice in my mouth and a pack of snack cakes in my bag for tomorrow. I don't mention history class. As awful as that holo-lecture was, it wouldn't be as bad as going back to Superior. And besides, I know how to think for myself. My grandparents met in one of those camps. I already know they were less than comfortable, less than humane. I don't need to sit in a school where I really don't belong so a teacher can tell me the same thing.

The boys tromp in, dropping their gear all over the floor, which Mom hates. But instead of yelling at them, she just watches them jostling through the front hallway, punching each other on the shoulders.

"Mom, you okay?"

My words break her gaze. She shakes her head and looks at me for a second before answering. "Oh, yeah. Yes. Just thinking about...just some things at work." She reaches out to pat my hand, and my shoulders stiffen.

Max tumbles into the kitchen dribbling a basketball and punches me on the shoulder. "D'you have to redo freshman year, Merrin?"

I snort and cuff him on the head. "Yeah, just like you need to go back to kindergarten." He laughs, grabs a bag of chips from the cabinet, and heads toward the stairs. Michael strolls in after him and leans in to smack a kiss on my cheek.

"Glad to see you made it through in one piece," he says.

"Thanks," I mutter, squeezing his shoulder and swallowing hard. Michael darts his hands out in front of him to catch the basketball, which Max has hurled at him so quickly I barely had time to notice.

"What have I said about no sports in the house?" Mom growls.

The boys stifle laughs and head up to their room.

Mom sighs and opens the newsfeed on the touchscreen

countertop. Julian Fisk, the head of the Biotech Hub, wearing his trademark impeccable suit, waves from the picture, flashing a grin back at me. The headline reads: FISK ANNOUNCES RENEWAL OF YOUTH OUTREACH INTERNSHIP PROGRAM.

The subtitle should say, "For Super-Extra-Gifted Super Kids Only." They're the ones who have been enrolling in mainstream Normal colleges like Harvard and Stanford in increasing numbers over the past few decades. Because, Normal or Super, smart kids are smart kids, and they want prestigious degrees in addition to working for the greater good at one of the Hubs.

It's not enough anymore for the United States government to pay us for using our Supers, Mom and Dad keep commenting over dinner — now people want to be more integrated into mainstream Normal society than they have been since before the Wars. So the Hub has to do "outreach" — wants to keep our most talented kids close.

The curve of Fisk's smile challenges me. It's like he's daring me to try for that internship. But if I'm getting that internship, it's not to impress anyone or meet anyone's challenge. It's to save myself.

I stare at the countertop feed. I think I catch the phrase, "uncovering decade-old research," but it's hard to read most of it upside down. I let my eyes glaze over until the letters blend together and run through the checklist of steps I have left before my application is complete. I already got my freshman year transcript, sat for hours completing the tests until it felt like my stylus would rub my finger raw, and typed the essay. Only two pieces left. Signatures from Mom and Dad — which I would fake if they weren't fingerprint verified — and a recommendation from Mr. Hoffman.

I sit there, gnawing on the candy and pretending I don't notice Mom raising her eyes from the feed. She looks sad.

"What?" I snap.

"I didn't know that still happened, sweetie."

I look down and groan. The stool is now about three inches below me, and I can see down into Mom's lap over the screen. I make myself heavy again and plunk down, scowling.

It happens when I lose control. Emotional control, that is.

It started three years ago in junior high, when I used to get teased for being so tiny. Before I knew it, I'd be freaking floating six inches above my seat, and everyone would laugh at me even more.

That day, I got home and Mom had the talk with me. Because she works at the Biotech Hub, she knows all the science behind it, and she talked me through it like most other moms talk to their daughters about boyfriends and birth control.

I would have killed to have been talking about boyfriends and birth control at that moment.

What I got was this: Supers have a genetic mutation that makes them do one awesome thing — lift twelve times their weight, light on fire, create or control electricity, stuff like that. The rest of their genes have to adapt to compensate or allow for that — be indestructible, conduct the spark. It's like in-person, real-time evolution. Normally, these adaptations show up by puberty.

In Ones, they don't show up. Ever. So there's basically a hole in our genetic code. That makes it — the One — kind of unstable. It could manifest any time we're freaked out, scared or depressed.

That was when I first figured out that having one power was way worse than having none at all.

Mom closes the news feed and reaches out to touch me. Her fingers half-rest, half-hover over my wrist, feather-light. She's always danced around me like this, like I'm a weak little baby bird that never quite got the guts to fly out of the nest.

Last spring, I saw one of those baby birds. It kind of flopped down from the tree, but it was really determined.

It kept hopping from its safe little nest to the street. Then it hopped all the way across, and it didn't get hit by a car. That bird couldn't fly, but it ended up okay.

I don't think that's inspirational — in fact, I think it's really sad. And I think that damn baby bird was really lucky. I wonder if it ever did learn to fly, there on the other side of the street, while its family sat around eating fat worms and trying to ignore it.

I'm not that determined. I don't think.

The little girl on the poster grins at me, and I stare at her, too tired to glare. The slogan makes my heart burn. "Saving the world," my ass. I hadn't heard that language at Superior ever. More like, "Building a better world for the poor Normals," even though no one would say as much. Not out loud, anyway.

Dad walks over from the stove where he's getting dinner ready. "Want to tell us about your first day?" Dad's smile is weird. Plastic and cautious. Like he doesn't expect it to be good news.

I wouldn't want to disappoint him, I guess. I launch into a diatribe about how ridiculous everything at Normal was, from the hologram teachers to the rusty lockers to the idiot calc students to the disgusting vomit-colored walls.

He's quiet for a moment. Then he asks, "So what really happened?"

"Nothing."

"Oh, come on. You don't expect me to believe that for a second. Not with that look on your face."

I go to my default — not saying anything.

"Were the other kids nice?" he asks gently.

I shrug. "They were just kids. I mean…there was this one guy in that sorry excuse for an art class. And…in the hallway." I rush the next sentence. "But I wouldn't say he was nice."

Dad looks at me, crinkling his eyebrows into a questioning expression.

"I don't know. Whenever he looked at me, all I wanted to do was leave the room. It's nothing. I'm just moving seats next class." *Or skipping class. Or moving classes altogether.*

"Doesn't sound like 'nothing' to me."

I grimace. "Yeah, well. That's what it was. Nothing."

He still watches me, but now he's got this weird smile.

"What are you grinning at?" I say, and my cheeks feel hot.

I look down at my tablet where I've been doodling during our whole conversation. The whole stupid screen is covered with letter Es.

I glare down at it and swipe it blank. "One good thing,

though. I think I saw Mr. Hoffman there. I think maybe he took a job at Nelson." I clear my throat. "Um. Or something."

"No. I know for a fact that he won't be at Nelson High this year." Dad's voice is gentle but firm. Final.

I look up at him, raising my eyebrows. "I saw him. He was talking to the principal. At least, that's who I think it was, and..."

"Merrin," he says firmly. Dad never interrupts, not anyone. I narrow my eyes. "Merry Berry," he corrects, immediately back to his old self. "I just know he won't be there."

"Well...okay." That reaction from Dad was so weird, but it's hard to keep the impatience out of my voice. "Do you think you could get him to tutor me or something? He was helping me with Orgo."

Mom and Dad glance at each other, and my chest squeezes again.

"They don't even have real teachers at Normal, Dad. They're all remote, holograms, and their lectures were ridiculous. I did all that stuff in class last year."

Dad squeezes Mom's hand. "We'll work something out."

He sounds reluctant, and something seems off about the way he looks at Mom. My chest falls.

Science phenoms like me are usually headed for a career at the Biotech Center — if they're Supers. That's really all I want to do — experiment with chemicals and formulas I've never even dreamed of, help make the Supers' lives better. Develop stuff to make the whole world better and maybe help myself while I'm at it. But Ones, and certainly not Normals, don't work at any of the Hubs — security and all.

The horrible Nelson history class was really just the last straw. I'm applying for the internship because I can't help but think that maybe I'll be the One who changes things. A One who can actually change herself. But I can't apply without Mr. Hoffman. He's the only high school science teacher I've ever had.

I cast my eyes down at my hands, which I shift around on the counter, trying to find a position to fold them into that'll keep me from punching something, or at least a comfortable place for them to rest. That place doesn't exist.

I bang the rickety screened garage door open and take a deep breath when I see it. My dinky little drum kit. My promise of relief.

Playing the drums works when I'm angry, or when I'm desolate, which are pretty much my only two emotions, so that's pretty much all the time. Which means — damn, I'm good.

I trip down the three concrete steps into the half of the garage reserved for me and my drums. Dad always parks his car out in the driveway, no questions asked.

I have an old twirly office chair to play on because that's the only one we could find to adjust high enough for me to play. I check the feet — all the way down. I grin because it means my veiled threat to Michael and Max not to mess with my freaking drums didn't go in one ear and out the other like it normally does.

I actually never mind when the twins mess with my drums since the set is so haphazard and cheap — $500 used and four years into my abuse to boot. Besides, at 10, the boys are still young enough to be cute when they know they're in trouble.

Doesn't excuse the fact that, at five foot three and growing like weeds, when they try to play my drums, they adjust them up. Then I usually stomp in the house, mess up their hair, and yell at them a little bit. Then I buy them cones from the Jet-Freeze down the road when they apologize.

I love those water-walking monsters.

I shake my shoulders, trying to loosen them, surprised at how creaky they feel. I'm sure it's because I've got a ton going on inside me, and I honestly don't know what to make of it. New school. New Merrin, maybe. One who's not scared of everyone and hiding it by being pissed off and banging on the drums so loud that no one dares come near her.

When I feel that rumble down the back of my neck, skittering across my shoulders, my hands itch to play. I crank up the speaker, and it screams out something heavy metal, fast and angry. I let my right foot warm up to the rhythm of the bass for two bars, and then my arms pump furiously, beating the crap out of those poor tired snares and cymbals. I'm going to have to give them a damn retirement party if I ever get a new set.

After three furious songs, the tightness in my chest has loosened, and I finally feel like I can breathe again.

I listen for the giant cricket that's made the back of the garage door track his home for the last few weeks. There he is. The sun must finally be setting. Time to practice again.

FOUR

Today, I'm looking forward to driving myself to school. A quiet morning drive is one of the few things besides my drums that can calm me. The car glides along the narrow road, and I breathe in deeply, taking in the sunrise, which is gorgeous even through the windshield. One good thing about living in the country is that there's lots of open sky.

Superior, Nebraska, is a tiny town situated right above the Kansas border, almost exactly in the middle of the United States of America. Cornfields and the wind turbines that live among the stalks line the roads as far as the eye can see, and millions more ears of corn live here than people.

Two miles north, in Nelson, there's one bar, one movie theater, and three restaurants, two of which are sad steakhouses. Nelson is centered on the same things it's been obsessed with for decades: 4-H and football. But on the Superior side, it's a whole different story.

Superior is the home of the Biotech Hub for the Super community of the United States. The money its inventions bring in from the United States government alone could fund more tech-advanced schools, movie theaters, and restaurants than the small number of Supers who visit and live in Nelson could ever want. It's kind of a shame that most Normals would rather die than set foot in a Hub-centered city — most of them are completely freaked out by Supers. Even though there are no formal structures or laws in place to keep them apart, everyone knows that Normals and Supers don't mix.

I've always thought that was weird. Supers are everywhere, and everyone knows it. People with powers are technically mutants, but everyone here calls them "Supers" — much more flattering. Mom told me we don't really have all the genetics nailed down yet anyway, and "mutants" suggests there's something the Hub can do, something they can manipulate about the genetics.

She assures me there's not. I asked her almost every day from sixth to eighth grade.

At the Biotech Hub they develop new vaccines, medical supplies, and foods for the general world population. At least, publicly. I know Mom has something to do with mapping the Supers' genomes and genetic research. That's what I want to get in on, too.

But Dad's happy to work in the part of the Biotech Hub that manufactures toothpaste. There's no hope for power or notability there, but he likes it that way. And after all, it's certainly a better fit for him than the Warfare Hub, down in Texas, where the Supers design weaponry, or Intelligence in DC, where Supers do all their society-helping good by way of dangerous spy missions. And even though he's a do-gooder, he'd really hate working for the Social Justice Hub in California, where the Supers spend their days coordinating rescue missions, conflict resolution, relief efforts, and other stereotypical hero stuff like that. He wouldn't want the attention.

I'm different. I wouldn't mind being recognized for doing something good.

The sun's gorgeous watermelon and orange display distracts me so much that I almost don't notice when Nelson High comes into view. Day two.

One of my first priorities at Nelson was finding the smallest desk in the most secluded corner of the library, which really should be called a study room since it doesn't have any books anymore. That's where I hide out whenever possible — especially lunch. Every morning, I remove the wrapping from my brownie or pastry and repackage them in quieter bags.

Today, something makes my stomach churn, and as I eye my schedule again, I realize what. Tuesday is art class day. Hopefully this won't be as awful as last Thursday.

I shake my head. What was so bad? A cute boy trying to talk to me? I need to get a grip.

I duck into my corner of the library and start working

problems in the organic chem textbook I found on one of the download catalogs back here. It's familiar, and it calms me. My mind runs through the questions like a computer, loving the rhythm of each one. Characteristics of a compound in: IR, NMR, visible spectrometry, mass spectrometry. Impurities. Stereochemical configuration. Next compound. Repeat.

They haven't stored paper books in here in decades, not since the Forestry Conservation Act prohibited printing them even for commercial purposes. This corner of the library still has a couple of creaking metal shelves where they once sat, providing me some kind of cover in the otherwise open study area.

All of a sudden, I hear one of them rattle slightly, followed by muted footsteps on library carpet.

I startle, nearly jumping out of my seat, and have to command my body to be heavy. No one comes this far back into the library.

"Still spending your lunch break studying, I see." A voice, soft and gravelly, comes around the corner a split second before I see him. Mr. Hoffman stands there, smiling his warm, encouraging smile.

I close my lips against a gasp — I feel like I'm looking at a ghost. I wouldn't have expected to see Mr. Hoffman at the grocery store, let alone looking for me at Normal

High.

After an impossibly long second, I say, "I thought... I thought you were..."

"Gone?" he finishes.

I nod, a grin flooding my face. Mr. Hoffman is the only teacher who ever put me through the paces in science class. I've needed that so badly here.

"I left my position as a classroom teacher at Superior High, yes. But I didn't leave Superior." He smiles. "How are you finding the classes here at Nelson, Merrin? I suspect they're not as challenging as you might want them to be."

"That's an understatement. Science is way too simple, and history is...weird. Did you know they don't even have real teachers?" I clear my throat, trying to control my smile. "Will you be teaching at Nelson?"

"That's part of the reason I'm here. A school full of teachers is expensive, to be sure, but impressive students like you, Merrin... Well, you thrive on individual attention. So, my entire job now is to work with you."

My eyebrows go up.

"And other students like you, of course. Here, at Superior and across the whole area."

My shoulders relax down the tiniest fraction, and I sit up straighter. "Like me? You mean, Ones?"

He nods. "Like you. Smart. Capable. Driven. Dedicated. You've always wanted to work at the Hub, right?" He smiles warmly. "This is your chance."

"The Hub?" It's a serious effort to keep my voice at library volume. I should have known he had an awesome new job. "Oh, right!" My hands shake as I get ready to ask him. "I'm applying for the summer internship. I need your recommendation... I mean, if you can give it."

Mr. Hoffman pulls up a chair and sits down across from me. He waves his hand in the air. "No need, Merrin. Your name's already in the running. Every student I'm working with is considered exceptional enough to be automatically considered."

Everything seems to spin a little. I don't know exactly where to look or how to sit in my chair. Besides the fact that he looks more polished today — crisp white shirt, blazer, and shined shoes, as opposed to his SHS-standard blue Oxford short-sleeved shirt and khakis — he's still the Mr. Hoffman I know. The same Mr. Hoffman who stayed after class to help anyone who needed him and whose eyes lit up when he talked about the freaking Periodic Table. He wouldn't have ditched the students there for just any job.

He picks up the corner of his tablet cover and lets it slap down, over and over, for a few seconds. "Don't look so surprised, Merrin. Right now the internship program is only for Supers, but President Fisk wants to change these things. He sees potential in Ones. He believes in what you can do. And with that brain, Merrin... I told him. You're at a college level of study without too much effort. Considering Ones for the summer internship is a great place to start the change."

"Yeah. I guess I thought... I mean, I'm smart," I say. "But I'll never be a Super."

Yes, I will.

Mr. Hoffman shrugs. "President Fisk believes you can do anything. You'd be an asset to us, Super or not. My job right now is to put you through the next level of testing."

"I thought there was just the one application," I say.

He pushes his horn-rimmed glasses up his nose. I smile. If anyone at Superior High wanted to do an impression of Mr. Hoffman, that's how they would start.

"This year, we're taking everything more seriously, Merrin. Raising the bar. You do think you can find the time to meet with me regularly over the next few weeks, don't you?"

I nod, my heart jumping. "Oh, yeah. I mean, it's only lunchtime. My friends will barely miss me."

Mr. Hoffman nods and looks at me, his expression unsmiling and intense. Not like him. "You should know that this is under the radar. If the board knew we were preparing Ones to work with us... Well, let's just say they'd never let us continue. Ones are still not as welcome at the Hub as we'd like them to be. So I don't want you to tell even your parents, Merrin. Or anyone close to anyone working in the Hub. It could put them in a very...difficult situation."

I nod, look down at my hands. "Okay. Yeah."

Something about the idea of not telling my parents makes me nervous. If I'm so great, why should I be kept secret? If it's a new era, what is the Hub ashamed of?

But then I think of the weird 3-D teacher projections in the classrooms and how the most important thing at this stupid school seems to be who's on what sports team. My chest feels tight, and I struggle to take a deep breath.

Mr. Hoffman watches me expectantly, waiting for me to say what should feel obvious to me — that I'll go along with this plan, no matter how top secret I have to keep it. He's so familiar, right down to the faint smell of the licorice he always kept in a barrel on his desk for the students.

I lock my fingers together and lean forward so my elbows rest on the desk. "When do we start?"

FIVE

When the bell signaling the end of class rings, I head out into the hallway to join everyone else. My chest feels tighter the closer I get to my locker. I get there, swipe my print, and open it in peace, but then I feel it.

An anxiousness, a humming feeling, inches its way under my skin. The feeling, warm and buzzing, builds up in my shoulders, gathering in my muscles. The energy begs to get out.

I slam my locker door shut, knowing Elias is going to be waiting there behind it. Yep. There he is, with his infuriating dimple, the one that makes my insides melt, standing there without flinching.

"How did you find me?" I realize a half-second too late that the question assumes he followed me here. So now I'm saying he is either a creep or way more interested in me than he probably is.

"My locker is next to yours. Fifth period art and all. That's how they're arranged."

Oh. So he didn't follow me. He was just going to his locker. I am a dumbass.

He sticks out his hand, and it sits there in the air, waiting for me to do something with it. "Let's try this again. Elias. Elias VanDyne."

"Related to…"

"The famous VanDyne twins? Yeah."

The VanDyne girls were seniors when I started freshman year back at Superior High. I don't know a lot about them, but I do remember their stunning almost-identical faces framed by starkly different hair, the same flawless skin with a spray of freckles, strong jawlines, and eyes sparkling with life. He does look a lot like them.

"I didn't know…"

"They had a brother? Yeah, no one back there at SHS does." He smiles a little. "No one back there cares about Ones."

My heart stutters. He's a One, too. "So…you never even got a chance at Superior Public?"

He shrugs. "I fit in fine here. I'm okay." The fact that he's smiling shows me he thinks he is, but the catch in his voice tells me the opposite.

No One could be totally fine, no matter how much they think they are. Not in Superior, Nebraska, with the Biotech Hub practically in our backyards, for sure.

He's wearing a thick gray hoodie with a giant N on the breast, looking pleased with himself. "What are you, the freaking quarterback?" I mumble.

His eyes widen a bit, his smile fading for a second, but

then he raises his eyebrows at me, not mad and walking away like he should be.

"Do I look like a quarterback?" He motions to himself, his hands running the length of his long, thin torso. He's right. He's much too thin to be a quarterback — or a football player at all, actually. But, I notice, his chest does curve his fitted shirt out slightly.

I narrow my eyes.

Elias laughs again. "And do you even know anything about sports? It's football season now. I would have been on the field every morning."

"Do you think I've been paying attention to what you're doing in the mornings?"

He quits smiling so widely, and his expression softens. He looks down at the floor. "No. Uh...no. I play basketball. I like this sweatshirt, that's all."

"Why do you keep looking at me? And talking to me?"

"I can't look at you? Or talk to you?"

I shake my head. "You're, like, everywhere I am. Classes...and...locker." I know I'm acting like a child, but now that I've started, I can't stop myself. I swing my arm up, and my knuckles scrape against the vent on the front of the locker. It hurts like hell. I push it down at my side and clench my teeth for a second, swallow hard, and say, "And I'm just the stupid new girl. Don't you have any friends?"

"So, let me get this straight," he says, the corner of his mouth tugging up. "We randomly get lockers next to each other, and you're smart enough to be in some of my classes, and this makes you think I'm — what — stalking you?"

I stare down at my shoes, shake my head to one side, then the other, slowly. I have nothing to say, but I can't move. It's like Elias is magnetic or something. I look up at him, hoping he'll say something to make me feel like I wasn't being a jerk to him for no reason.

"Hey." He raises his hand up like he's going to touch my shoulder, pauses it in midair, then lets it drop again. "There's a good energy coming off you or something. I feel this buzz. I don't know." He shrugs.

A warmth floods me. Slowly, the anxiousness starts to turn to relief, the feeling that I can suddenly take a deep breath.

"I just want to get to know you." He flashes me a smile that must work really well on all the other girls who are probably all over him all the time.

Okay, so I feel it, too.

Is that because it's real, or because I really, really do want to hang out with him? My eyes flash up to his face, and my cheeks warm faster than I can cover them with my hands.

~ 45 ~

"You felt it, too! You just did!" The excitement on his face at my expression does not match what he's supposed to be — a high school jock who hangs with the cheerleaders and only cares about getting a seat at the right lunch table.

"You sound like a hippie." I shut my locker and tear myself away from him, walking out the exit and all the way to my car without saying a word. But he catches up. When I unlock the door with the stupid manual key — the remote broke a long time ago — Elias reaches down and pulls the door open. Our fingers brush, and I swear a shock of electricity travels all the way up to my shoulder, fast as lightning.

I turn to thank him, but when our eyes meet, I can't get any words out. The sun pours into the parking lot in angled rays. Sunlight glints off the rims of his glasses, and he looks at me, patient. Waiting.

I want to tell him how I've been pretending to be okay but really I'm not at all — can't everyone see how I'm not okay? — but now that I'm looking at him, really looking at him, I can see my sadness reflected back in his eyes.

It's humbling.

It reminds me that I'm not the only One around. There are hundreds of us, for all I know, on a farm somewhere or going to soccer practice or walking right

~ 46 ~

beside me through the halls of Normal High.

I can't be the only One who feels so wrecked because she's only half of what she's supposed to be.

I take a deep breath. "My brothers walk on water. Speed on water, actually."

He nods, still listening, waiting for me to say something else. I don't.

After a few seconds, he says, "My sisters can teleport."

"Whoa. Are you serious?" It occurs to me that I never knew what those girls' Super was. They were really popular, so I assumed it was something awesome. That power actually involves more than two abilities. Seeing where you're supposed to go by either clairvoyance or seeing through the walls. Breaking your body into molecules. Sending them where they're supposed to go. Putting the pieces back again.

"Yeah." That look is back in his eyes, the one that's telling me that he wants me to think he's doing okay. Nice trick, but I don't believe it for a second. I know how it feels to have Supersibs when you're not. It sucks.

"They're away right now, actually. Gap year at some top secret program at the Hub, I guess."

I feel at this moment like I really truly know him, and I know that he needs to talk to me.

And somehow, Elias needing me is a bigger threat than

if he had grabbed me by the shoulders, held me against a locker, and tried to kiss me.

"Listen. A couple of my friends are sitting over at one of the picnic tables. Let me introduce you."

I stare at him like he just asked me go skydiving or eat worms with him.

He smiles again. "Just come sit with us."

I eye him suspiciously. "You mean, the team?" No way I'm about to hang out with a bunch of jocks who all tower over me. No way in hell.

I look up, and he's doing it again, that smile, closed-lipped. Dear God, that dimple. I still haven't figured out my reaction to most of this, but I do know how that dimple makes me feel. Generous.

He gestures back toward the school and there's a cheerleader — an actual, honest-to-God cheerleader in the ridiculous blue and white uniform with the pleated skirt and pristine white sneakers and everything — sitting at one of the concrete tables outside next to a guy in designer jeans and a button-down shirt. The girl waves like she's on a freaking parade float, and the guy jerks his head upward, acknowledging Elias.

"Right out there. We're studying for calc after school — don't you have Davis, too? — and you should come with us. Tuesday is pizza night. Rosie is great at pizza."

Rosie? Who the hell is Rosie? I know what I want to do and what his expression makes me want to say. The girl smiles at me, and when she does, I roll up my sleeve and punch Dad's number into my cuff.

"Let me text my Dad," I grumble.

He looks at me with a smile behind his eyes and walks toward his friends at the table. I trail behind him, tapping a quick message to Dad into my cuff.

The cheerleader is beautiful, the sort of beautiful that knows it can stop anyone in their tracks. She's tall, with strawberry-blonde hair so brassy-bright it almost glows. Her skin is touched with gold and dotted with a thousand freckles.

She looks like the freaking sun itself blew kisses at her. She is the kind of girl that guys like Elias want to be with, always *are* with. She is a prize.

Elias beckons to her, his fingers bending in at the end of an outstretched arm, and she bounces over, her orange ponytail swinging level with Elias's shoulder, her perfect, glossed lips beaming. A funny burning feeling creeps up through my chest, and I try desperately to make my mouth smile, though I know it turns down anyway.

I hate her.

"Len, this is…uh…"

"Merrin," I say, acknowledging his cleverness with a

humoring smile.

He grins back at me, triumphant. *"Merrin* is new, and she's gonna tag along to study."

"Hi, Merrin." She leans forward and shakes my hand, smiling warmly. Why is this girl being so nice to me? At Superior High, she would have raised her eyebrows and sniffed.

Theoretically, I don't care, so I force the full-on smile I rehearsed on my first day and stick my hand out, play the fake voice I rehearsed in my head. "Nice to meet you."

"And this is Daniel," Elias says and walks over to clap his friend on the back.

Daniel, nearly as tall as Elias, sits at the concrete table with pebbled legs and looks up from his textbook, jerking his chin up in greeting again. His hair is jet black, and his skin is the color of cinnamon mixed with coffee. His eyes are black, too, but they flash fiercely when they look at me.

"Hey, Merrin. Welcome to Nelson."

SIX

On the drive over to Elias's house, I take a lot of deep breaths through my nose. I feel like there's no space in my lungs, or maybe there's no breathable air in the car. I try blasting something metal with a heavy drum line through my speakers, but that only makes my thoughts skitter around in my head, banging on my brain and making my limbs jittery.

I roll the window down and try to steady my arm on the door. The sun beats down on it, warming my chilled skin with its light. A whisper of humidity lingers in the air, a fleeting remnant of summer. It weighs everything down.

Exactly what I need right now.

My breathing slows, and I can think again. Elias's house for studying. Two other kids there. Pizza. Totally normal. Nothing to worry about.

I believe these self-reassurances while I drive through the suburb where everyone in Superior lives, where the houses all crowd together like an army lying in wait. When we cross through the suburb with the newest, largest houses, on the outskirts of town, my mind goes wild again. Where does this guy live?

I follow the caravan — Elias in his car, and Leni and Daniel riding together — over some rolling hills until we're surrounded by cornfields. The sun makes them look golden too, and for a minute, I really love Nebraska. Even though I still think I would love it more if I could fly over and out of it.

I wish I had given Dad Elias's address when I talked to him or even known one myself. No one really lives out this way, and there are no malls or groceries or anything out here, so I've actually never driven down this road out of Superior. Which is pathetic.

Anyway, Dad's text sounded so freaking happy that I was doing anything with anyone after school, I didn't want to kill his buzz. He didn't even ask Elias's name, which means he failed the overprotective parent test when I probably most needed him to pass it.

Elias's bright blue sports car and Leni's rattling station wagon turn into a long gravel driveway, which, when I check my odometer, is actually just a mile or so from our school. A sprawling ranch stretches out at the end of it. The central part of the house has the frame of an old farmhouse, but it's been given a facelift to look far more modern. Aside from the slick black solar panels that line the roof, there are long extensions on either side of it, each of them about the width of our little house back in the Superior suburbs. All the outer walls are made of glass, and it almost doesn't even look like a home — more like an office building or a lab. The dipping sun glints off its surface, and the whole damn house looks like it's winking at me.

The driveway outside his house, protected by a large, domed carport, is the size of a small parking lot, which it certainly looks like right now. One of the seven cars is Leni's and one's mine, which leaves five cars belonging to Elias's family. And they're all late model and high model — I don't even recognize some of the symbols they bear.

Elias's family is swimming in cash.

"Okay, there, Merrin?" Elias looks up at me after bending down to plug his car into the charger strip, a fancy one that's built into the concrete instead of the wire-jumbled hack job Dad rigged on the side of our garage. Once again, I can't make anything come out of my mouth.

When I finally pull myself together, I swallow and say, "Never really driven out this way, I guess."

Leni and Daniel are halfway up the driveway. They stop at the door to hug a middle-aged lady who I assume is Elias's mom. Her cardigan matches the sweater underneath, and she's wearing khaki pants and loafers. She's even got a string of pearls and a perfect bob. When I get close to her, she smells so good, flowery and sweet, that I can almost see the perfume wafting off of her.

Along with the cash-swimming, Elias's family also

looks like a freaking department store ad.

Elias waits for me to walk all the way up to the house and then falls in step beside me. He puts his arm out behind my back, guiding me up to introduce me without actually touching me. In theory, I really appreciate him not being presumptuous, but as he walks closer to me, that stupid warm buzz is back. My instincts tell me to slow, half a step even, to make his arm touch my back.

Instead, I speed up.

"Mom? This is Merrin," Elias says, and his mom flashes me a smile with the whitest teeth I've ever seen, especially on a lady her age.

"Merrin..." She's still smiling.

She wants my last name. Okay, I'll play. "Merrin Grey," I say, trying hard to maintain eye contact with her.

"Yes, we've heard about you. Just transferred to Nelson?" Her smile continues but looks more inflexible.

"Yeah, I..."

"Hey, I want to introduce her to Dad. Is he on his way?"

"Oh, honey. He called and said he'd be home very late tonight."

"He's home very late every night lately," Elias says under his breath. He clears his throat and turns his head, but I don't miss the frustrated shake of his head. "Anyway, we're swamped tonight, Mom," Elias says, and he brushes the outside of my shoulder, so lightly, to signal that I should go in. I feel his touch across my shoulder blades, down my back, and in the base of my spine.

Yeah, there's a buzz. But what the hell is it? Whatever it is, and as much as I hate to admit it, I really like it.

When Elias crosses over the threshold ahead of me, a pleasant voice rings, "Welcome home, Elias. Who's your friend?"

"Oh! Rosie, meet Merrin."

I look around and don't see a soul.

"Welcome, Merrin," the voice says.

Then it dawns on me. My mouth gapes open. "Rosie is...your house?"

Elias chuckles. "Yeah. R-O-S-I-E. Stands for 'Residential and Office Service and Identification Engineer.' Mom's working on it for the Hub. The one over there doesn't talk, yet, but we get the prototype. You'll get used to her."

I seriously doubt that.

The inside of the house gleams nearly as much as the outside. Not a scuff anywhere, not a smudge on a mirror or the perfect, shining glass walls. I smell something warm and yeasty and completely wonderful. Of course —— Rosie's great at pizza.

His mom calls behind us, "Mr. Davis hitting you with the homework already?"

Elias calls back, "Yeah. Be down for dinner." We head down the hallway to the right where I can already hear Leni and Daniel settling in.

Elias's room feels more comfortable than the rest of the house. Instead of white walls against mahogany trim on wood floors, his room has high-piled carpet and posters on the walls. Giant throw pillows are scattered on the floor. There are a couple sweatshirts strewn at the foot of the bed, and I like it. It makes me feel at home.

He settles himself on his bed but doesn't offer me a place to sit, so I just stand. Now I'm only a head taller than him.

"Can she... Can *Rosie* hear what we say?" I ask.

"Only if you ask her to listen," Elias says as he grabs a folding chair and sets it out for me. "You have to address her."

Somehow that information makes me feel better. I sit down and start pulling my tablet and reader out of my bag.

"So," Leni says from the desk chair, "Why did you transfer?"

Normally I would have frozen at a question like this, but her smile is so genuine and she looks so much more normal now, especially since she changed out of those ridiculous white shoes and pleated skirt and into yoga pants and a hoodie.

But I still can't come up with an answer, not one that sounds normal anyway. So I glance over at Elias.

He jumps in, saving me. "Leni, can you show her your, uh…"

"Wait, what? She's a One?" She turns her head up to look at me. "That's a late transfer." She's still smiling, but her look is even more knowing now. I'm in some club of secrets that I really, really don't want to be in. Even if it does mean, for the first time in my life, that I'm — well, *in*.

He eyes me meaningfully. "I didn't say she was a One. But she's spent all this time at Superior as a Normal and come out relatively unscathed. And now she's here."

I raise an eyebrow at him. This is what he thinks "unscathed" looks like?

"And she thinks I'm creeping on her, but really I'm just trying to be nice." Did I see his cheeks flush red?

"But, um…" I interrupt. "I *am*. A One. My parents…or I thought…maybe a second would show. Obviously it didn't." I try to keep my face from falling. "No big deal."

Except that it's the biggest deal ever.

"Oh. Yeah." Leni nods knowingly. Her eyes aren't sparkling quite so much now, but still she turns around, unzips her hoodie and lets her shirt dip down off her shoulder an inch. An ugly, puckered, white and pink scar, about two inches wide, snakes from her neck, across her shoulder, and down the back of her arm.

"What..." I ask, my head shaking, suddenly feeling sorry for this bright girl I hated only seconds ago.

"I have combustibility. But not indestructibility or regeneration. Or that skin-oozing-plasma thing that some combustible Supers have. Even though that's slower, it would have been... Anyway. Learned that the hard way in second grade," she explains, her smile the same sad smile that Elias first gave me a few days ago when we first met. The idea of flames ripping through my flesh, and it not healing or protecting itself... I fight against a horrified shudder.

"Whoa," I say, a lump rising in my throat. The question's out of my mouth before I can keep myself in check. "How do you keep from — you know — " and I make a flaming motion with my hand in the air. "When you're upset, or whatever?" I finish in a lowered voice.

"Oh," says Leni, "You know. Antidepressants. They tend to, uh...dull things."

Everyone's quiet, watching me.

~ 58 ~

Daniel starts the round of nervous laughter, changing the subject. I wonder how often he comes to her rescue like this, how many times he's saved her from comments by jerks like me.

"Are you the only three?" I ask.

Now Leni's mouth turns down even more. "There are other Ones, but they won't admit it. We're the only Ones we know of around here who have kept trying."

A wave of intensity throbs through my chest. I'm not the only one who hasn't stopped practicing my One in my free time?

I turn to Leni, asking the question that I don't want to put words to. "Wait, so you…you still can…"

"Yeah." She smiles, and there is a glisten to her eyes. She kind of rubs her fingers together, then flings them open. I see the hint of a dancing orange glow hover above her whole hand, centered on her palm. One second later, she winces, sucks in a breath, and claps her hand shut, putting out the fire. She shows me the redness of her fingertips and the scald in the dip of her hand. "Still hoping the Second will manifest kind of. I really don't have any fingerprints left. So, if it never does, I can always turn to a life of crime."

"That's my girl," says Elias, and her eyes turn from sad to grateful.

Yeah. I hate this girl, even if I really, really like her.

I shake my head, trying to distract myself. "So, wait," I say, looking over at Daniel, who's sitting on the floor against the wall, absorbed with something on his cell. "What can you do?" I silently scold myself for talking about these Ones like they're a freaking parlor trick. I would have spit at anyone who suggested the same to me.

"I'm indestructible." The tone in his voice is weird, and I'm not sure if he's trying to make a joke.

"Really? But nothing else?" Every kid I know who's indestructible also has super-strength or could combust or was super-fast. If Daniel's telling the truth, his One is like a Second — the physical traits that make the Ones possible.

"Yeah. Pretty lame, huh? I've cut myself more times than any of the depressed emos or cheerleaders here, and nothing." He stretches out his arms, insides up, to show me. He's right. His skin is completely flawless.

"Shut up about the cheerleaders," Leni says. Her eyes dart between the floor and her hands, which she twists and untwists over and over again. I can tell that she's torn between fitting in and being a One, between being loyal to her Normal friends or to this ragtag group of Ones. Whether she wants to take a natural place in the world or fight to make her own.

I've never done anything but fight, never even imagined another option. But then again, I'm not like Leni. I'm not beautiful or sweet or smiley. Even if I should be on antidepressants, I'm not.

I'm just Merrin. And my only option is to get that Second. Because the only way I'll ever be worth anything is if I figure out how to fly.

We don't study any calc. When Rosie announces, "Fifteen minutes till dinner," the three of them flip open their readers, and their styluses fly across their tablets, working the problems. I follow suit, plopping myself down on the floor.

Daniel switches off his reader no more than 10 minutes later, and I'm next to finish. He grins up at me, eyes flashing again, and I can't help but smile back. "Brought us a genius, here, man. And you said she's a sophomore?"

Elias snorts and looks up at him, his eyes darting to me first. "Your ego's so huge you don't think it's possible that an underclassman is smarter than you?"

"No," he says, still smiling. "Just because she finished almost as fast as me doesn't mean she got the answers right."

"He probably hacked his tablet to work the problems

for him," Leni says, flipping the cover back over her reader.

Daniel snorts. "Please. I could do that, but then I'd have nothing to do while you losers take your sweet time."

Well, I'm impressed. It took me days to hack one thing about the ID file on my cuff, and I'm not sure it wasn't a mistake.

Leni smiles at him with an unmistakable fondness, then hoists herself out of her chair and looks down at Elias, who's still scribbling. "Gotta go," she says. "Family game night." She rolls her eyes and smacks Daniel on the head. "Coming, genius? Or are you going to make Merrin drive you home?"

Daniel gives me one look and says, "Nah, she's had enough of me for one night. And maybe the extra few minutes will keep you from the 'pick a Monopoly piece' drama."

She laughs, the sound of it like a bell. Real, not like the stuttered laugh she gave off at school.

"See ya, Elias." She throws a glance at him over her shoulder on the way out.

If they're letting themselves out, they must be here all the time. This is the Nelson High crew of Ones. And they've just let me in.

"Glad you were here," Elias says, jotting down one last

answer before finally closing his reader and sliding it onto the bed next to him. "I was really starting to feel like a third wheel."

Did he just read my mind? "What are you talking about?" I ask.

"Len. She's been crushing on Daniel for ages. Somehow my room turned into flirt central last year. I think you helped."

New visions of friendship with Leni flash through my mind.

Mrs. VanDyne's voice rings through the staircase and into his open door. "Elias? You still have someone up there? I have dinner for you two!"

"Yeah, Mom," he calls down. "Be right there."

He stands up and reaches down for my hand, and I give it to him without thinking. His hand is so huge that his fingers and thumb overlap a good inch when they wrap around mine, and he hoists me up with no problem.

"After you," he says, motioning me down the stairs. I try to think of an excuse to get out of there, back to the safe familiarity of my car, but Elias's mom is standing at the kitchen island, and when she smiles at me, it's too late. She presses a button, and the counter opens and pushes up two huge, gorgeous, incredible-smelling homemade pizzas. His mom pulls a giant green salad out of the fridge and throws on what must be the last of the season's tomatoes.

"Thanks for dinner, Mrs. VanDyne," I say.

"It's no problem. Rosie made it. And you can call me Dierdre, sweetheart."

Sweetheart? No adult's been that affectionate with me for ages, not besides Dad, anyway, but somehow this presumption, coming from her, doesn't bug me.

"Okay. Um, thanks, Rosie." I look up and around, uncertain of where to say it.

"Elias, honey, I've got some things to finish up. You two going to be okay here?"

"Yeah, fine," he says.

She makes herself a plate and heads off to another room, picking up a leather ladies' briefcase on the way. Elias sits on one of the stools at the island and pulls out one for me.

Elias puts a piece of pizza in front of me, and I start on it right away. Hopefully my chewing means he won't try to talk to me for a few minutes. I wrack my brain for anything we've already talked about, anything I know for certain we have in common.

The kitchen is lit up, but the house has an open floor plan and I can see that the rest of it is dark. The living room sits pristine and empty, and the two hallways leading off of it are dark too. There's a spot of light from some

French doors at the corner of the living room, which must be Dierdre's office.

We always feel cramped at my house, especially now that Michael and Max are shooting up so quickly, but it never feels empty. I'd rather feel full than empty.

"Is it weird without them here? Your sisters?"

Elias still chews on his first piece of pizza, even though I finished mine a while ago. He puts another one on my plate, and I pick it up to take a bite. He puts a napkin to his mouth and wipes his fingers too, and finishes his mouthful before he speaks.

"Yeah. Yeah, it is. I mean, I expected them to be gone for college anyway, I guess. They didn't get into any of their top choices, of course — Normal Ivy Leagues. I wasn't surprised when they took the option to spend the year at the Hub. But they don't call."

"Never? Are you guys close?"

"Never. And, yeah. Really close. They're awesome. They never treated me like I was an annoying little brother, even though I was, you know?"

"Yeah, I know." I smile. "I try to treat my brothers that way, too." I can't imagine I would ever leave them without word from me for that long.

Elias's eyebrows furrow. "I haven't gotten an email from them, even. Should see them at the Symposium, though."

I had almost forgotten about the Symposium. Every year, the hob-nobbiest Supers flood Superior to check out all our advances in Supers' biotech. I'd always wanted to go to check out what it is exactly that Mom and Dad do. But you only get to go if you work there or if you're rich or important. Then I remember. Elias's family is all three.

I clear my throat. "I'm jealous," I say, smiling.

"I'd trade places with you in a second," Elias says. "That biotech stuff bores me to death."

My stomach twists. He has no idea how lucky he is, but I'm not going to hold it against him.

My eye sweeps along the living room walls and catches on a photo on canvas, a huge one. It's a portrait of the three VanDyne kids hugging each other and smiling. The setting sun kisses Nora and Elias's blond and Lia's brunette hair with gold.

"My brothers are too young to be that close to," I say, nodding toward the picture. "I'm still training them to do simple things, like take showers and pick up their damn dirty socks. And be nice to girls instead of picking on them."

Elias laughs while chewing, puffing air out of his nose. He swallows and says, "Their wives will appreciate it one day."

"Guess so," I say, reaching for a third piece of pizza.

Elias raises his eyebrows at me. "A little thing like you can put away that much pizza?"

I don't like being referred to as a "little thing," but he looks at me with admiration, so I let it slide.

We eat in silence for another minute. Then he says, "It's mostly the quiet, you know? They used to freak me out by teleporting into my room, and I always threw something at them. Scared the hell out of me and reminded me that I couldn't do the same thing."

I grin. That's what I do with the boys when they cruise across the water — use them as targets for pool darts. I never hit them, but sometimes I get close enough for them to catch one and bring it back, dripping water all over me. Punks.

"It's weird, but I'm still kind of...I don't know...expecting them to show up one night, you know?" Elias continues. "But they never do. One reason I'm glad you're here." He looks at me, puts his napkin on his plate. I swear I see his cheeks flush, and he stares at the napkin. "I mean, Len and Daniel, too."

I look at his face, and I understand him. He's jealous of his sisters, but the love is stronger than the jealousy. We're the same.

Suddenly, I'm afraid to look at him, afraid he'll see

something in my face that I'm not ready for him to see. Fondness. Sadness instead of anger.

I don't want him to see that we're the same even though I think he already knows.

I stare out the glass kitchen wall. The sun's setting earlier and earlier as Nebraska moves from summer to autumn. Thinking of it, the warm familiarity of it, makes me feel comfortable in my own skin for the first time in a long time.

I feel a rush of bravery, enough to make me look over at Elias again. "Why didn't you show me yours? Your One?"

Elias lowers his voice and says, "Mom doesn't know I still practice." I can't keep myself from smiling for a second. His shoulders lift once, then drop again. "And I didn't want you to feel alone."

Affection for Elias creeps into the corner of my mind. He's not a showoff. He didn't use his One to impress me, and because of that, he really doesn't have to. I'm impressed with him. Just him.

Elias slides our plates down the counter and on top of a large square section built into it. He taps the counter twice and says, "Thanks, Rosie." The panel flips, lowering the dishes to below counter-level and sliding a perfectly clean surface in their place.

"My pleasure, Elias." Rosie's voice comes from two round speakers in the kitchen ceiling.

"Maybe a little less garlic next time, huh?" Elias smiles and winks at me.

"My apologies, Elias. I'll put that in the log."

"Oh, Rosie, I'm just kidding. It was perfect." He looks at me. "She's still learning to pick up on humor."

I shake my head at him, look up at the speakers and clear my throat. "It, uh...it was great. Rosie."

"Thank you, Merrin."

He smiles at me, and I feel warm all over. "It's good for her. Recognition of stuff like sarcasm in the human voice helps refine the AI tech. Right, Rosie?"

"Yes, that is my understanding."

"Wanna see the rest of the house? I've got to...uh...I'm not allowed to have people over too late, so if you want to..." he says.

"Uh..."

Elias's eyes crinkle into a smile — since when does "uh" mean "yes"? — and he stands up and calls, "Mom? I'm giving Merrin the tour."

"Okay," his mom shouts back from her illuminated corner.

SEVEN

The sun has almost completely set now, and the last of the daylight flares the deep blue sky with purple at the top layer. It makes me look at my watch. It's quarter to nine. How long did we spend eating pizza?

We walk toward the main corridor of the house. Now that it's dark, I can see that the floor tiles light up as we walk across them. Just as we're about to step into the darkness, Elias says, "Lights please, Rosie," and a low, warm glow fills the hallway. My breathing eases. "You've seen the other wing," Elias says. "Just my bedroom, the girls' bedrooms, and a bathroom. Here," he motions to the first door on the right, "is the master suite. Nothing else on this side besides a bathroom on the end."

"I don't need to see that," I say.

He chuckles. "No. Although the shower in there is pretty sweet." He turns a handle to the room on the other side of the hall. "Here's the movie room." There are rows of leather chairs on a tiered floor, and a huge flat-panel TV suspended against the glass wall. "Rosie, turn on my favorite, huh?"

The screen glows to life with — of all things — Superman, who pushes his way through the clear, blue sky and fluffy, white clouds. I plop down in a black leather chair.

"When you just have the TV on, it's kind of like you're watching the movie outside," he says. "Rosie, lights down." The lights dim, and Elias rolls his eyes, reaches out and taps the wall. "Sorry, Rosie. Lights *out*."

"My apologies, Elias," Rosie says, and suddenly, the room is pitch black.

If this evening hadn't been so strange on its own, this house robot would be seriously weirding me out.

But soon as the lights go out, the familiar beauty of the outdoors is the only thing I can see or think about. The sky is a deep indigo now, and a few stars wink at me.

"Oh, yeah," Elias says, like he read my mind. "The view from here is incredible. Check it out. Kill the screen, Rosie." The TV dims, and all of a sudden, the sky sparks to life, its intoxicating sapphire studded with a million diamonds. I can see hundreds of stars, and I gasp with the wonder of it.

Growing up, I would have loved to have had a view like this. But I probably would have laid on the floor of this movie room, staring so long at the hazy-white cloudless summer sky, or the gray and brooding autumn one, or the bright white moon and stars against the black night, that I would never have done anything else.

I'm totally lost in it until Elias clears his throat. "Rosie, lights please."

I realize that my eyes are wet and turn to leave ahead of him so he can't see.

We walk further down the hall, and he points to the next door. "This is the music room, and that down there at the end is the gym."

I turn the handle to what Elias lamely called "the music room." He follows right behind me.

"Lights, Rosie?"

The room fills with a warm, golden glow, and I look inside. This is no music room — it's a concert hall. Three of the room's walls are glass — two sides and the front. Whoever plays in here has the stars or the clouds or the sun itself as their audience.

The hardwood floor, the color of honey, gleams at me. Even though I'm only wearing rubber-soled flats, my steps echo gently. The acoustics in here are incredible.

A baby grand piano sits in the center of the room, flanked by three electric guitars, two basses, and the sweetest amps I've ever seen. They're all lined up and waiting for some action. But something more amazing than all that catches my eye. It's shining and winking at me, I swear, and begging me to come sit and play.

My freaking dream drum set.

"Yeah, so that's boring." Elias says.

"Wait," I say, and it's the first time I've said something bossy that's also pleading, or nice in any way, in a very long time. Maybe ever.

I move slowly over to the drum set and sit down, positioning my bony bottom over the seat that's way too low, adjusting it to meet my body at the right height for playing. I let my hands hover over the spotless cymbals, not even touching them because they're so perfectly shiny and gorgeous. I stare at the toms, painted a gleaming red, their clear tops unblemished. Never been played. The snares are the same color with star-shaped vents.

"Wait a minute," Elias says. "You play?"

My voice shakes now, and my hands, too. "A little," I say. "But my set is… Well, it's not like this."

Elias crosses the room and rummages inside a drawer, but the drums are so beautiful that I can't tear my eyes away from them, not even to look at him. I push my foot lightly down on the bass pedal, and the most satisfying boom comes from the soft contact. So firm and quick.

I giggle again. That's twice in one week I've giggled within twenty feet of this guy.

My hands fumble for the screws on the tom holders and floor legs, lowering them enough so that I get a sense of what it would really be like to play. I let my foot hover

over the high-hat pedal and twitch it, imagining.

Suddenly Elias's hand is on top of my left one, and his other hand puts something in my right. He brings my hands together. I stare up at him as my fingers clench themselves around two brand-new sticks.

"The smallest ones we have," Elias says. I want to tell him it doesn't matter what size the sticks are, but thank you. Something stops the words from coming out of my throat, so I nod dumbly.

He smiles — for real, not sadly — and says, "Go ahead. Let's hear it."

I shake my arms around, loosening my shoulders, and I spin the stick in my right hand. My wrist adapts to the action like that's what it was made to do. Elias's eyebrows go up, and he laughs like he's never seen anything so awesome.

Heat floods my face, but as soon as that stick hits the tom's clear head, making the first mark on it, I am in another world. The ends of my sticks explode with a long note on the side and then crash against the cymbals, their sound so crisp and clear that I can practically see the shimmers they send through the air. I bring it down to a steady beat on the snare and side for a few bars, and I'm stunned by how beautiful these drums are, how strong and solid. They don't tremble or budge a bit.

After twenty seconds, I start a driving thrum between the snare and the high-hat, my right foot bouncing my leg along to the rhythm I pound out on the bass.

My whole body moves with the rest of the band I can only hear in my head, letting my drums shine, making them sparkle.

I hear Elias's feet shuffle. He must be getting bored, I think, but I don't really care. Then, all of a sudden, a low chord progression plays over and over again to my drumbeats. I look up for a split second through the blur of the sticks, which are now playing at exactly the same rhythm as my heartbeat.

Elias is standing there in his t-shirt and jeans, having shed his bulky sweatshirt, holding a deep blue electric, playing along with me.

A grin so wide spreads across my face that I swear my cheeks will crack off and fall onto the floor. I don't even know why Elias playing along makes me so happy, only that I start to bounce my shoulders on purpose now and play a little faster.

Elias keeps right up. He grins now, too, and as our eyes meet, I start to drum more gently, letting him riff. His fingers are moving so fast right at the base of the guitar's neck that I almost want to stop my drumming so that all I have to do is listen to him play, but I don't want to make him stop. I close my eyes, feel my body move almost of its own accord, feel it absorb the drums' vibrations, and let the sound of us playing — together — wash over me.

A lump rises in my throat, and something hot and wet slides down my cheek. I'm crying. I'm playing the most beautiful drums ever and crying.

A second after I realize it, I decide I don't even care.

For the first time, I don't have to drown someone out. Elias is meeting me where I am. He's the only person who's ever been willing to do that — *able* to do that. Now that he has, I'm not so sure what to make of him anymore.

Elias stops playing and basically ditches the guitar on the floor. He crosses the room to me in a handful of long strides. He's looking at me like he wants to touch me but doesn't know where or how. I let the sticks clatter on the floor and stand up, turning toward him.

It's almost painful how far back I have to tilt my head to look at him. He stands there, looking at me, his eyes a little worried, and he's so close that all I need to do is lean my head forward and I could just fall into him.

My stomach feels tight but I don't know if it's from embarrassment or nervousness or him being so close to me or me wanting to be closer to him.

It takes me a split second to figure it out. I let my head

fall, and then his arms are around me, letting me decide how close he holds me. Breathing in the scent of his t-shirt — sunshine and aftershave and detergent — is the only thing that could stop my tears now. I step closer to him.

He's touching me, body against body in so many more places than I ever imagined letting a boy ever touch me. But it's warm and okay. The feel of his skin and bones reminds me that he's just a boy, a sweet one. Not a threat.

I sniffle, and I'm horrified at myself, but something about being in his arms is so warm and wonderful that I start to laugh. It's not a giggle, and it's not nervous. It's relief, to be standing here in this room being held by a boy who understands me without words.

He laughs, too, and we stay there for a long moment. He pulls back and looks down at me.

"Mom really wanted me to take lessons," he says, his voice low. "I didn't have the heart to tell her when I finally decided I wanted to quit. You?"

I laugh once. "Pent-up anger, I guess. Sucking at being a Super pissed me off more than anything else. No one cares if you beat drums, so…"

He laughs again, and he's so close I can feel his breath. His eyes focus on some part of my face in such a strange way for the briefest instant. Then, like a switch has been flipped, he stands up straighter, takes the slightest step backward. I try not to make my breath too audible.

"We've, uh… I've gotta be back," he says, his voice gentle and affectionate. He motions toward the door at the back of the room, which leads outside. "Let me walk you to your car."

I'm suddenly shy, but I have to say it. "Only if you promise I can come back. You know…to play again."

He nods and smiles that smile of his again, the one that's small but real, and I shake a little.

"Done," he says. There's a pause, and we just kind of stand there looking at each other.

Elias walks me out the door. On the way down the steps, he reaches out and gently takes my hand.

"What are you…" I say, and he guides me to the outside wall and presses my hand — palm first and then finger by finger — to a shining black panel there. It glows to life under my skin.

"Rosie," he says to the panel, "Give Merrin full house access, okay?"

"Full house access granted to Merrin Grey," Rosie says.

I lean in toward the panel. "Um, thanks?"

"You have to say her name." The grin on Elias's face is so infectious that I want to laugh.

"Thanks, *Rosie*," I say, looking at Elias.

"My pleasure, Merrin," she says. I shake my head and look back at the house.

"When I say 'come back any time,' I mean it," he says softly.

"But I don't even…"

"Know me? Well, maybe you do a little better, now, huh?"

The idea of driving all the way to Elias's house to sneak in and play drums sounds enticing and silly at the same time. I shake my head in a way that could mean either "maybe" or "no, I wouldn't do that," depending on how he wants to see it.

He beams. Guess he really does want me back.

We walk back to my car, and the gravel crunches under our feet. My body shakes with the sudden chill in the air — the sunlight is the only difference between warm and chilly in the autumn.

"Whoa," I say. "I should have brought a jacket."

Elias picked up his sweatshirt on the way out of the music room but never put it back on. I can see goosebumps on his arms, but he swings it around my shoulders. The sleeves reach to my knees, and he smiles.

Oh my God. He thinks I said it to flirt with him or get his sweatshirt or something. "No, I didn't… I mean, there's heat in my car."

"And there are more sweatshirts in the house. No worries." He smiles at me, but there's a hint of disappointment hiding behind it.

Elias unplugs my car from the strip. I duck into the driver's seat without looking at him, push the startup button, and shiver into the sweatshirt one more time, cranking up the heat. When I start to back up, I roll down the window.

"Thanks. Um, you know. For everything." Suddenly, I can't make eye contact with him. Or I don't want to. Or I'm afraid to.

He starts back toward the house and waves over his shoulders with two fingers extended.

That night, I have vague dreams, dreams that involve flashing golden light. It's the only thing I can see. Something makes my hair lash across my face, blows it back again, and then it catches on my skin. It's the wind, rushing past me. I only feel it on my back, even though my whole body is moving.

The front half of my body presses up against something, but I don't know what. It should freak me out — I don't like being pressed up against anything, not even tight clothes — but it doesn't. I know how I always expected flying to make me feel — freaking over the moon. But now that it's happening, now that the feeling is mine to taste, prickling across my skin, I don't know how I feel, really — confused and euphoric and terrified all at once.

All I know is that my smile is so wide I can feel the wind against my teeth.

The flashes of light fade, slowly, but for a long time, the wind keeps whipping around me, and I speed through the blackest night, pressed into the mysterious solid heat. Eventually, the combination of speed and warmth lull me back into a deep sleep.

EIGHT

The alarm on my cuff screeches, ripping me out of the most vivid flying dream I've ever had. I realize I'm lying on my stomach and think — in my fuzzy half-awake haze — that that makes sense. That's why I was dreaming about being pressed up against something. I never sleep like that. My body normally takes up the whole bed, limbs flailed every which way.

I roll over and turn my face toward my window, soaking up the early morning sun. This is my morning's guilty pleasure and why late spring into summer into early autumn is my favorite season. First thing in the morning, I bask in the gorgeous, glowing rays that invite themselves into my room. I'm obsessed with it.

There's something new to the ritual this morning. A foreign scent, unfamiliar and enticing, a little woodsy, a little musky. I open my eyes, reluctant to give up the sensation of the orange glow of sunlight filtered through my eyelids.

Oh, God. I fell into bed last night still wearing Elias's sweatshirt. I can't wipe the smile off my face.

I stumble out of bed, finding my flip flops — the bathroom I share with the boys is always gross — and wash my face and run a comb through my hair, still wearing the stupid sweatshirt. I look up in the mirror, and sure enough, I'm still smiling. Still.

It's the drums, I tell myself, the drums that were so beautiful and sounded so amazing and felt so solid and responsive. But every time I say the word "drums" to myself, all I can think of is how Elias looked, how he felt, in that damn concert hall of his. How his voice sounded when he told me to come back any time, cautious but inviting. The look in those stupid, gorgeous, multicolored eyes of his as I drove off.

I take a deep breath, unzip the sweatshirt, fold it up, and stick it in my bag.

I flip through my closet and pull on a stretchy jersey skirt that swings around my knees, red flats, and a t-shirt that clings instead of hangs. I own a ton of skirts because I always liked the way they swung around and let the air move around my body, but after the incident last year, all I wanted to wear was old jeans.

Today, I feel a little safer.

I run downstairs, and Mom raises an eyebrow at me. "You look nice, sweetie."

I'm not feeling *that* generous, so I kind of raise an eyebrow at her and make a lot of noise unwrapping my brownies so I don't have to talk to her. I shift my weight from leg to leg, fidgeting while eating, impatient with the slowness of my own chewing.

To avoid eye contact with Mom, I pull my reader out and pretend to be reading something. Really, I'm watching the news feed on the countertop. An image of Julian Fisk, President of the Hub, with his arm around a woman in a white coat and holding a beaker, stares at me from the screen. The headline screams, "A STEP TOWARD ADVANCEMENT FOR THE SINGULARLY GIFTED?"

Holy shit. Are they working on Ones now? Finally?

Maybe it's a sign. I should ask Mom and Dad for their signatures today. That application for the Hub internship is due before winter break, but I want to get it in as soon as possible. My heart jumps. I swing my bag around to my front to reach for my tablet.

Suddenly, Mom clicks the feed closed.

"Don't worry about that, Merrin. It's nothing but marketing. Feel-good stories. I work there. I know."

I look up at her, narrowing my eyes, and her face is tight, her stance tense.

"I'd be one of the first to know," she says again.

"I made some eggs, honey," Dad calls from the stove, breaking the tension.

I swallow hard and call, "Thanks. Gotta go though." I would rather die than eat the jiggly yellow-and-white grossness that is scrambled eggs, and Dad knows that. He doesn't want to feed me. He wants to hear about me studying with other kids. Like I'm normal or something.

"Oh, and by the way," Dad says, stepping over to the table and handing me a plate anyway. "I called Mr. Hoffman. A couple of times. Left messages, but I still haven't heard back."

"Um...yeah. Okay. Thanks, Dad."

"Do you still want a tutor? I can ask around..."

"No," I say, pretending to be very focused on getting my reader in the pocket inside my bag. If I look up at Dad, he'll be able to see the lie in my eyes. Plus, I'd rather not give him something else to worry about. "I'm okay. I'm doing better, Dad. Just like I said, remember?" I glance up to check his expression as I shove some snacks in my bag. He's watching me so carefully, with a tight half-smile on his face.

"Really," I say. "Remember? Friends? Studying for calculus? The holo-teachers aren't as bad as I said. I was just being a brat."

I snap my bag closed and look up to see Dad's familiar sympathetic smile. As much as he loves me, even he wants me to be a Normal. Pick a side already, stop moping around, live like a regular person. Stop hoping for something I'll never be able to have. I can hear that much, at least, in his answer. My fingers mechanically snap my bag shut again.

I slug back a glass of chocolate milk, throw it in the dish sterilizer, and stride out before I even get to hassle Max and Michael for the morning.

There's a damp chill to the air made up of the first days of autumn and the dew from the grass. I slump into my car and fumble through my bag for my keys. My fingers fidget like I've had too much coffee, even though I haven't had a drop since yesterday morning. I crank up the heat, rub my hands together half to warm them and half for something to do. I briefly consider digging out Elias's sweatshirt and then decide that wearing it would make me look like a tool or, at least, like one of the girls crushing on him. No chance.

Only then do I glance down at the time on my cuff — quarter to seven. Half an hour before I have to leave for school.

At least being this early to school means I can sneak into the classroom ahead of everyone else. I duck into the bathroom and spend two minutes checking my makeup.

The halls are still empty when I get out, even though a few kids are starting to trickle in from the parking lot. I'm halfway to my locker when Mr. Hoffman practically crashes into me from an adjoining hallway.

"Oh, Merrin! I'm sorry." But neither his voice nor his expression indicate that he's surprised at all to be nearly knocking me over. I guess he was always pretty chill in class. He adjusts his glasses. "You're here awfully early."

"Oh, yeah. I'm a little weird with time today, I guess. I was out kind of late last night."

He raises an eyebrow.

I laugh even though most teachers by now would have told me to have a nice day and been on their way. "Just studying with some kids." He doesn't say anything, just keeps looking at me with his eyebrow up and a half-smile on his face. "For calc. No science stuff."

A relaxed smile spreads across his face. "Good. We'll be studying some high-level material, and I wouldn't want it slipping out in your study sessions. You understand."

I nod. I don't know if he understands how low-level the science classes are here, but nothing I learn with him will ever come up in a Nelson High classroom. I'd bet my drums on it.

"I'll contact you about our next meeting, alright?"

"Thanks, Mr. Hoffman. It'll be a welcome change of pace."

I don't even think to ask him what he was doing here so early before he turns and continues on his way.

Calc is fourth period, and I'm pretty sure Elias has it second. It takes me longer than usual to pack up my reader and tablet at the end of that class. The first students for second period trickle in and give me weird looks — most of the juniors haven't seen me around much — but no Elias. I walk out, frustrated with myself, and bump shoulders with Daniel. He lifts up his head in greeting.

I stalk toward my next class through the thinning crowd of students, staring at my shoes, watching them flash across the speckled floor. Where is he? He seemed fine last night.

Someone nudges shoulders with me, and a flash of orange hair swings in front of my face. "Merrin!" Leni says, smiling. "Lunch with me today?"

I'm not fast enough to come up with an excuse for why I can't possibly have lunch with her. She catches my arm, nods, and smiles wider. "Come on." She drags me through the lunch line while pointing to a table populated with half a dozen girls as gorgeous and confident as she is.

I punch my lunch choice into my cuff and scan it at the screen at the beginning of the line. I glare down at the tray that rises up on the platform in front of me.

I don't care what anyone says — that gloppy, pale yellow mush is not mac and cheese.

I sit down and crane my neck toward the door,

waiting for Elias to show up and stride toward his seat at the table.

"Hey. Have you seen, uh…"

"Elias?" Leni smiles at me, like we share a secret.

"Yeah. I have something to give him," I say, pointing to my bag to show that it's not just an excuse.

"That's cute," one of her friends — another cheerleader, I assume, with shining brown locks — says.

"Is she crushing on Elias?" another brunette asks. "Save your energy, honey. Elias VanDyne has only dated one girl at this school, and that was back when we were little freshmen."

I raise my eyebrows at her, silently questioning — I can't help it — and she suppresses a grin and points at Leni, her index finger making a circle in the air.

"Yep. Helen and Elias, sittin' in a tree…"

Leni rolls her eyes, pushes the girl lightly on the shoulder, and says, "Quit it. You know I was too good for him." She laughs, and all the other girls eye each other, responding with lighter, shorter laughter.

So Leni's the ringleader of this group. That could be really good or really, really bad. Depending on how much she feels like sticking up for me.

"Yeah. Too good for all the boys at this school, apparently."

"You know it." Leni's smiling, but it's the same smile I've seen on her before — and on Elias. Faking it.

One of the brunettes points at me. "She's not really going for Elias, anyway. Not dressed like that." My chest burns, and I'm sure my cheeks do, too, but once again I've got nothing to say. I don't want to be the Girl Who Stomps Out of the Lunchroom. Not if I've got three more years here. I concentrate on feeling heavy, on staying in my seat.

"Oh, lay off, girls. I'm trying to save Merrin from eating lunch in some classroom and being hassled by the janitor." Now they laugh on cue.

I manage a smile at Leni, grateful that she's deflected the attention from me. She reaches down and squeezes my knee. The contact surprises me, but it's not too bad.

It's an art day, and I'm sure I'll see Elias in that class, but he's not there, either, or at our lockers afterward.

All the students seem like they're normal height now without Elias's head bobbing around the hallways above everyone else's. It's weird, and I don't like it.

After I fidget through the rest of my classes, it's like I'm on autopilot. Get in the car. Text Dad: "Going to study again." I already finished all my mindless homework in sixth period study hall anyway.

I tell myself I'm just going to drive by his house, see if

his car is there. I don't know. Make sure he's okay.

I zoom in one side of Superior's suburbs and out the other, feeling lighter and freer when my car hits the dirt-and-gravel roads of the bonafide country.

Even though it's only a couple miles out of town, everything feels so huge out here. Like it's mine to reach up and grab if I want it. The clouds roll across the gray-blue autumn sky in billowing mammatus puffs, and for a second, I'm not thinking about Elias, but about the pictures I used to draw as a kid — illustrations of myself stretching out across the clouds like they were pillows.

I spot the glass walls of the VanDyne house reflecting bright patches of sunlight out into the road. The glare blocks my view into the house, but my eyes train on the music room at the end of the wing anyway. I think about the drums in there, waiting for me to play them again.

What I'm really wondering, I admit to myself, is whether Elias is in there too, thumbing over the guitar strings, remembering what it was like to play with me, missing my angry, loud pounding.

Because I know I'm thinking about the way his fingers looked playing that guitar, the relaxation on his face when he looked up at me. Like, in that moment, he was really home.

No, I realize, as I pull into the driveway without really

realizing it. He's not in there. He's not here at all. His sleek blue car isn't in the driveway, and neither is anyone else's.

Perfect.

Suddenly, I feel very brave. I crank up the brake on the car and trudge toward the step we walked down last night.

I plunk myself down and let my hand wave through the grass, resting my chin on my knees. I can see my drum set gleaming in there. I look up at the handprint sensor panel and wipe my palms against my skirt to wipe off the sweat. But I can't make myself go in. It doesn't feel right somehow. Not without him.

My chest aches, and it feels like loneliness and emptiness and missing something, which I suppose are all kind of the same thing.

The swaying blades of grass make breathy rustling noises in the late afternoon breeze — it must be five o'clock by now — and I can almost hear them talk to me. *You don't belong here*, they say.

Yeah, I think. *Except I don't belong anywhere else either.*

The sound of a rolling crunch interrupts my conversation with the freaking weeds. Dammit. Someone's here. I look up and see a flash of blue. It's Elias.

The tension in my chest deepens to a knot, and now it

feels something like excitement. I tamp it down, willing it not to push my face into a smile. Last night with Elias was a dream world, and I'm still not sure whether I can imagine it into a reality.

I watch him unfold himself from the car's seat, see me sitting there, and grin. The slowly setting sun throws a sharp shadow of him across the driveway, exaggerating his height. As he gets closer, the shadow almost touches me. When it does, I stand up.

"Hey," I say.

"Hey," he says back, still smiling and watching me. "I see you came prepared today." He reaches out and flicks the hood of my sweatshirt. He doesn't stand that close to me, but his arms are so freaking long it's easy. Not threatening.

"Oh. Yeah," I say, motioning toward my car. "Yours is in there."

"Keep it," he says.

"Uh..." I really don't know what to say to that.

"My parents aren't here." He says it tonelessly, implying nothing. Just wanting to let me know.

I shrug.

"Want something to drink?" he asks.

I smile, relieved, and nod.

"Good." He grins. "Wait here."

The sun dangles over the horizon, orange and glowing. It protests like a kid who doesn't want to go to bed, angrily flinging its light at anything it can.

Elias walks out with something in mugs. The steam coming from it wafts, fruity and spicy, toward me — hot cider. He's framed in bright-against-dark shadows that make me blink into the sky and tent my hand over my eyes to look at him. Something about his fingers wrapped around the handle of a mug for each of us makes my heart swell.

We sit there, blowing ripples across the surface of the cider and letting the mugs warm our hands.

"You weren't in school today," I say. *Thank you, Captain Obvious.*

"Doctors' appointments. Uh, physicals. For basketball. Starting practice soon." He eyes me curiously.

Then I feel brave. "Well, come back tomorrow, okay? Leni's friends are a pain in the ass."

He laughs again, and this time the smile lingers for a second. Then he nods, looking out across the farmers' fields that stretch miles and miles in front of his house. Like he knows what I mean.

"They don't matter," Elias says, staring at his hands, his fingers gripping each other. "I learned that a long time ago."

Suddenly, I'm angry at his passivity, like I want to shake him by the shoulders and scream some sense into him. He's a One. He's a freak. He should be suffering just as much as I am.

"Yeah? Well, if your One doesn't matter and they don't matter, what does matter?" I clench and unclench my jaw over and over again, wavering between feeling bad about saying that to him and feeling powerful for finally unleashing this on anyone besides my poor parents.

He doesn't respond right away. Oh, God, he must hate me. But then he speaks, and his voice is soft and patient. "There's something beyond Superior and the Hub, Merrin. Someplace where no one expects anything from me. From people like us. Somewhere I could be myself, without the One and without the stupid school and basketball team. Those are just things I'm using to get by. Leni...she really fits in there at Nelson. But I don't."

"Somewhere you can be just like a Normal, you mean. But your One will never leave you." The words come spilling out, like I couldn't stop them if I tried. Still, I don't look at him, focusing instead on twisting a long blade of grass into a knot over and over. "You can always leave Superior, leave other Supers, but you'll always be half like them." I can't keep my voice low and measured like he can. "You'll always be doing...whatever it is you can

~ 95 ~

do…and wondering if there's more. Don't tell me you would ever give it up, that you'd give up practicing whatever your One is. We're meant for more than Normal life."

A smile teases at his lips, like he wants to tell me about his One but knows there's no point. Like he doesn't even care whether I know or not. And because of that, I really do want to know. Finally.

I can't stop my legs from fidgeting. They bounce up and down, making my skirt swing against my calves. But I can't make myself leave him. Even though he makes me feel like screaming at him and sobbing into his shoulder at the same time.

A few lone fireflies flit around a bit too early. The top three-quarters of the sky are only slightly dark. I reach out to swipe one from the air and watch as it staggers across the back of my hand, testing its legs after a stretch of flight.

I wish walking felt more foreign to me than flying.

It flicks its wings out, and they tremble. Green-yellow light sparks at its back end. It pulls them back in, waits to be encouraged by the slightest bit of wind. A breeze curls through the air. The bug pushes its wings out and is off, victorious.

Nice work, I think at it.

I look over at Elias, and he's doing the same thing,

catching lightning bugs and letting them go. The tendons in the back of his hand flex lightly, coaxing the one teetering there to fly. He looks up at me, his eyes gentle.

"Hey. You know how to smile," Elias says, and there's something different about his voice, something distracted.

"You knew I could smile," I say, leaning and nudging into him with my shoulder. I sit up straight, my back rigid, as soon as I realize what I just did.

"You're right. The drums made you smile for sure. Now I just have to figure out how *I* can do it."

For a second, I can't find my breath. A few ideas flit through my head about how he could make me smile, but they are vague and terrifying — Elias's arm around me, his lips against my skin, his voice speaking softly in my ear.

Our breathing is the only sound besides the crickets' chirps, and I try to force my breaths into a steadier, slower pattern, one that shows a calmer me than my erratic heart rate would betray.

We sit silently for a while. The harsh shadows have softened into a burning golden light that sets the tips of Elias's hair on fire and casts a glow over everything — the porch, the glass walls of the house, and the waving wheat and rigid cornstalks in the fields beyond.

"Wanna walk?" Elias asks.

No. I want to fly. "Yeah," I say and hoist myself up from

the step before he can help me up because I feel like touching him, just having his skin against mine, would really put me over the edge. What edge, I don't exactly know. But I'm terrified of finding out.

"Let's head down this road. The fields are beautiful this time of year." Elias motions down the dirt road that passes his house, framed in barbed wire that I always thought was ugly. But now that it's glinting gold-orange, it's actually breathtaking.

The fields call to me, too. I've imagined soaring over them a million times, how the burning gold of the sun would scoop down into the husks and bounce back in curves, how the lazily turning turbines would shrink to the size of pinwheels.

Someone's bonfire, miles away, scents the air with a sharp smokiness. A chill settles over everything as the sun retreats, making way for frost. For the first time this year, I realize it's solidly autumn, and I shiver, fighting it.

He's so close to me, so very close. Maybe a foot away. I really feel it — his closeness — but it's not scary. The slender shape of his body feels familiar, feels just like mine. Only a foot and a half taller.

"Is there a reason you still won't tell me?" he asks.

Our hands swing past each other as we walk, not brushing but close. I want to memorize the arcs they make through the darkening light.

"What else do you really need to know about me besides my mad drumming capabilities?" I push my eyebrows up at him and smile a tight-lipped smile.

"There's more to you than being a drummer," he says, watching his hand too, not moving closer. "Yeah, you're cute and smart. Everyone knows that. You're also angry, and I get that. But I want to know more."

He stops dead in his tracks, and so do I, turning to face him as if by instinct.

"I'll tell you mine if you tell me yours," he whispers.

I can't tell if it's a tease or a challenge, so I press my lips together, waiting for his face to tell me what to say next.

He looks down, right at me. There's this weird feeling in my chest, and I've honestly never felt it before. It seems ridiculous, even to me, that a sixteen-year-old girl never felt her heart beat like crazy, but I am not kidding, this *is* the first time. I stare back at him. My mouth hangs open, waiting for my heart to fly out of it.

He drops his gaze to the ground. I thought that was all I wanted him to do because at least it would stop my heart from running circles inside me, but now the damn thing thuds to a stop and drops into my stomach. Now I'd give anything for him to look back at me, say anything. I honestly think my life depends on it.

"I float," I say, and he turns to look at me again, but oh my God, now he's looking *up* at me because I'm freaking floating. This is the first time this has happened in forever, and it's because I let my stupid head get away from me and my stupid heart drop into my stomach and this stupid, stupid boy get to me. "I just..."

And then he reaches his hand up to me. His fingers make a ring around my wrist. They barely touch my skin, but where they do, there's this electricity, warm and melting and vibrating through my skin. And then my face follows his up because now he's floating, too.

My heart really pounds now, so hard that blood thrums through my veins. The sensation is so horrific and so energizing at the same time that I can hardly stand it.

"Another One who floats?" I whisper.

He shakes his head, staring at the place where his fingers meet my wrist. He breathes in so deeply that his chest pushes out, making him even closer to me, and brushes the underside of my forearm with his fingers.

He wraps one arm around my waist, then the other, and pulls me close to him. His heart races against mine.

And then we're moving. The wind brushes my cheek so gently it's a whisper, but I watch as the gravel moves a foot below us. The pebbles all blend together, into stripes, then into a big gray blur. The wind pushes out from my face, making a bubble all around my skin, and the tension of it pushes my body to the side, so gently that if it weren't for the gravel stripes I wouldn't believe it was happening.

We go higher — four feet off the ground, then six, then ten — but now we're really moving, too. My hair whips around my face, and we start going so fast the corn stalks blur into a striped gold-and-green backdrop.

I hold onto him so tight, my arms around his waist and my fingers bunching up his shirt. It's not because I'm afraid or even because I need to. It's because that's what my body wants to do.

I start laughing, and I haven't laughed like this in so long, not since I was a little kid, that we fly even higher, so high the air tastes thin.

Then I shriek like a freaking sixteen-year-old girl, and when I stop to realize that's exactly what I am, I laugh even harder.

Elias whoops, and my heart stops pounding and soars with his joy. His sad smile is gone, replaced with the real Elias smile. This is really him, I know, suddenly and completely.

He's taken us in a circle, around a corn field that must have been four miles square at least, and my skin buzzes from the feel of the air whipping against it, like when I was a kid and I stuck my hand outside the car window on the highway. I used to imagine that's what it felt like to fly. I laugh one more time when I realize that, aside from his body keeping mine from the wind on one side, I was right.

When we land, the ground underneath my feet buzzes, too, like it's too solid to handle me, like I don't even belong there. Not anymore.

We're standing so close together. His shirt is bunched together at the sides, right above his hips. The wrinkles are lined with sweat from where my hands held on to him. I should feel mortified, but I don't.

It's getting dark. Since we walked out here, someone's painted the sky with broad, bright strokes of cotton candy pink, glowing amber, and deep purple. Fireflies dot the musty air with bursts of glowing green. This is just like a movie, it's so perfect and magical. Which makes it all the more impossible that this is actually happening.

We look at each other for a long minute, grinning like idiots, like the people in the movies do when they've just kissed for the first time. Not that I would want to do anything like that.

Except, now that I think of it, I really, really would.

He looks at me with mischief in his eyes, and I wonder how I look, with my hair even more messed up than usual.

I'm sure my cheeks are red. I know I'm blushing, but hopefully, he just thinks they're windchapped.

He looks right into my eyes for a moment, then nods, like he's decided I'll be able to handle what he's about to say. "I push the air. Only from around me which is why it's my One. I can't control it from far away."

"But you floated," I say. I furrow my eyebrows, glare at him. "You *flew*." But that doesn't make sense because, in order to take me with him, he would have to be super strong, too. Or maybe I'm so light that my weight doesn't matter at all.

He shakes his head, still looking right at me, and I swear his gorgeous freaking eyeballs are going to burn a hole right through me. "Only with you. I saw you go up, and I...I wanted to touch you. Again." He looks down, then back at me, his eyes wide. "And when I did..." He makes a swooping motion in the air.

The buzz from the ground moves up through my body, and it feels so good, I know if I stand here any longer I'll get addicted. I won't be able to get enough of this beautiful boy and the beautiful power he can give me.

All I've ever wanted is to be more than a One. But no matter how fun it is to finally, finally fly, and how good it felt to hold onto Elias while I did it, this is not okay.

It feels so incredible to fly, but it's not okay to need

him to do it.

I wonder if he's doing his air-pushing thing right now because all I can feel is the tension of the space between us. He steps in and brushes the hair off my forehead, looking at me in that infuriatingly patient way he does.

I reach up to touch his face, brushing my thumb across his cheek because I have no idea what else to do with it. All I know is that I have to touch him. He circles his arm around my waist, pulling me in to his body and my face up toward his, and I push up on my tiptoes.

He kisses me, and I'm even higher and farther away from everything than I was when we flew.

His lips are soft and warm, and I ache for wanting to be closer to him. My feet lift off the ground again, but this time I don't care because now our eyes are even. I sigh, realizing how badly I needed that. His lips part against mine, and I gasp, and I'm so excited that I bite the bottom one a little bit. He kisses me deeper, wrapping his fingers around my waist, and my hands rake through his hair, palms hugging the sides of his face. He pulls back and looks into my eyes, then down past our feet, and laughs.

"You're doing it again," he says, his voice lower than it was a minute ago. "Um, *we* are." I look down and sure enough, we're a good four feet off the ground. Terror rushes through me. Not because I'm floating — he already knows all about that now.

It's because now that he's gone and kissed me, I might need him for more than flying.

We sink down, down, down, and by the time, my feet touch solid ground again, I'm torn between tackling him in the cornfield and getting away from him as soon as possible.

He looks down at me, smiling a gentle smile that tells me he'd appreciate the tackle. I look at him for one second, two, five. I open my mouth and stammer something that doesn't make sense.

And then I do the only thing that *does* make sense — I turn around and run home.

NINE

I know that most girls would cry at this point. Most girls would sprint down the dirt road, running so fast they kicked up a cloud of dust around them, stopping when they were out of the boy's sight. Most girls would crouch down and weep in the middle of corn fields under a canopy of painted sky, feeling sorry for themselves.

But I speed down the path as fast as my legs will carry me, desperate to feel the wind whip against my face again, willing to do anything to relive the dream of soaring through the air. I am fast for a Normal. The air breezes against my face, through the tunnels made on either side of my body between my arms and torso, but it's not fast enough, not by a longshot.

Eventually, the dust I'm kicking up rises past my waist. I hate it so much. Not because it's making me cough, which it is, but because it breaks the fantasy that I'm flying.

You can only kick up dust if you're on the ground.

My lungs start to really burn about a quarter mile from home, and that's when I drop to the ground, pull my knees against my chest, bury my face in my hands, and weep with everything in me.

I want Elias — kissing him was enough to tell me that, and I'm not stupid enough to deny it.

I want to fly more than I want him. Way more.

As unbelievable as it was, it wasn't — could never be — it's *not* flying on my own. If I fly with Elias, I can't fling my arms out to the side and feel the nothingness speeding between me and the earth. Not unless he carries me.

And no matter how good it felt to kiss Elias, to be so close to him that I felt his heart beating in my chest and the vibration of his speech against my skin, I don't want to let him carry me until I know I can carry myself.

I pound up the driveway, where my brothers are playing basketball even though it's almost too dark to reasonably see the ball. Max nails a free-throw and does a victory dance. Michael has always been a little slower, less agile. That's why they link arms when they speed across the water. They go so much faster together.

I bend at the waist, digging my elbows into my knees, trying to hide that I'm gasping for breath. I stare at the dull gray coating of dust on my legs. I could drag a white line through it with my finger.

Michael's voice interrupts my panting. "Merrin, you okay?"

Max is next to me in seconds, probably glad to

abandon the game. "What happened to you? Was it a guy?"

Their baby faces are so serious, staring down at me. I grimace when I feel a cramp start to form in my calf, and that just makes Michael look more outraged.

"We'll kick his ass, Mer. Just tell us who." He's still a little boy, spouting threats in his high-pitched, just-starting-to-crack-sometimes voice. I want to laugh — for his incorrect assumptions and for how sweet his concern for me is.

Then a clear thought pierces my mind. Did the boys hear about what happened at SHS last year?

"No, guys. No, uh…but thanks," I say, trying to keep my face as serious as possible. "Long night. I'm going to bed."

The cerulean-and-magenta flashing of the TV from the living room lets me know that Mom and Dad are still up, but I don't want them to see the dirt on my legs and the redness in my eyes. Don't want them to think the wrong thing, not after what happened to that girl at Super. Not after what they knew, without asking, that I was afraid of.

I yell into the living room, "Home, guys!" Then I hurry up the stairs, duck into the bathroom, and turn the shower on so they know not to bug me. I toss my clothes just inside my door, adding to the pile of dirty socks and wet washcloths, and glance at the hall clock on my way into the bathroom. Eight o'clock already.

The shower has steamed up the bathroom, and I step in, inhaling the hot fog and blowing it out in a deep breath. I close my eyes, tip my head back just enough for the stream of water to tug my hair back, and feel the steam caress my face, my arms, my neck. This is what it's like to be inside a cloud. It must be.

I step backward and let the hot water pour over my face. It's scalding hot, just the way I love it, but as much as I do, it's still too hot for the skin on my eyelids and lips. I drop my head forward, and the water pounds my muscles until it turns from scalding to hot to tepid, and the change sends goosebumps rippling across my skin.

When I get out, I look down at my body, at my ghostly white skin striped with red on either side of my neck and down to my belly and thighs from where the steaming water ran its course. Exhaustion hits me, envelops my body seemingly from nowhere, and I feel my legs tremble slightly.

I reach for my white waffle-weave bathrobe and wrap it tight around my body. I head toward my room, but when I'm just about there, Dad calls up the stairs, "Mer Bear? Sweetie?"

"Right here, Dad," I say. His head cranes around the banister, and I swear I see his shoulders relax significantly when he sees me. Then he basically sprints up the stairs to stand beside me.

"Everything okay, honey? Where's the car?"

Oh my God. I am even more out of it than I thought I was.

"I, um. I walked home. I guess I left it..." I give myself over to the trembling in my legs and sit on the top step, look at him, and shrug. I can't say anything because I know I'll burst into tears.

Now my lip trembles, too, and I must looked wrecked because Dad sits down beside me, looks at me sadly, and wraps his arm around me.

"Is it...a boy?" He actually sounds hopeful. Maybe that I have enough of a social life to even be upset by a boy at all.

"Yes...no...I don't know, Dad." I turn my head into his shoulder and really let loose, soaking his shirt with my tears. I'm so overwhelmed with emotions — excitement and confusion and frustration and exhilaration all knocking together in my head — that I can't even figure out how I feel. Maybe letting the tears loose will free up some room in there so I can think. Dad rests his chin on my head and just sits there for a few minutes, squeezing my arm occasionally, letting me cry.

"Did he hurt you?" Dad asks after a moment.

"No... Elias? No. Not at all."

"Elias." Dad turns his head into mine, kissing the top of it.

A bright blue-white light pans through the front windows of the house, and I hear the hint of a car door slamming. Five seconds later, a light knock on the door.

He is too perfect.

Dad runs down the stairs, and I listen to his gruff voice exchanging with Elias's younger, velvet one.

"Good evening, sir. I just wanted to get this back before the morning."

I hear the clink of keys changing hands. How could I have been so stupid as to leave the keys in the car? Or did I leave them in the dirt next to the house? This boy takes my head away from me.

"Thank you...uh... I didn't catch your name, son."

"Elias VanDyne, sir. I have the same calculus teacher as Merrin." There's a pause, half a second too long to be normal. Then, "I won't keep you any later, sir, and my curfew is almost up. But please tell Mrs. Grey I say hello."

"Can I drive you back?"

"No, thank you, sir. It's not too dark for an evening run. No one out there but the crickets and owls anyway."

Great. He runs, too. Of course he does.

"Thank you, Elias. Be careful."

"Thank you. And good night, sir."

Dad closes the door softly and walks with measured steps to the bottom of the stairs, and looks at me for a quiet moment. I'm not crying loudly anymore, but tears still roll down my cheeks.

After a few moments, Dad says, "Well, he's hardly a monster. Right?"

I respond with a hiccuped laugh, covering my mouth with the back of my hand and shaking my head. "No," I manage. "No, he's not."

"I'm going to let you go to bed," Dad says. "If you want to talk more in the morning, you know where to find me."

I use the banister to pull myself up and collapse into bed — wet hair, bathrobe and all.

TEN

The next morning, when I try to turn into my golden-sunshine-bed-bath, I can't.

My whole body is heavy and thick, like lead runs through my veins. There's a vague ache, but it sort of courses around the heaviest layer of my body, the one stuck to the bed.

I feel the glow of the sunlight at the edge of my bed, can glimpse it out of the corner of my eye, but there is no way I can move my body to reach it.

It must be 7:15 already. I've slept way too late. I should be getting in the car right now. I let my eyes close as the dull ache turns into pain and bleeds in a wave up from the small of my back to my shoulder blades, and for a few minutes, it's all I can think about.

There's a knock on the door, and I manage to croak, "Come in."

Mom sticks her head in, says, "Honey? You feeling okay?" Her voice sounds like it would if I were underwater, like I'm in the bathtub instead of in bed.

I move my head a bit, trying to shake it, but I'm not sure if it's a "yes" or a "no." Mom's eyebrows furrow, and she steps in gingerly and sits on the very edge of my bed, her body not touching mine. She presses the back of her hand to my forehead, looks puzzled, then bends in to kiss it.

"That's quite a fever," she murmurs. Then she puts her hands on either side of my face and says, "What's going on?"

"My back hurts," I say, "and I'm so...exhausted."

Mom sits up straight, and her eyes widen. She clears her throat, stares at me for another second. Her eyes dart to the box of tampons on my desk. Then she swallows hard and speaks again, her voice weaker. "Does this happen every month?"

Oh. She thinks it's *that*.

"Um. Not usually this bad."

I turn my head to the side, closing my eyes, indicating that I want to rest. She pats my arm. "Well, if you have the flu, too, I guess... You'll feel better in a day or so."

Great. Mom's bonding with me over girl stuff. Or thinks she is, at least.

Later that morning, I manage to sit up, even though my body still feels heavy against the pillow. By eleven o'clock, I really, really have to go to the bathroom, and I walk so slowly it feels like it takes me a week to get there, even though it's only a door away.

When I get back in bed, I feel like I've just run a marathon. I stay there the rest of the day, drifting in correspondence with the waves of pain, in and out of sleep.

I dream of the air rushing all around me, of punching Merrin-shaped holes through the white cumulus clouds against a brilliant blue sky. Every dream ends with me plummeting, suddenly, through the sky, but I don't hit the ground. Elias is always there to catch me.

I want to read, but I can't open my eyes or concentrate long enough to make any sense of the words on my reader. I manage to get my ear buds into my ears and listen to some hard, pounding tracks. I imagine they're beating the pain out of my body. Maybe it works or maybe the pain actually leaves, but I feel better by the time Mom gets home.

I realize now that I'm sweating, soaking the sheets. Gross.

Mom does the concerned face again, and I guess this doesn't fit with her normal experience of monthly pain. I hear her and Dad talking about something in the hall outside my room, but I don't pick up much — just the verdict: "Tylenol. Check on her a couple times tonight."

Mom comes in and asks me if I want to eat. My

stomach feels empty. It doesn't growl, but I don't feel sick either, so I say, "yes." She brings back chicken noodle soup, and I eat all the noodles, one by one — my jaw feels like it's been wired shut — but leave the broth, weird cubed chicken, and carrots.

Her voice is much clearer than it was this morning — almost too clear now, her words rattling around in my brain long after she's let them out of her mouth. She asks, "Feeling better, honey?"

I nod my head and realize that the range of motion is much better than what I had this morning. I'm not sweating nearly as much either.

"Is there anything I can get you?"

There are two things I want: to talk to Elias and to feel better. In that order. Maybe he has a clue as to why I have a freaking full-body flying hangover.

My heart sinks when I realize that I don't have Elias's number. I don't have anyone's number, actually, besides Mom's and Dad's.

I click open my reader instead, but before I can look at what's on the screen, my eyelids push themselves down and I am caught in a swirling, black sleep.

The next day, I shake and tremble whenever I move, but at least I can move without too much extra effort. At least that heaviness is gone. Progress is good, especially if it means that flying won't kill me. Mom's left a note on my bedside table.

Didn't want to wake you. Your fever seems to have broken. Water, Tylenol, snacks on your nightstand. Call if you need anything. Love, Mom.

I roll my eyes at Mom's assumption that I wouldn't realize my own fever had broken but smile when I see what she left me. Cupcakes and brownies and some licorice. She must be worried if she's leaving me all the stuff she normally bristles at me eating. I see that she left some protein bars for good measure. My cheeks feel like they'll crack when I grin at that.

I manage to scoot my body out of bed and get to the bathroom. Then I come back and lie down right in the middle of my bed, where the sun shines so brightly that it warms my whole body, and sleep more.

Sometime in the late afternoon of the third day, Mom comes and sits on the edge of my bed again. I manage a small smile and say, "Hey." I'm surprised that my voice sounds clear and strong, and from the look on Mom's face, she is, too.

"I got an email from Professor Fitzsimmons just now," Mom says.

"Who?"

"Your science class coordinator. Honestly, Merrin, you could bother to learn her name."

Oh. That must be the freaking holo-teacher in my sorry excuse for a science class. "Why? With a thousand students, there's no way she knows mine."

Mom sighs. "Well, she's very interested in her Nebraska students today. It's going to be an exceptionally clear night, and the National Weather Service is predicting a...geomagnetic storm, I think? Which means..."

"The aurora," I gasp.

"That's what she said." Mom grins. "The whole school's meeting out near Blakely Creek tonight to see it."

An anxious energy vibrates through my chest and arms. "I've gotta get ready." My hand flies up to my hair, which is a greasy mess after two days of lying around without a shower. I swing my legs out of bed, but they wobble beneath me and Mom has to catch me by the forearm. I shake her off after a couple seconds, give her an obligatory smile, and say, "Thanks," on my way out of my room.

"Dad'll drive you," she calls after me.

"Yeah, okay!" I say as I wave her off. I'm seeing the Northern Lights — in freaking Nebraska, which never happens — and Elias tonight. I really don't care how I get there.

I still feel weak the whole car ride out to the clearing in the next township where all the science classes are meeting to gather around radio telescopes and watch the aurora borealis. Dad keeps glancing at me but doesn't say a word. The car glides soundlessly down the country road. I lean my head against the window, pretending to watch the horizon as usual. Instead, I close my eyes and try to steady myself.

When we pull up to the clearing, Dad unclicks his seatbelt. I roll my eyes. "Dad, you can stay in the car." I open the door and find the ground with my feet — still unsteady.

"Do you even know where your class is?"

Looks like Dad's more than making up for his lack of overprotective parenting skills from the other day. Weird. But okay.

"Really, Dad, it's fine. In fact," I pull back my sleeve and tap my cuff, "I'll call you when we're done. Okay?" He raises an eyebrow at me. "There are chaperones, Mom said. We're fine."

Dad nods and re-clicks his seatbelt but still scans the crowd through the car window. I put a hand on either side of the door frame and take one deep breath before a gentle touch brushes the inside of my arm and a strong grip closes around my hand so quickly it startles me. My head pounds again, and I stand upright to see Elias smiling down at me.

He cranes his neck down to look at Dad. "I can bring Merrin home, sir, if you'd like."

I haven't seen Dad look so pleased in a very long time. "If that's okay with you, Merrin," Dad says as he turns the key in the ignition.

"Um…" I check Elias's expression, and he gives me the slightest nod and smile. I'm short of breath for a moment. "Yeah, okay. See you at home, Dad. We might be here for a while — we don't know when the lights'll start, and they can last for hours."

Dad drives away, and Elias and I are once again standing together under the sunset. Leni and Daniel are with the rest of the students about 50 feet away, talking to a lady with mocha skin and a shock of short, kinky hair.

"Is that some teacher I haven't met?"

Elias laughs. "No, that's Leni's mom." I raise my eyebrows and look at pale-skinned, bright-haired Leni. "Stepmom, I guess. Her mom died when she was little — five, I think. Her dad remarried a couple years later — she's been mom to Leni as long as I can remember."

Leni grins and waves at us, and Elias raises a hand in greeting but doesn't move toward them. Neither do I. He looks back at me, and my mouth feels like cotton.

I want to ask if he noticed I was gone the last few days. Want to tell him that I hate how I ran away that night. Want to tell him how he makes my heart pound, even now when we're not alone.

Most of all, I want to ask him to fly with me again.

Instead, I say, "Hey," and stand there staring up at him like an idiot while my stomach flips and twists. "Um...thanks for waiting for me. I mean...were you waiting for me? I mean... Wow, I sound stupid."

The corner of his mouth teases upward. "Hi."

I grin, unable to break my gaze from his. "Hi."

My heart races again, begging me to move, to join the rest of the students. But instead of propelling me away, like my head wants it to, it pulls me closer to him, so close that the buzz between us raises the hairs on my arms.

And then he is kissing me, lacing his fingers through my hair, and oh my God, it is so nice and warm and sweet and totally not what I wanted at all.

Suddenly, it hits me: why there was ever a minute I didn't want him. I wanted to blend in, wanted to be all alone in my Oneness forever, because that's what I was used to. There's no way I can blend in if I'm with Elias because he is so handsome my heart breaks when I look at him.

My Oneness has always been the only thing I've

thought about, stressed about, fought against, and now —
when I'm standing here with his arms around me — it's
the last thing on my mind.

His fingers loop around my wrist lightly. This touch is
tender and somehow so much more intimate than holding
my hand, and I want his fingers to run up my arm and
down my back and...

There are a few low wolf whistles from the crowd of
students, and some guy shouts, "Hey, E, who's your girl?"
but they all sound like they're worlds away because Elias is
so close to me, resting his forehead against mine and
grinning, even though I'm just a pale, plain girl whose only
real superpower is playing the drums louder than anyone
can stand.

Finally, he pulls away.

"Why did you do that?" I'm trying really hard to look
away from him and not let him see my face because I'm
pretty sure I look like an idiot, twitchy and half-smiling.

"It was the only way to get you to stop."

"Yeah. Well, next time you kiss me, make sure no one
else is watching," I say.

As soon as the words come out of my mouth, I regret
them. I look at him, expecting him to look hurt. But
instead, a slow smile creeps across his face, his shoulders
begin to shake, and then he's laughing.

"What are you laughing about?" I ask, indignant.

"You said *next time* I kiss you."

This is not the time to hold anything back, I realize. "Look, I'm just pissed off because you wouldn't...if we were..."

"You mean I wouldn't have kissed you if we were both Normals?"

I flush when he says "kissed." A lot. "Yeah," I say to the ground.

"That's ridiculous," he says.

"You're ridiculous," I huff, even though I can't hide the smile that has touched my cheeks along with the blush. He touches my arm, and the buzz stops me dead in my tracks, pulls my gaze back up to his.

"I would be nice to you if we were Normals, yeah... I'm nice to all the new kids 'cause I'm a nice guy. Especially the transfers because...I know what it's like. To be an outsider. But I'd never kiss you, Normal or One, unless..."

I look up at him, and his smile is gentle, and he's looking at me like I'm a rainbow after a thunderstorm, a breath of fresh air, a promise of hope. Like I'm the best thing ever. And I think he's probably the best thing ever, too. I try to look him square in the eye, but he's so tall and so freaking beautiful, and there goes my stupid palpitating heart again. I want to say something, but all I can do is smile.

He grins and reaches down to weave his fingers with mine. I let him.

And I know, right then, that he would do anything for me and that I can trust him. And that right there is my breath of fresh air. If being attached to him is the price of being able to fly — *if* it is — I may be willing to pay it.

"I missed seeing you the last couple days," he says.

I really can't get my head around how boldly he says it, like he either knows what my response is going to be or it doesn't affect him in the least what I say.

But I know from the way he kissed me three days ago, floating above the cornfields, that he must care what I say. At least a little. I want to stand on my tiptoes and touch his jaw, stare at his eyes some more, check them for reassurance that this is real.

"I would have called," he says, "but I don't have your number. Besides, the first day I could barely get my head off the pillow."

"Wait. You were sick, too?"

"Too? What happened to you?"

"A lot of heaviness," I say, rolling my shoulder. "And pain, the aching kind. Mostly in my back."

He nods, like he knew what I was going to say. "And

fever?"

"Yeah."

"My dad was really worried," he says.

"Oh. Well, my mom thought it was...um...you know."

He looks at me, puzzled. He has no clue.

"Uh, a girl thing. I think."

"Oh! Right. Right." His cheeks blaze red. "Sorry."

If it were anyone else, I would run from the embarrassment, but I can't stop looking at him. "Anyway," I say, "The fever was bad, the end of day one. I think they decided it was the flu. They mostly left me alone."

"Wish my parents had done that. They just paced in front of my room a lot and talked about me when they thought I couldn't hear."

One of the chaperones calls, "We're expecting things to start in the next few minutes, so gather around a telescope. We only have a dozen or so, and we'll need to take turns."

"I think we could see them closer without a telescope if we need to, huh?" A nervous laugh rolls up from my belly and out my nose, and he laughs, too.

He cocks his head toward a cluster of trees silhouetted against the horizon behind us and says, "Come on."

The air cools by the minute with the setting sun, and I

zip up my hoodie a little higher. Elias reaches out his hand, folding it around mine.

He glances at me, wondering if it's okay, I think. I smile and nod, squeeze his hand, and he beams. He's so brilliant, I might die.

I fall in step with him, and we don't speak. As we walk, he shifts his hand to intertwine his fingers with mine, and my heart jumps, flits around in the upper regions of my chest, and it's almost painful how good it feels. His fingertips, which stretch out across the back of my hand almost all the way to my wrist, brush lightly against the knob of bone there.

This is almost as incredible as flying. Almost.

ELEVEN

The sky has darkened to a dusky charcoal gray, and it's the clearest I've seen in a while. I can already count dozens of bright stars. The chatter of the crowd fades into the background, and when I look back to where half of the school has gathered, I realize we're a quarter of a mile away at least. With the light fading by the minute, I'm sure no one will even notice that there's someone moving around beyond the tree line.

I still feel weak, but I can't tell if it's leftover sickness or from being with Elias or from wondering if he'll agree to fly with me again. And then it hits me — he might not feel the same way. He might be freaked out.

Or worst, it might all have been a dream.

But the way he looks at me is so intense, even through the thickening dark, that I know he's thinking the same thing.

He takes a deep breath in, then out again. "Are you okay?"

"Um, besides being knocked on my ass for the last few days? Yeah."

He doesn't laugh at my joke. Probably because it wasn't funny. "No, I mean…the way you left and all."

"Oh. Oh." It all comes back to me in a rush now — my shock, my panic, my indecision. I've been so focused on flying and so focused on kissing him that I've almost forgotten that the two of them are linked. And it was that link that terrified me.

He looks at me, waiting for me to respond. Then he looks down at our hands, still woven together. I smile at them and then back up at him. Even though I don't know what to say, I hope he gets it.

"Yeah." I say. "Um…thanks for bringing the car back."

He swallows hard. "Of course."

"If you don't want to, we don't have to…you know…anymore," I blurt out.

I actually don't know exactly which thing I meant — the flying or the kissing. I'm dying to do both but terrified of both at the same time. I look at Elias, and my cheeks flush again. Then, thank God, he raises his eyebrows questioningly and makes that same swooping motion with his hand in the air. My heart wants to burst with excitement. It's going to happen again.

We're going to fly.

The slightest breeze rustles the trees' leaves, pushing their sibilant whisper through the air. It's like they're acknowledging that we have this secret and that they'll keep it safe for us. Between the tree trunks separating us and the growing darkness, I can barely see the crowd.

He turns to face me and drops my hand. "How should we do this?" His voice wavers, and I'm lost in wanting my face to be closer to his for just a moment.

"Um. The way we did it before, I guess?" I giggle. Again. This giggling is getting ridiculous.

"I mean," he stammers, "did you want to turn around or something? So you can look down?"

Something like defiance rises up in me. I shake my head, automatically. The image of Elias's arms around my waist with him behind me is not okay. I don't want to be carried.

"Or do you want to go behind me?" He shifts his balance, looking everywhere but at me.

I wrinkle my nose more at that image. I'd be...riding on his back? I can tell he's picturing the same thing because we both laugh, then say at the same time, "No."

"You know," he says, "we don't even really know how it works. We don't know if we'll be able to make it happen again."

I put my hand out, palm toward him, and sure enough, it buzzes with the same electric energy I felt between us when our hands swung innocently in the twilight blue, three days ago. I nod my head, look at him boldly.

"We will," I say.

He puts his hand out, too, his palm facing mine, and a puff of air gusts against my palm.

"That is incredible," I say.

"You know what's incredible?" he asks. He clasps our hands together, closes his eyes, and his feet hover off the ground, even as mine are still firmly planted there.

"How are you doing it?"

"I don't know," he smiles. "There's a buzz, like I told you, and I kind of let it...go through me. I don't know."

I reach up, snag his waist with my arm, and imagine myself weightless, just like every other time I've ever practiced, and then I'm at eye level with him. He hugs me to him, and I grin.

God, this feels so good. So good. The floating, of course, but most of all being smooshed up against him. His scent is so heady that it almost makes me forget everything.

It doesn't hurt that he's so cute.

We hover there, grinning at each other again, and suddenly I feel the need to make some small talk. "Are your glasses going to be okay?"

"Oh, yeah. They got a little messed up last time."

Feeling bold, I unhook them from behind his ears, fold

them up, and put them in the front pocket of my hoodie.

"Thanks," he whispers.

I close my eyes and imagine myself as a balloon — or even something lighter and more ethereal, like a cloud. We float up, up, up, twice as fast as we did outside the cornfield, and I hold back a shriek, gasping instead.

Elias screws his face up in concentration, and I feel it again, that bubble-like feeling around my skin, but this time it's so tense I can feel it actively pushing air away from me. We move, staying below the treetops, but just as fast as the last time.

But we're only up for a couple of minutes this time before a tremble rumbles through my limbs, along with an edge of the aching pain from the day after.

"Do you feel that too?" I say in his ear, my neck stretching to put lips right up against it. It's the only way he'll hear me against the roaring of the wind.

"Yeah. We should get down."

How will I ever tell the difference between feeling weak and feeling the way it feels to be close to him?

Our feet pound down on the ground, and immediately my head starts to throb. My legs feel like rubber. I double over, elbows on my knees, and then my legs give out completely. I plunk down on my bottom right there in the tall grass, which rasps against my arm and face while Elias does the same right next to me.

Elias peers at me, his brow furrowed. "You okay?" Then he says, "Whoa," and lays flat on his back.

I close my eyes and tilt my head back, trying to calm the spinning and throbbing. When I open my eyes, I see two silhouettes tromping toward us through the tall grass.

"Hand check!" a low boy's voice calls, and Elias laughs.

"Daniel. Jerk," he mumbles. Then he calls, "Did you drag Leni out here, too?" Leni's laugh rings out like a bell in the clear, cooling night.

When they reach us, Leni stretches her hand down to help me up. "Yes, moron, I'm here. There's nothing I love more than ditching our class, in the dark, when my mom's the chaperone, to make sure you're not getting in trouble." I grunt and wince as I get to my feet, and Leni eyes Elias, who pushes himself to sitting, then to standing. "But, really, what were you two doing out here?"

"Check this out," Elias says, and I see his whole body tremble a little. He grabs my hand, and his feet hover off the ground a few inches, maybe a foot. Then he lands and takes a deep breath.

Daniel's eyes narrow. "What is going on, Elias? What have you two been…?"

I beam. Elias's gaze shifts between me and the tree

line. He seems on edge.

"Is it okay if we show them?" I ask.

"Uh…yeah. I just…let's do it fast. I don't want anyone to see…that we're not with the class."

I nod. "His One is pushing air and mine is floating, right?" I say to Leni and Daniel, bouncing with energy now. "So when we touch…" I loop my arm around his waist and look up at him.

Elias stops looking so worried and flashes me that damn dimple. I can't help but smile back.

We shoot up 10 feet and zoom around in a little circle. We land quickly, just as my muscles start to twinge, right in front of Leni and Daniel. Something glints in Leni's eyes — tears I can't make sense of. She kind of leans against Daniel, like she's having trouble standing up on her own.

Elias watches the tree line for another long moment. "Okay, guys," he says, his voice hushed. "I want you to try something. Hold hands."

"Okay…" Leni shakes her head slowly, but she turns and reaches her hands out to Daniel's waiting ones. Of course she trusts Elias — they've been friends forever. Daniel bobs his head, smiles, and takes Leni's hands.

"Do you feel something?" Elias asks, his eyebrows high.

"A…it's like a tingling?" Daniel says, but his black eyes flash warmly at Leni.

She smiles back and then gasps. "Oh! Yeah. I feel it."

"Like, a buzz?"

Daniel nods.

"Okay." Elias beams. "Now don't let go, okay?"

"Elias? What do you want me to do?" Leni knows — I can tell by the tone of her voice. She knows what he's going to ask of her, and she's asking herself how much she wants to trust him, how much she wants to believe in this guy she loves like a brother.

"Flame on, Len."

"Elias, I haven't…you know…for a while now. Weeks."

Daniel looks at her, his eyebrows scrunching up. I know what she means. She's just about given up on her One.

"Use that feeling, okay? The buzz. Just picture it moving through you, making you do it, okay?"

She shakes her head again, stands up a little taller, and breathes in deeply through her nose. I gasp as wisps of smoke rise from the place where she's touching Daniel. They twist themselves around the point where their skin touches, then curl upward, disappearing into the air. Then, with a quiet whoosh, their hands light on fire.

Leni's arm shakes and her voice along with it. "Daniel?" she says, and Daniel has a smile playing at his lips, and then the flames fully engulf his hand and snake up his arm, licking through the knit of his sweater.

Leni gives a gasp, breaks contact, jumps back, and stares at her hand. It's not red, not raw, not burned. She touches it to her own face and doesn't pull it away immediately. It's not even hot. Leni pitches forward and grabs Daniel's forearm, inspecting it for sizzling skin.

"Oh, man," Daniel says, shaking his head at Elias, the same smile on his lips. "Oh, man. How did you..."

Elias takes a long breath, in and out, and then answers, "I have a theory. I've been thinking about this a lot," he says.

Of course he has. While I've been basking in sunlight, eating brownies, and having dreams of flying. Without him.

"I don't think Ones are just Ones. I think there's, like, this hole. In the code maybe. There's a hole because there's something we could fill it with."

Daniel nods. "Keep going."

I listen just as attentively as he does. This reminds me of the talk with Mom.

"The genetic code. And the hole sends out signals to someone whose code is close to what is supposed to be filling it. Compatible Ones. Normal people — or normal Supers, I mean — would have both the powers needed. But we're not normal Supers. So our bodies are looking for another body that it can adapt to. Combine powers with, I guess."

"So she completes you? You've gone all soft, man," Daniel teases, even though his voice sounds uncertain.

Leni shuffles her feet and smiles at the ground, biting her bottom lip. I'm pretty sure that if it wasn't so dark I could see her cheeks turning bright red.

My heart rushes, but it's not from excitement. It's more panicked this time. I've known Elias for a week and a half. I am sixteen years old, and he is handsome and kind, but if someone told me that for sure he was my other half, I would throw up.

"I don't know. I suspect that another One who could make herself weightless might have this effect on me. Just like another One who pushes air or can create a pressure vortex might make Merrin fly, or another indestructible could make our girl Len into a human blowtorch."

I don't say a word. I'm trying to decide if I want to be the only One who affects him in that way. And whether I want him to be the only One who does the same for me.

Thankfully, Leni breaks the silence with a sniffle, then a short laugh. She's smiling and crying.

"Leni? Helen. You okay?" Daniel's voice is soft, concerned. He pulls the arm she's been inspecting from her hands and loops it around her neck, hugging her to him. She covers her laughing mouth with her other hand, then hiccups. She falls into him and throws her arms around his neck. His grin is so wide, probably a bigger smile than I've ever seen from him, and then he closes his eyes and turns his face into her neck.

Suddenly, I feel like I'm intruding on something. I know Elias feels the same way because he looks down at the ground and grabs my hand at the same time. For a second, the warmth of his skin distracts me, and I don't care one bit about Leni and Daniel, and then I hear Daniel say, in such a low voice, "Let's try it again."

Leni pulls back, arms still around his neck, like they're slow dancing or something. She steps back and holds both his hands in both of hers.

For the first few seconds, it's a low burn, orange-red flames snaking up their arms again. Then the flames start to get lighter and brighter and jump out from their elbows. Bright yellow flames tinged with white and blue heat shoot up three, four, five feet above them, forming wide columns in the air.

The fire roars, but above it I can hear Leni's laugh, taking on a new tone from deep in her belly. Daniel's laughing, too, and they look at each other like nothing and no one else exists in the whole world.

Elias squeezes my hand and says in my ear, "Let's get out of here."

I can't tell whether it's his warm breath or the way he says the words, but either way, I totally melt with his lips that close to my ear, especially when we're not flying, when they don't need to be.

All I can think about is how I want to take this straight to the Hub, to see if they could make it stick. Then I remind myself that my fantasies about the Hub could be just that — fantasies, stories I've been telling myself even though Mom's told me a million times they're impossible. I don't even know if the Hub has thought about Ones combining.

What I do know is that the space where my arm touches Elias's still feels charged, and the buzz that made us fly is only a small part of that. The rest is warmth, excitement. Wanting to be nearer to him.

Hundreds of bright white stars pin a black velvet curtain to the great arching dome of sky. All of a sudden, my eye catches a ripple of emerald green at the corner of the horizon.

"Elias!" I gasp, tugging at his hand. When he sees it, the biggest grin spreads across his face, and his hand wraps around mine, warm and steady.

The Northern Lights stretch and twist upward, like lazy coral, jade, and crimson flames from an impossible fire somewhere below the horizon. I clear my throat.

"It's that geomagnetic storm thing," I say. "A big solar wind — when a stream of charged particles breaks away from the Sun's gravity. When they run into the Earth's thermosphere..."

"The oxygen and nitrogen atoms de-excite at different frequencies. The unique combinations make unique colors."

"Yeah." I grin. "You're a sky geek too, huh?"

"You could say that." He laughs. We watch for a while, smiling stupidly at the Lights. "I really don't know anything more about this whole Ones combining thing than you do," he says. "But I do like you. I mean, I like being with you."

I fight to keep the corners of my mouth from turning up. I count five breaths in and out, then say, "I've wanted to fly my whole life. Dreamed about it."

"Me too. And also about being not so alone at Nelson High. So this has been a pretty good week, personally."

I start laughing, full-on laughing, even though it brings the headache back and makes my ribs ache. Before I can even think about what I'm doing, I turn and smile at him.

When our eyes meet, it's like I'm looking into his soul. I'm a goner. I reach out and grab his waist, which feels so natural now I can hardly believe it, and pull myself toward him. We alternately press our lips together and smile at each other, cheeks pushing against cheeks, until our headaches are gone, or at least forgotten.

TWELVE

The next couple of weeks fly by in a haze. Go to school. Rush through homework at lunch. Suffer through every other art class, sitting close to Elias but never close enough. Skip one every other week to fly. And kiss. And fly some more. Skip study hall every day to do the same.

The afterpain of flight is brutal at first. It's a slicing feeling, like a knife shimmying beneath the skin on my back, all the way up through my arms and neck, then a pounding in my head, and an aching heaviness. The first few days, we have to lie down to recover. After that, we just stagger a bit or have to bend over to catch our breath. After a couple of weeks, it's like shaking off a trip and a skinned knee. Elias thinks that whatever makes the powers of Ones work together forces our bodies to grow and stretch — maybe even all the way down to the genes. I've studied some stuff on epigenetics, the adaptability of existing genes for in-generation evolution, and that makes sense to me. The fact that the pain lessens each time is proof, at least in my head.

I can't remember the last time I've been pissed off. I haven't slammed a door in weeks. I shuttle Michael and Max to soccer practice without complaining because most of the time Elias sits in the front seat next to me. I play the drums sometimes — the ones in my garage, if I don't mind Elias standing there looking at me. If I want him to play, we hang out in the VanDyne concert hall, but when we do that I normally play slower, softer, so I can hear him play, too. Now it's happiness driving the sticks instead of anger.

Over the next few weeks, I scan the news feed every morning for any information about what they're doing at the Hub. When nothing about Fisk shows up for a while, my eyes perk up at anything that could refer to the internship — an experiment, a new hire, the gap program...anything.

But after so many weeks of him showing up on the front page at the beginning of the year, nothing does now.

I meet with Mr. Hoffman twice a week during lunch. I never hear him enter the library, and he always slips out again without anyone else noticing.

All this time, I never get an official communication from the Hub. Not one. I ask questions, try to clarify things. Mr. Hoffman tells me that everything is under wraps, that what we're doing still isn't official. That even exactly what *they're* doing at the gap program, for the Supers only, isn't public, and that the board barely approved that.

The exercises seem pointless, at first — more organic chem problems to work, more models to build, more theoretical situations to run each molecule through. What would its characteristics be in the various spectra: Mass spectrometry? UV? IR? NMR? I jot down the answers faster than Mr. Hoffman can get new questions to me, with such intense concentration my fingers ache from holding the stylus so tightly.

Late summer turns into fall, and by early October, we're solidly into hot chocolate and hayride season.

When I finally get sick of flying over fields, now mostly harvested, we go to Lincoln Park and fly there after closing hours. It's small, but the blur of red and orange and yellow and green from the trees takes my breath away. When the sky dims to a dark enough blue for twinkling pinholes to cover it, I tilt my head back and try to count the stars, knowing I never can, reveling in how luxurious it feels.

I let Mom take me shopping and buy lots of cute sweaters and fitted jeans, swinging skirts and tights. I can tell she wants to ask if this is about a boy. I know she knows it's about Elias. Mom and Dad tell each other everything. But she never does ask about him, and because of that, it's not annoying to be around her, because I'm happy and she's not meddling. For the first time in my life, I can just be with Mom.

I still practice my One. Now, instead of imagining only weightlessness, I also think of Elias, of being with him, when the buzz is strongest. It's when there's tension between us — the delicious kind of tension, like when he's going to kiss me, which is amazing, or when he's going to grab me and shoot off into the sky, tugging and lifting me until I catch the buzz and fly along with him.

Now, instead of just floating, I drift a little, so slightly that it might be the wind.

One night, we walk from my car in his driveway to the edge of our cornfield, silently, like we always do when we know we're about to fly.

"What's the backpack for?" I ask.

"Surprise." Elias bends down to kiss the top of my head, breathing in deeply.

"Why are you always doing that?" My voice sounds annoyed, but I lean into him. In the couple weeks Elias and I have been together, he's learned to read my body language instead of my voice. Thankfully. It means he understands me. I'm getting a little better at it, too — understanding myself.

"Um. I like how you smell?" He stands up, looks to the side, and smirks.

I stick my elbow straight out to the side and hit his ribs. "Weird."

"I mean, your shampoo. Your hair always smells so good. And since your head is, like, pretty much at my smell level…"

"Shut up," I say softly, floating up to his height and grabbing his face in my hands, slamming a kiss on his mouth. Even my One is good for something with Elias around.

He wraps his arms around my waist without having to bend down, and the noise he makes leaves my lips tingly. Then he pulls back so his lips move against mine when he talks. "Whenever you're ready."

When he buries his face in my neck, I catch the buzz, and we shoot up into the sky, toward Historic Superior. He pushes the air much more strongly than I can, and he almost always controls the trajectory.

When I realize how close we're getting to town, I yell, "Are you crazy?"

He grins. "Everyone's at Homecoming," he reminds me.

"Go Raiders," I say, smiling.

Everyone's at the big football game, including Leni,

who's cheering, and Daniel, who will go to watch Leni cheer even though he hates football and revelry and painted faces and general high school happiness of any kind. No one will notice us soaring around old town Superior. We're supposed to be at the game, too, actually. Lying to my parents about what we're doing is second nature now, but I rationalize that on any given night we're not doing anything that regular teenagers wouldn't do — calculus homework, sharing an ice cream cone, making out in a cornfield.

Except for the flying. The flying is not normal.

If Mr. Hoffman hadn't already brought the Hub to me in the Nelson High library, my first reaction would have been to bring this straight to them. But Elias doesn't suggest that we tell anyone, and his dad works there. I don't know who's supposed to know what — all I know is that I want to keep flying with Elias, I want to keep my application for the internship intact, and I don't know if anyone finding out about the flying would ruin that. So, even though we never talk about it, neither of us tells anyone about the flying either.

It's weird, a bit laborious, to haul the backpack with us. Unexpectedly so, but as I think about it, we're just a couple of floating, air-pushing kids. So it's basically like we've run three miles holding that pack, with only Elias's muscle to back it up.

My mind puts it all together — backpack, Homecoming night, not telling me where we're flying. He's been planning this for a while. A vague sensation scuttles along my shoulders, setting the hairs at the back of my neck on end. It's worry, something I haven't felt with Elias since that night at his house when he wanted to give me the tour. I had to figure out what he really wanted, whether it was really okay to be alone with him. For the first time since then, I feel it again. It kills me. I don't want to feel that way about Elias.

We land on the roof of one of the historic houses. If we look out to one side we can see old Superior, but if we turn around we see the fields, the sky above them dripping with colors, so bright they're almost unreal. The silhouettes of some old phone poles reach, spindly and graceful, into the watercolor backdrop.

"Which way to do you want to sit?" Elias asks.

"Do you have to ask?" I grin as I fight to still the trembling in my knees. This time it's not from the aftereffects of flying. I place my hands gingerly on the shingles below me and settle down, sitting Indian-style, tucking my skirt around my legs. "Away from Superior."

Elias smiles, a little sadly, I think, though I can't understand why. "Of course." He unzips the backpack and sits down next to me.

Then he snakes his hand up along my shoulders and down the back of my neck, all the way to the base of my spine. His long fingers clutch at my waist, and his lips press against the sensitive skin just below my ear, then my collarbone. Electricity skitters through me and ties my stomach into knots. For the past few weeks, I've been working under the assumption that Elias is different from other boys. But when a boy takes you on a mystery date and the two of you are all alone, it means something, doesn't it? Means he wants something, the thought of which still reminds me of Sean Cooper, standing over me in the hallway last year.

Being with Elias, really *being* with him, would be just as close as flying but wholly different. My stomach twists. I honestly can't tell whether it's from anticipation or apprehension. I try to remind myself how much I love being with him, how he makes my heart race when I so much as see him walking toward me in the hallway. I close my eyes and try to lose myself in the breathtaking burnt orange of the sky and the warmth of this boy. I try to tamp down the fear rising in my chest. I want, more than anything, to remember how he's always made me feel — like I am absolutely perfect and exactly what he wants, just the way I am.

I want to because I know he wants me, and I know I want him, and I don't know what the big deal is. I want to, but no matter how hard I try, I can't.

I do know one thing for sure — I've never felt afraid with Elias, and I don't want to start now.

He holds my face in his hands, and his fingers push through my hair. When the wind blows against my face, I breathe in, trying to center myself.

This is okay. This is perfect. This is Elias. He would never hurt me.

His lips part mine, and I deepen the kiss, pushing my chest against his. I try to concentrate on how sweet he tastes and how he makes me feel — like I'm the only person in the whole world.

But a second later, he moves his hand down my side and under my shirt, his palm hot against my skin, his thumb pressing into my ribs. He leans us back against the slope of the roof. There's no breeze now; there's only heat, engulfing my whole body.

Completely overwhelming me.

When his fingers move just under the waistband of my skirt and he kisses the hollow of my throat with insistent lips, I push my palms against his chest, just hard enough to get him to stop.

"What — what are we doing?"

He pulls back and crinkles his eyebrows, a slight smile on his face. "We're watching the sunset."

"No, I mean…" I sit up. Now that I'm looking down at him, I feel stronger. "What do you *want* us to be doing?"

My lip starts to tremble, and tears threaten to spill from my eyes. His expression softens, and he cradles my face in his hand, reaching up to wipe a single escaping tear with his thumb.

"This is okay, right?" he asks and sits up next to me when more tears roll down my cheeks. "Mer? What's up?"

I tell him all about last year's incident in the hallway. When I mention the bruises, he stiffens and shakes his head, glaring off into the distance. His grasp on my waist becomes protective, and he draws me close to his side, hugging me there until the tears stop.

"But this is okay," I finish, looking up into his waiting eyes. "This is different."

Elias gives me another gentle kiss. "This," he says, "is just you and me and whatever both of us are one hundred percent comfortable with. And, it's dinner."

Elias pulls cheddar cheese and crackers, some slices of tart green apples, and a loaf of bread out of the backpack. My shoulders relax, and I know that I'll never worry about anything like that with Elias ever again.

"Come on. Dinner's getting cold."

I laugh at that because it was always cold. "You know I don't eat any of that junk anyway," I say, and he nods, leans forward, reaches into the bag.

"Which is why I brought these." He brandishes two jars, one with hot fudge and one with caramel topping. "These should at least make the apples edible for you."

"Oh, don't underestimate me," I say, reaching for the caramel. "Now I can eat the bread, too."

He laughs and makes himself an apple-and-cheddar sandwich, then leans back on the roof. I sit forward, seeing how high I can push the caramel-to-bread ratio, and we gaze at the deepening colors of the sunset together.

"Basketball starts soon," I say. Elias has already been in practice most school nights and half of Saturday, just enough time to force me to spend my free hours with Michael and Max and sometimes Leni and Daniel, too. Enough to keep me from being that girl who everyone thinks is obsessed with her boyfriend.

He sighs. "Yeah. Weekend away games. Tournaments. And, uh...my dad set up some private coaching for me, too."

I can't read his expression at that last one. "Are you hiding, like, some secondary One that makes you awesome at basketball? That you're not telling me about?" I tease, trying to hide my sadness that our weekends together are pretty much going to be gone between basketball and homework. Trying to make it sound like I'm not curious about the private sessions.

He sits up and looks at me, right into my eyes. "I would never hide anything from you. Over the last few weeks... You're my best friend here. My best friend ever. I'm so glad you transferred to Nelson, so glad I found you. Mer, I..." But then he trails off and stares at his hands, shakes his head like he's frustrated.

My heart races again because part of me knew what he was going to say, what he decided not to say. A peace floods me because I know it, but I don't have to deal with it. Not yet.

I don't know what I would say back.

"Me too," I say. Nelson High would suck without him. I don't let a second of dead air pass because neither of us wants it. "I'm so glad you refused to quit stalking me."

He smiles, takes my hand, squeezes it, and leans in to kiss me, softly, teasing me with the combination of his nearness and distance. I turn toward him, swing my leg over, and settle myself on his lap, facing him. He holds his hand a few inches from my face, and a pretty good puff of air comes from it and brushes my hair out of my eyes, away from my lips.

"Showoff," I say. I grab his hands, which he's still

keeping carefully outside my shirt, and remove them. He looks at me with one eyebrow up, and I float up and away from him. The wind takes me backwards, and I check that there's still roof below me. I don't want to make him jump off to get me or anything.

"Yes, I get it." Elias rolls his eyes, grinning. "You're very impressive, too, Miss One."

I smile back, but something twinges in my heart. I know I'm still a One, but something about being with Elias has always made me forget it. I don't need anyone to remind me, especially not him.

He stretches his arms up toward me, his smile softening. "Now come back down to me before I have to make camp up here for the night and call someone to get me down in the morning." His fingers curl in, beckoning me, and weirdly, the wind blows in another direction now, bringing me right to him when I let myself descend.

He draws me close. The feel of his arms against mine makes my skin warm all over, and when he buries his face in my neck and breathes hot against it, I feel warm on the inside, too.

The rest of the bread and apples roll down the steep slope of the roof for the birds and ants to eat tomorrow. Elias kisses my eyelids, my nose, and I let my head fall back so he can kiss my throat, too. We sit there for a long while, kissing eyes and lips and ears and necks, until he squeezes me against him, his signal that we're going to take off. And we do, and it's perfect, and maybe better than it was the night before.

Mr. Hoffman and I have been meeting for months now. Slowly, it's changed from me doing lots of written work to him quizzing me orally. He drills me on theories about mutations, which gene components match up with which, which chemicals and treatments would push further mutation. When we talk about these things, especially, my arms and legs fidget with excitement. During these sessions, the words I want so badly to say sit on the tip of my tongue. *I know, firsthand. Elias and I can fly. We're Ones who have been Seconded.*

As amazing as Elias is, though, he can't give me the Hub. He can give me some of what I've always wanted, but not all of it. Flying around Nebraska with my high school boyfriend is fine, but what happens when we have to grow up, want to go to work, make a difference?

I want to know how it works — the One-plus-One-equals-Super mystery. I want to figure out what it is about Elias and me that makes us work together, makes us absorb each other's powers so seamlessly. I've always wanted to find out about the Oneness, and this adds a whole new layer, a whole new mystery.

A hundred years ago a kid in my position would have raided my parents' files from work or some books they had lying around. But no one's had paper books or files for decades, and my parents always have their readers with them. Even if I could snag one, they're password-protected, especially the work stuff. I'm sure there are some really old books on what I'm looking for somewhere, but they've got to be locked down at the Hub.

Freshman year, they took our class on a field trip there, but I pretended I was sick that day. I couldn't stand to look at it and know that I could never really see it — not the parts I cared about, anyway.

The whole time I meet with Mr. Hoffman — doing pointless exercises; answering rapid-fire questions; staying up so late working the exercises he's given me that I fall asleep in English class and yawn on walks with Elias; keeping everything from my parents; and worse, keeping it from Elias — one thought keeps piercing my mind. This is how I'm going to do it. This is how I'm going to get there. And the one comfort in the whole thing (or the rationalization — I don't know which is which anymore) is that when I get there, I'm going to take Elias with me.

And we're going to be the first Ones who get fixed.

THIRTEEN

That night, Elias and I head to his house after school and basketball. Elias hops in the shower while Mrs. VanDyne feeds me some kind of Chinese food dish that I suspect she's asked Rosie to doctor to make it healthier. She talks to me about my classes and my grades, what books I've been reading, what TV I've been watching, but she never asks any questions about Elias and me. Good form, Mrs. VanDyne.

Unfortunately, I don't have such tact. "I haven't seen...uh, Mr. VanDyne around here. Like, ever," I say between bites.

She smiles, exactly the same sad smile Elias has. "He's preparing for the Symposium, dear. Being the Vice President and all... I thought Elias would have mentioned it."

"Elias isn't really one to brag. About anything."

A fondness sweeps over her face. "No, he isn't. Well, anyway, Andrew is the Vice President of the Hub and oversees experimental operations. Between the Symposium and keeping an eye on the girls after hours, he's been working quite a lot." Her gaze sweeps over the rest of the house, which is, as usual, dark except for the kitchen and her office off the corner of the living room area.

She nods toward my plate, clean after two huge helpings — her plan to get some nutrition into me worked, but not unnoticed — and I say, "Thanks." She takes it away and turns to put it in the sterilizer, saying, "Speaking of Elias, he seemed very…happy after your class met to see the Northern Lights. Did you four make some earth-shattering discovery or something?"

I look at her curiously. Maybe he said something to her about the flying. With his dad being Vice President of the Hub and all…

"Did Elias tell you what we can do?" I ask, scrunching my eyebrows together.

"What you can *do?*"

"Yeah. We figured out that if we stand close together…"

"The image from the radio telescope looks different to each of us," Elias's voice interrupts from the other side of the kitchen.

"Oh," his mom says, as if she was only half paying attention to begin with. "Very interesting."

He strides up to me and takes my hand in his. "Thanks for waiting around for this long. What did Mom do to you?"

"Horrible things," I say. "She fed me lo mein. But I think it was whole wheat. Right, Rosie?"

"No, Merrin," Rosie responds.

I narrow my eyes. "What were those noodles made of then?"

"Technically, they were a sixty percent wheat blend."

"She got you there." Elias laughs, but it sounds hollow. "We've got a bunch of calc to finish up, Mom. Can I take a plate of that back with me?"

"Rosie already made one up for you." She hands it to him, and he leans in to kiss her on the cheek.

"Oh! I almost forgot," she says as we turn toward Elias's room. "From the twins." She hands him a long white envelope addressed to him by hand.

I wrinkle my nose. "Snail mail?"

"They're not giving any of the gap year participants computer access, not yet," she explains.

When we reach Elias's room, I whisper to Elias through tight lips, "What gives? Why didn't you want me to tell your mom? About the flying?"

Elias smiles down at me, and this is one I've never seen. Some cross between genuine and faking it. Tense and strange. He shrugs.

"I don't know. We don't really know what's going on, you know? Why it even works." His voice is even weirder

— the tone is assertive, but the words are not. "And I kind of wanted it to be just ours, I guess. For now."

"Just ours" is something I understand. Keeping secrets as delicious as ours makes sense to me, in a way. So I nod slowly, say, "Okay."

"Besides," he says, pulling me close to him, his scent distracting me for a split second, "we don't want them to mess it up."

"Them who?"

He shrugs and plunks down in his desk chair, turning his attention to opening the letter. Clearly he doesn't want to talk about this.

I fall backward on his bed, doing a quarter-turn to bury my face in his pillow. I know my expression shows how upset I am, even though his explanation makes sense to me, I guess. I don't want him to see it. I try to think of something that makes me happy. Flying over a field with Elias, the wind whipping through my hair. The burning recedes from my chest a bit.

Then I remember I didn't practice a damn thing that day, power-wise. I go light, levitating over the bed. Here in his room with his scent, I can imagine what it would be like right next to him, without him holding on to me. It feels awesome, being completely untethered to anything and anyone. Even *imagining* it. I can almost hear the slap of tree branches whipping by and the sound of cars or animals or people or whatever is around, distorted by my motion.

Elias murmurs, "Hey, Floating Beauty," and pecks me on the lips.

My eyes snap open, and I shriek, plunk down onto the bed, and slap at him playfully. He interrupted my daydream and scared the crap out of me.

He sits down, puts a hand on either side of my face, closes his eyes, and kisses me properly, slow and lingering for a few seconds, then pulls away with a satisfied, "Mmmmm."

"Me too," I say, and he smiles.

He glances at the time on his cuff. "You've gotta get out of here in a few," he says, bringing his lips to mine again, the intensity of his kiss not matching his words.

I sit up next to him and swing my legs over the side of the bed because I am dangerously close to offering to hide under the covers until lights-out time. And as much as that idea attracts me, I know I'd probably just have another Homecoming night-style freak out and embarrass the both of us.

I stand up, and Elias does, too, slinging his bag onto his desk. I step into my shoes, and Elias shrugs out of his sweatshirt, handing it to me. "Got cold out there, Mer."

I roll my eyes. "Yeah, and the drive home is so long."

My collection of Elias sweatshirts, nightgown-length on me and used for just that purpose, grows by the week.

I pull the sweatshirt down over my head and smooth the static from my hair. "What'd your sisters have to say?"

His face falls, but then he gives me a smile. The sad one again, with a hint of worry. The faking-it one.

"What is it?" I ask.

"Oh, nothing."

"Elias. I haven't known you for that long, but I know that look."

He eyes me for a minute, then says, "The girls and I thought security might be tight at the Hub. We were right. No internet, no TV, no calls. So...it's an inside joke." He holds the paper out toward me and points at something on the back corner.

I lean in to read the tiny, perfect cursive writing, which does not match the print on the other side. I read aloud, "Doris locked. You've got to break it down." I look back up at him. "What the hell?"

"Inside joke. Uh, knock-knock joke," he says, taking off his glasses and pressing the heel of his hand against his right eye. "Knock, knock. Who's there? Doris. Doris who? Doris locked, that's why I'm knocking."

I still look at him, one eyebrow in the air. "Is that supposed to be funny?"

He smiles. "It was always kind of our code. Because they can teleport in, you know? So if they wanted to let me know they were coming in, it would be, 'Doris locked, but I'm coming in.' Or whatever. They're the ones who started the joke a few letters back, in little writing like this, on the flipside of the paper. Barely caught it the first time. And now…this answer…I don't know. Worries me. That's all."

I want this look on his face to go away. His love for his sisters is coated in worry, and I want to make it go away. I walk a few steps to him, stand on tiptoes, and tug on his arm so he'll bend down to kiss me. He does, but it's distant, distracted.

"I'm sure they're fine. Just want a visit, probably. Right? And you'll see them soon at the Symposium."

"Yeah." He forces another smile. If he thinks he's getting away with that without me noticing, he either thinks I'm stupid — and I know he doesn't — or he doesn't realize how much I care about him.

He glances at his cuff again and then pulls me toward him by the waist for another hug. I squeeze his hand and smile at him as he walks me down the hall and out the front door. But instead of smiling back at me, he trains his eyes on the horizon. He's not normally this quiet — doesn't usually focus on anything but me, kissing me goodbye.

"You okay?" I finally ask.

"Oh. Um, yeah. Just preoccupied."

"About what? The girls?"

"No. I mean, yeah. But…"

"What? What's going on?" I search his face.

"The other night we…uh… The police came to my house."

My breath catches in my chest. "Why?"

"The local police found my backpack, Mer. From Homecoming night. Still on that roof we landed on."

"How did they even know…?"

"I had an old flash drive in there with my name on it. Stupid. Anyway, they brought it to the house and talked to my dad because he's my dad, you know, VP at the Hub and all, and they didn't want to press charges against me."

"Okay. So what's the big deal?"

"They thought I was climbing it, you know, vandalizing it. But they…they don't know."

"About your One?"

Elias nods.

"Okay. So?"

"So my dad does. And he's still watching me to see when I'll develop that second power. He's been dying for it to manifest for the last 10 years. And now he thinks this is it."

"So…maybe this *is* it, Elias. Maybe this is our chance to…"

"No," Elias says, his mouth set in a hard line. He shakes his head quickly, then stares into my eyes. "No, we're not telling them about you."

"What's the big deal, Elias? We're amazing. Maybe they could figure us out, you know? Why we work. Maybe they could…"

Maybe they could fix us.

He shakes his head to each side sharply. "I don't…" He trails off for a second, looks off in the distance. "I don't know what's going on with Nora and Lia. I haven't heard from them for a while, until now. I don't know if what's going on over there is good. And until I know…" He draws me to him, squeezing me tightly to him.

"You don't want them to know about me."

"I don't want them to know about you." He nods and presses a kiss to the top of my head.

A burning acidic feeling creeps around my stomach and floods my chest. Elias is worried about me being at the Hub, the one place I've always wanted to go, where Mr. Hoffman thinks I belong.

Elias rubs my upper arms, whispers, "I'll deal with it. I promise. Don't worry about it, okay?"

The warmth of his words tamps the burning down and makes my heart jump in the way that reminds me that, at least for now, he's more important than all that.

I get in my car to head home, and Elias bends down to toss his sweatshirt on my lap and kiss me while I put my seatbelt on. He shuts the door for me while I start the car, turns, then looks over his shoulder and flashes me that dimple and wink. But I can't shake the memory of the cloudiness to his eyes instead of the sparkle I love.

FOURTEEN

Frost has started to decorate the Nebraska grass overnight, and Elias is deep in practices and private coaching now. Personally, I think it's weird, and he doesn't seem too excited about it. But I think I know what's going on. It's hard for Ones to find a way to fit in and especially hard to figure out how to make our parents happy. Especially if they have crazy kickass twin Supersibs.

God knows the closest I ever got to appeasing Mom and Dad was driving Michael and Max to practice, getting out of the house, and accepting the transfer to Nelson without a fight. And if I didn't like Elias so much, they'd be getting an earful about that, too, because these holo-lectures that pass as classes at Nelson are so boring they make me want to crawl out of my own skin.

So if this makes his dad happy, if it's their thing together, then I'm not going to argue. Especially since working with the coach more often was part of the deal after Elias admitted to climbing that roof. Scaling historic buildings and not using a Super to do it pissed his dad off twice as much, and Elias picked extra hours in practice over being grounded. I think he's nuts — I'd rather spend time alone in my room than do a forced workout any day

— until he reminded me that he could stop by to see me on his way home from coaching.

It's early November now, and we're in the few weeks between autumn soccer and winter soccer for Michael and Max. Instead of going to practice, they've been spending a couple hours three nights a week at the Hub. I kind of freaked out when I first found out because they're just kids. They deserve a break, and whatever they have them doing at the Hub has them coming home even more exhausted than soccer. But Mom explained that they're starting the period of adolescence where Supers see the most dramatic changes, and they're just going for checkups and testing of their abilities.

I wouldn't know about that stuff. I was never an adolescent with a Super.

I'm hanging out at our house with the twins today since Elias is in another private coaching session anyway and has no idea when he'd be back. I watch them closely because they dragged an awful lot when they came home yesterday and had pretty big bandages on each arm. Blood tests, Mom said. They both collapsed into bed, which is strange for them.

But today, they're mostly their normal selves. Compared to yesterday, "mostly normal" is good enough for me.

The three of us spread out on our worn brown sectional, each of us curving against a different part of it under throw blankets. I balance my reader on my lap and tap more organic chem models into shape on my tablet.

Some stupid cartoon show where the characters knock each other over the heads with stuff and make farting jokes blares on the TV. Max snorts, sniggers, and pops cheese balls into his mouth. Michael is absorbed with something on his tablet, and knowing him, there's an equal chance that it's a stupid game or some classic literature he's plowing through at the speed of light. The only reason that Mom and Dad are more impressed with Max's super and not his IQ is that mine is still way higher than his.

I reach over into Michael's bowl, grab a cheese ball, and throw it at Max's head.

"Whatcha doin', nerdface?" I ask.

"Reading," he says and locates the cheeseball, which bounced down and wedged itself under his leg. He pops it in his mouth for a second, takes it out, and lobs it back at me. I raise up my blanket and deflect it onto the floor.

"You are gross, Max," I say, brushing my fingertips over my hair to remove invisible drool that didn't fall there.

He shrugs and flashes a grin. "You called me nerdface. Besides, what you're doing is way nerdier. Who reads textbooks that aren't for class?"

I stick out my tongue and glare at him. He sticks his tongue back out at me and goes back to his book.

There's a knock at the door, and I sit up straight, rubbing my lips together. Too late for a delivery guy, too frigid for door-to-door salesmen. It's got to be Elias. I check the clock — 8:15 — still an hour before he has to go home.

Mom strides down the hallway to open the door. From the looks of her, she's almost as excited to see Elias as I am — we try to avoid parents at all costs, with our limited hang out time, and she barely ever sees him.

Elias's voice floats down the hallway. "Good evening, Mrs. Grey."

"Come on in, Elias. Can I get you anything? Something hot?"

"Yeah, that would actually be good. Some coffee?"

"If you don't mind the dregs."

"Thanks."

By this time, I've sat up and run my fingers through my hair, trying to smooth it.

"Yeah, Merrin, better try to look nice for your boyfriend." Michael draws out the last word, and I roll my eyes and kick him under his blanket.

"'Try' is the best she'll be able to do," Max cracks, and

I glare at him before looking down to straighten my shirt.

Elias strides in and stands behind the couch over my head. I look up and back at him, grinning. He pulls his glasses off to wipe off the steam that formed there from coming into the warm house so quickly, and my heart stutters at seeing his eyes, open and bare, the way I normally only see them when we fly.

"Hey," I say, my voice way different than it was when I was yelling at my brothers. Lighter and softer. Just like I feel when he's around.

He puts one of his huge hands on either side of my head and bends down to kiss the top of it from behind, then strides along the back of the couch and peers down at Max's reader.

"Ah, awesome, man. Classic."

Max beams. He ruffs Max's hair, and the adoration on Max's face is plain. He nods like Elias has just spoken the Gospel, and he's hearing it for the first time.

Elias sits on the floor in the center of the semicircle the couch makes. Does he look thinner? It's hard to tell when he's got such a huge sweatshirt on. But he's definitely pale, and big bags carve out dark circles under his eyes. Mom comes in with the coffee, in a travel mug of course — can't risk staining the carpet — and Elias smiles at her gratefully.

When she walks out, he leans in toward me, lowering his voice and waggling his eyebrows like a conspirator. "I've got a surprise for you."

Michael groans. "Aw, we're leaving. Don't wanna be here for this."

"I'm not gonna kiss her, doofus," Elias says, finding a cheese ball on the carpet and lobbing it at Michael's head this time. "Surprise for all of you." He pushes some buttons on his cuff, and mine beeps. "Check it," he says, smiling.

I push up my sleeve and read the message scrolling across my wrist. "The Biotech Symposium?" I shriek, launching myself off the couch and into Elias's lap, throwing my arms around his neck. "How did you…"

"Dad's VP, remember? He got me five tickets to give to whoever I want. So that's you, Leni and Dan, and…"

"My brothers," I say, shaking my head and giving him a soft smile.

The Hub hosts a Symposium every two years where it rolls out all the new Biotech achievements. It's for Supers only, and mostly only adult ones. Officials and insiders. The part that the press and general public gets invited to — what these tickets are for — is a two-day affair, super fancy. Even though Mom and Dad work there, us kids have never been, and me and Max are geeky enough to be really excited.

Max fidgets where he sits, grinning. He's got to be totally psyched for this. Michael couldn't care less, I know, but he's no impolite kid, not by a longshot.

"Thanks, Elias," he says.

"Yeah, man. No problem," Elias says, but he keeps his gaze fixed on me.

I lean in to kiss Elias. Can't help it. Retching noises fill the room in dual surround-sound, and Michael says, "Now we're really getting out of here."

I wave them off behind Elias's back, mid-kiss. After a couple minutes of that, I draw back.

"Wanna...you know?" I make the swooping motion with my hand. "You could use one of my dad's coats," I say, shivering when I move my hands over his back and feel how cold his sweatshirt still is from being outside. Thinking about the Symposium energized me. I want to fly, even though I know the grass outside seizes with frost and the sun went down long ago. We'd probably get frostbite.

"Nah," Elias says, wrapping his fingers around my waist. "Less than an hour till I have to go. I just want to see you."

I peel myself off his lap and get back on the couch, pulling the blanket up and patting the space next to me. The same stupid cartoon still blares in the background, but

I don't care enough to change the channel.

We sit there, cuddled up together, and he stretches his arm across my shoulders and plays with my hair. He presses his nose to the side of my head and breathes in deeply like always.

Mom walks down the hallway, clears her throat way louder than normal, and says, "Just keep the lights on, kids."

Elias turns around, grabbing the couch back with both hands to show Mom where they are without making her ask anything embarrassing. "I've gotta be home by 9:30 anyway, Mrs. Grey."

"Good to see you here, Elias," she says and walks up the stairs.

I sink further down into the couch cushions and slap my palm to my forehead. "Sorry about that," I mutter.

Elias sinks his body down too, harder for him because he's so tall. I pull the blanket up over our heads, and we are in a world of our own making, one I never want to leave. We talk and kiss and laugh, and Elias sneaks his hand around my waist, under my shirt this time, and I don't shake or get nervous at all. I love it, all of it, being this warm and close to him. He kisses my eyelids, behind my ears, and my lips, lingering there for awhile.

"You make everything else go away," he says, and I

figure school or basketball was pretty stressful today, so I just put my hand on the side of his face and look at him as sweetly as I can manage.

We stay there so long that Elias has to speed home and call me on the way just to say "Goodnight" one more time.

Today's session with Mr. Hoffman is different. Finally, something other than chem. Mr. Hoffman's taking a vial of my blood so I can look at it under the microscope. He wants to talk about genes and knows me so well that he can tell I'm dying to see my own.

I wince and take in a sharp breath through my teeth as the lancet bites into the skin of my index finger. It's not the pain that bugs me. It's picturing that tiny needle attacking me at the click of a button.

He pulls out a slide and some solution while I set up the microscope he brought for the purpose. I run my hands over its surface, distracted by the high-tech brilliance, when he says, "You and Elias are together a lot."

I nod, slowly. He hasn't brought up Elias, hasn't talked to me about anything but chem, since that first day.

Suddenly, Mr. Hoffman looks up from preparing the slide. "Why do you spend so much time with that boy, Merrin?"

I sit up straight, removing my hands from the scope.

"Well, I…" I clear my throat. "He's my boyfriend, Mr. Hoffman. I thought you knew that." It feels weird to refer to Elias that way since we never defined our relationship as "talking" or "going out" or "together." We've always just been "us."

"And yet you don't go to many school activities together."

"We're…uh…we're both quiet," I say in a rush. "We like to hang out at home, I guess." I would tell him what we've really been doing in our free time. I would. I want to. Every cell in my body wants to get closer to the Hub, and I know this is the way to do it.

But the way he looks at me, his eyes burning, prying, desperate — it's not okay. And I know it's not okay to tell Mr. Hoffman from the Hub about us, about what we can do. Not here, not like this. Not without Elias next to me. This is the one thing about meeting with Mr. Hoffman I would have to tell him.

After all, he is half of it. Half of us.

Mr. Hoffman prepares a second slide with the last of the blood from the tiny vial and slips it in his bag.

"What's that for?" I ask. I swear the twisting in my stomach makes my words waver.

"The last piece of your application."

"You need my blood for me to work there?"

"Well, yes, of course. It's for security, among other things."

I laugh, and my stomach stops twisting so much. They can do twenty different tests for drugs if they want. I slide the stylus back into the side of my tablet and start packing up to go.

"Do you...love him?" Mr. Hoffman asks.

My heart seizes in my chest. I don't know if it's because of the question or the way he asked it, but I suddenly want to get out of there, more than I've wanted to get out of anywhere in my life. Even more than that summer morning in the kitchen with Mom and Dad when they told me about the transfer to Nelson.

"I...I have to go," I mumble and start shoving stuff in my bag.

"I'm glad you've applied for the internship, Merrin. Glad you've been able to keep this quiet. You could help a lot of people by being at the Hub, Merrin. People like me."

I catch my breath. "What? You're a..."

He nods, sitting back, a small, sad smile forming on his lips. "I'm a One."

I throw my bag over my shoulder and stand up abruptly, making the chair shudder as it tries to slide along the carpet. Some combination of Mr. Hoffman having kept that from me, the secret meetings, and the slide with my blood on it makes even his Oneness irrelevant. He's gone too far, creeped me out too much, for me to care about even that commonality between us.

"Thank you," I say over my shoulder on the way out. Tears burn at my eyes. I'm glad the application is complete now because I don't think I could bring myself to go back to studying with him.

FIFTEEN

About half an hour's drive out into the cornfields of Nebraska lies a 100- acre plot of land on which nothing but tall grass grows. It waves unassumingly against the graying November sky. The hawks still circle above, waiting to pounce on any mice that have delayed going into hibernation.

The Hub is a city underneath it all.

"It's completely subterranean for a couple of reasons," Dad explains as we drive through the endless parking-garage-style ramps to the entrance, mostly to Michael and Max because I'm so obsessed with Hub that I've known this for years. "One is for security. Even if Nebraska was struck by a nuclear bomb — highly unlikely in the first place because not many people know exactly where the Hub is — it wouldn't have much, if any, impact on the structure and lab materials."

"Nuclear bombs. Awesome," Michael mutters from the back seat, and I reach over to smack him. Mom rolls her eyes.

"The other reason," Dad raises his volume, and I know he wants the boys to hear this one, "is for subtlety's sake. There's been a lot of money and time poured into this place, and we've come up with some amazing discoveries. But we're not here to brag. Gifted individuals are no more important or valuable than anyone else. It's important that we all remember that."

I try to imagine what kind of building the Hub must be that, if it were built above ground on the Nebraska plains, would intimidate anyone enough for them to get angry.

A security booth at the entrance scans our cuffs, electronically bleating out "Verified: Grey" or "Verified: VanDyne" for each of the tickets that have been programmed there.

When we park, the garage is just that — a garage, like in the airport or the hospital or any other place. I itch at the button on my cuff, impatient to get out and see the Hub. And hopefully see Elias, sooner rather than later.

We squeeze into an elevator and lurch up a few floors. I brush some lint off the black suit pants Mom made me wear and roll my ankle toward the outside of the black, pointy-toed pumps she handed me to go with it. The elevator dings, and we step out into the hugest, whitest, most glowing room I've ever seen.

Everything shines with its slickness, from the tiles to the walls. A solid white ceiling stretches down the wide corridor almost as far as I can see, and it's tiled with rectangular fluorescent lights lined up in perfect diagonal rows.

"Welcome to the Biotech Hub Symposium," a Hub worker greets us. "This is the center room, where we'll be having the resources fair. Check out what's available for the average Super and our scientists out there." He turns and motions toward the stages. "On either end, we'll have demonstrations.

"The Symposium schedule is programmed into your cuffs, and you'll need to scan into each section of the building. Different clearance levels for each participant. You understand. They're on high alert with so many non-personnel here."

My heart sinks. I knew, of course, I wouldn't be seeing the whole Hub. I guess I just didn't think about it. But something in me knows that this might be the last chance I get, especially since I ditched Mr. Hoffman and haven't heard from him since. All the formulas and equations and experiments of this place have been calling me since I was little. Ever since I wanted to be more than a One.

"Thank you," Dad says to the worker and turns back to us. "Now, go anywhere, do anything you want. Anything you're *allowed* to do, which I think..." He checks his schedule. "...is pretty much just the resources fair today. And a few demos."

He clears his throat. "No leaving the Hub without us, obviously. You can text us as you normally would, so no excuses for anything. Meet back here at 4:00, boys, so we can take you home before the dinner, and so Merrin can go with Mom to change."

Dad turns to me. "Merrin? You are staying here until the end of the dinner. You can ride home with Elias, but you must let us know if that's what you're doing, and you must go straight home. So you let us know when you're getting in the car and when you arrive at the front door."

I roll my eyes, thinking how if Elias and I really wanted to spend some alone time in the house, a requirement for texting wouldn't prevent that. At all.

But I smile and say, "Sure, Dad."

Mom gives us all hugs, seeming even more distant than usual, and hurries off to wherever she needs to be. Dad gives me a hug and walks off, too, and the boys start buzzing around the tables, checking everything out.

I stand by myself, Supers spilling in all around me, and the energy of this place is so intense, I want to close my eyes and breathe it all in. So I do. I must look like an idiot, but I don't care.

A hand rests on either side of my waist. Elias.

I turn, and he's in a dark gray suit with a white shirt, no tie, the top button undone. My heart drops into my stomach. I thought he looked good in his hoodies and jeans, but clearly I hadn't imagined all the possibilities thoroughly enough.

"Uh," I manage before he sweeps me into a bear hug.

"Excited?" he asks, grinning down at me, clearly just as charged as I am.

"I guess." I let loose a small smile. That's the understatement of my life.

Elias squeezes my hand as he walks me down the hallway along with hundreds of others Hub visitors.

About 40 feet down, right before the second security check, hangs a gilt frame with a painted portrait of a boy, about Michael and Max's age. I drift over to look at it, bringing Elias along with me.

A name plate beneath it reads, "Charlie Fisk. Inspiring us to make the world a better place." I run my finger over the letters, repeating the words under my breath, trying to grasp at why they're so familiar.

I look up at Elias. "Fisk?"

He nods. "President Fisk's son. He would have been in his mid-twenties by now. Died when he was a kid, about our age. Some fast-moving cancer."

"What was his Super?" I wonder out loud, then feel guilty for being so morbidly curious.

Elias shrugs. "They, uh...they say they never knew. Hadn't manifested by the time he got sick."

I quickly do the math of years in my head. "Would have been late."

Elias shrugs. "I don't know. Maybe they force the kids too quickly now. Especially with the Supers' classes starting earlier... I don't know. You want your kid to fit in, I guess. They never said it, but I think my mom didn't want that for me. She never cared if I was Super. Just Dad."

We stand there, staring at the portrait, ignoring the rush of bodies behind us. I squeeze Elias's hand so he knows I heard what he said. So he knows I care.

He clears his throat and says, "That's the slogan. The one they've been using ever since Fisk was elected. Fifteen years now. He thinks... Dad says he wants to be more than just a biotech service for the Supers. He wants to make the whole world better."

"Cure cancer," I say.

Elias nods. For a second, I stare at the portrait of Charlie, his dark hair and evergreen eyes so alive. I wonder if Fisk wants to cure anything else. I wonder if curing cancer made him think about curing people like me, too.

After a cuff scan and a facial-recognition identity

verification, we stand in another huge, cavernous white room turned into a maze of tables, vendors, and info booths.

"What do you want to do first?" Elias asks. I think he has gotten even more excited now that he sees my eyes roving and body itching to check everything out. "There's a demonstration, we can watch some other kids test their powers against their parents,' um, I think there are some lectures..." He taps through the schedule on his cuff.

"I think I really want to stay here. Is that weird?"

"Wanting to hang with the biotech reps all afternoon?" He wrinkles his nose, still smiling. "Yes, it is weird. But I should have known."

"Yeah, you should have," I say, punching him on the arm. The twins barrel over toward us, pushing through the crowd to greet Elias.

"I'll drag these clowns around while you check everything out," he says.

"They're twice the trouble," I tell him and give the twins a warning look, my eyebrows in the air.

"You think I don't know? I grew up with twin Supersibs, too. Conniving ones. These guys are cake." He slings a long arm around each of their necks, putting them in a lock, and both of them protest, laughing.

They walk off, and Elias yells over his shoulder, "Meet

you back here at two, okay?"

I shake my head at the three of them, smiling. The boys' dark curly heads bob up and down next to Elias, and they look up at him like they've just won the freaking lottery. Boys. They'll probably find some incredible underground basketball court and waste a whole afternoon at the Symposium doing that.

After an hour of browsing the booths, stuffing flash drives full of information and other swag into my bag, and buying a t-shirt — magenta with an illustration of a drum set the artist has turned into an lab for liquid solutions, with every drum bubbling and half-filled with bright color — I realize that Elias has never really been to the Hub, just like me. So how does he know his way around here so well?

Finally, Elias and the boys find me. It takes everything I have not to stretch up and kiss Elias — I almost never wear heels, and I'm even closer to his face now — but there are too many people here. The boys decide to go to some static electricity demonstration, and I drag Elias to a lecture I've been eyeing on the schedule all morning titled, "New Horizons: Malleability of the Gene Structure and Real-Life Improvements for Gifted Individuals."

The word "improvements" catches my eye. I could use

some of those.

The presentation isn't so much of an exposition as a teaser.

Like everything else about this building and this Symposium, the background of the movie playing glares stark white. Friendly figures show up on the screen, though, softening it. A woman in a cardigan and khakis that reminds me of Elias's mom. A kid and her dad playing catch. She has a pink baseball mitt like the one I have stashed in my keepsake box at home. The girl catches the ball and then dashes to the other side of her dad in half a second, standing 20 yards from him.

"Getting faster every day, sweetie!" the man calls and then turns to grin at us from the screen.

This time, a middle-aged man sits reading a newspaper at a breakfast nook in a warmly decorated kitchen. A woman stands at the counter making pancakes in a waist apron. I snort, and Elias reaches over to hold my hand.

"Grab the milk for me, hon?" the woman asks.

Without looking up from his paper, the man flicks a finger at the fridge, and a gallon of milk floats out and goes straight to her hand.

The woman turns over her back to the screen and beams. "A year ago he would have dropped it."

A little girl reaches for a candy jar, trying to grab a

piece of chocolate inside, and starts crying when the tips of her fingers disappear. A teenaged girl who's supposed to be her sister or her babysitter comes over to comfort her, and then gives her a pill. She pulls her hand out and the tips of her fingers rematerialize.

The older girl turns to the screen and says, "Without this patching solution from the Hub, this singly gifted little girl would have lost her fingers."

I squeeze Elias's hand hard. "They fixed her," I whisper. "Now can she…?"

Elias shakes his head and sets his mouth in a hard line. He leans in and whispers, "Just a patch."

The man in the suit steps to the front of the screen again.

"Genetic improvements are being made every day, thanks to new discoveries at the Hub regarding the malleability of the gene structure. Think of the implications. For the elderly gifted, for the worker who wants to step up in her career, even…" It switches to a photograph of a sad-looking young boy. "…for the singly gifted individual. The Hub isn't only here to help. It's here to make your whole life better."

And for the first time in a long time, since I met Elias, I feel it, strong. I can see it in this man's face. There's hope for people like me, for people like Elias. We'll be more than just Ones. I know it.

SIXTEEN

After we leave the presentation, Elias says, "I told Mom and Dad we'd sit with them for coffee." He jerks his chin toward the hallway, and I look up and see a tall man with wire-rimmed glasses and sparkling eyes headed our way.

"Hey, Dad." Elias shakes his hand. Mr. VanDyne nods toward me, smiles, then turns over his shoulder.

"President Fisk." Mr. VanDyne pulls a figure in a dark suit, impeccably pressed, over to where Elias and I stand. The man has short hair cropped close to his head, the same length as his goatee. He's almost as short as I am, and that alone is a total shock.

"Miss Grey," he says, tilting his head back a bit to get a better look at me. "I've heard a lot about you."

Mr. VanDyne turns his head to President Fisk, his eyebrows pushed up in a silent question. Elias raises an eyebrow at me, and I can't help but think I see hurt in his eyes.

"I've heard about the late transfer to Nelson High," Fisk says, "and that you've shown a lot of promise in your class exercises. Mathematics, especially biology. Organic chemistry."

For the first time ever, I wonder who else can see the

answers I punch into the computers at school besides the remote teachers. I wonder who else is watching. Paranoia skitters over my shoulders.

Fisk lowers his voice and leans in a bit. "A second round of application testing with Mr. Hoffman during your lunch hour. I'm sorry you never felt...comfortable at Superior. Unfortunate, really, since we expect so many of your classmates to work and be quite influential at the Hub. I assume you plan to pursue a career with us."

Something about the way he draws out every "S" freaks me out. I feel the familiar skin crawling sensation but tamp it down.

"Oh." I blush. "I'm flattered that the Hub selected me for the second round. But...I'm just a One, sir." *But maybe you can fix me. Can you?*

President Fisk waves a hand in the air, as though he's never heard about what a disappointment Ones are or how they never get picked for a Hub internship, certainly not one as important as Biotech. Like he's hardly ever thought about it. Like everyone doesn't know.

"Yes, I know. And there is a place for everyone, I believe, Miss Grey. Especially if what Mr. Hoffman tells me about your intelligence and drive is true."

Drive? At least the intelligence part is right. My grades are nearly perfect, even though I'm not really trying. I know I'm crazy smart, probably smarter than a lot of the kids who made it into the Hub internship.

I must have been quiet too long because President Fisk speaks up again. "Can you really tell me you'd have nothing to contribute to the Hub?"

"Well, sir, uh, President Fisk, I do. I think I would." I clear my throat and use the most mature voice I can muster. "Biotech is a fascination of mine. And I'm working at a graduate school level in organic chem."

"A young girl this enthusiastic about biotech when her peers are only worried about boys and shopping? And a Grey girl at that? Andrew," he says, turning to Elias's dad, "make sure she gets in."

Mr. VanDyne's eyes flash down at me, and he stammers for a second before he nods his assent. And then, as quickly as they got to us, they disappear into the crowd again.

After that, I basically float on a cloud for the rest of the afternoon. It's all I can do to keep from smiling and fidgeting as Leni and I get ready for the dinner in one of the fancily furnished ladies' rooms.

I don't own a single formal dress and shopping before the Symposium was the last thing I wanted to do. Thank God for Leni who volunteered to bring a few things for me to try on.

"A few things" is more like a dozen gowns. I rifle through them, ignoring anything floor length — I'd need six-inch heels just to avoid stepping on the hem — or strapless — no boobs to hold it up.

Then I see it. "Len," I gasp.

"Oh, I forgot about that one! Mom got that on clearance, post-prom last year." She waves her hand in the air toward the pale blue dress. "Too fluffy, too tight, way too short. Made me look like a freaking lollipop. Too cheap to bother taking back though."

I stick my arms up the skirt through what is, admittedly, a lot of fluff. I shimmy it down over my head, and the skirt comes all the way down to my knee. Leni zips me up, and I look in the mirror.

It's strapless, and the bodice hugs tight to my torso, hitting just at my waist. The fabric is a little shimmery but not shiny. The most incredible thing is what Leni hated about it — the ruffles. An airy, finely netted fabric peeks out in a row all around the top, covering whatever cleavage I might have had, and the same stuff lies in layers under the skirt, puffing it out and making it sway if I take a few steps.

I look like I'm in the middle of a cloud. Elias will love it.

I smile so wide I think my face will break.

"Well, hell." Leni gives a low wolf whistle at the sight of me in it. "Obviously, it's yours."

"Yeah. Obviously," I murmur, doing a quarter turn in front of the mirror. A minute ago, I was a plain, slight stick figure. Now I'm curvy and luminous. The blue of the dress makes my hair look richly colored, almost with golden highlights, and there's a bit of pink in my cheeks that I didn't notice before.

I launch myself at her, throw my arms around her neck, and whisper, "Thank you."

"Okay," she laughs, "but now you owe me. Blow-by-blow account of the entire dinner. Including," she wiggles her eyebrows, "after." I know Leni's been dreaming pretty much nonstop about spending the evening with Daniel, but it doesn't mean she's not going to be nosy about Elias and me on the side.

Mom's waiting for me outside my dressing room. She wears a burnished bronze ballgown with a strapless bodice, covered by a velvet short jacket and topped off with a string of pearls. Seeing her in that, you can't help but think of her Super — this is what a flame-thrower *would* wear. I wonder if every woman in the room is as in love with her Super as I am with my One and dressed to symbolize it, like I did.

Dad meets us near the entrance to the ballroom and extends both his arms. Mom and I each take one.

"Two beautiful girls on my arms tonight," Dad says, stepping through the doors.

Mom cranes her neck forward to grin at me, while she talks to Dad. "You're a lucky man."

Elias stands right inside the hall, and I know the moment he sees me because his mouth gapes. After a second, he closes it, and I can see his Adam's apple bob when he swallows hard. That makes me smile even harder.

We approach him, and I'm proud because I don't wobble at all in the silver three-inch heels I dug out of Mom's closet before the Symposium. And because I look amazing and I know it. Thankfully, seeing Elias in a button-down shirt and jacket prepared me for seeing him in a tux. He looks only slightly more incredible than he did this afternoon.

But my Elias will always be in a t-shirt and jeans, flying with me through a Nebraska cornfield. One hundred percent himself, one hundred percent honest. One hundred percent happy. The tux is great, and the Hub is great, but my Elias will always be mine to keep, away from all this Super stuff.

I kiss Dad's cheek and then join Elias at the VanDyne's table. We sit through a dinner with a fancy salad, about twelve utensils at each place setting, and some kind of delicious, melt-in-your-mouth steak. The only thing more intoxicating than the taste of the food is the way Elias brushes his hand against my knee every now and then, between listening and responding to his dad talking about Hub business.

Mr. VanDyne mentions something about artificially engineering the chemicals for a suit that would be able to withstand the intense wind speed and pressure on the skin of a Super who could project the mass of her own body into a pressure vortex — basically, float and fly. I launch into some theories and formulas I've been kicking around for a year and a half. Hoping one of them would be useful for my own Super one day.

Mr. VanDyne sits back and looks at Elias approvingly, but Mrs. VanDyne just gives me a polite smile. "Clearly a young woman this brilliant has earned a pass into the program. And to think Elias only ever mentioned how good you are at calculus."

Elias leans in, lips against my ear, and whispers, "You are truly amazing," and I know he's talking about my conversation with his dad, but the feeling of his breath against my neck makes me think that he means a couple other things, too. If I don't get up and move, I'm going to jump on him right there. Or at least drag him down some dark corridor outside this ballroom, if those even exist in the Hub.

The way Elias looks at me now, I know he's feeling the same thing. He folds his napkin, puts it on the table, and grabs my hand. "Dance with me?"

He smiles, and I glance at everyone around the table, murmur an "excuse us," and follow him to the floor.

We try to mimic the way everyone else dances, hands on waists and shoulders. I glance over at Leni tugging Daniel to the dance floor, and he holds her at quite a good length — confusing, I think, since they've been even more inseparable since that in the woods. But then I see why: His parents, the Doctors Suresh — both influential in the genetics department, I know — watch them dance with dead faces. Poor Leni.

The big band plays "Blue Moon," a song I love, naturally. The beat is faster than I'd like, but we take it as slow as we can. My arm snakes up along Elias's. Because my heels give me some height, my hand rests comfortably wrapped around his shoulder, and I don't have to crane my neck quite so much to look at him.

Elias reaches his arm out, still holding my hand, and makes me spin under it. He pulls me back to him, hugging me tight, and I clutch at his waist. It can't get any better than this. It just can't. Not in a crowd of people, anyway.

I remember that my parents are somewhere around here, and I pull back and smile at him but don't get close enough that I want to stand on my toes to kiss him for real because that would be beyond embarrassing.

He spins us in a circle, pressing my body to his. "So, what do you think? Can we skip prom now?"

Even through his glasses, the colors in his eyes stand out, like a kaleidoscope, and they completely mesmerize me.

"I thought that was always the plan," I say, my voice low. "Skip prom. I'd rather be flying." I flash him my most charming smile.

"You and me flying in prom clothes? Tux and gown?" he asks, chuckling. "Mer, you're gonna make me feel like Superman. Give me a complex or something."

I laugh. "No way. You're as handsome as Superman," I say, brushing my fingers at the hair right above his ear, enjoying my extra height, "but if you even suggest that I'm anything like Lois Lane ever again, I'll kill you." Then I lean in, lowering my voice. "Plus, you'll always need me to fly."

There's something behind the slight smile he gives me in return, but I can't put my finger on it. It's not sadness. Maybe resignation.

"So what did you think of Fisk?" Elias sways with me

to the music. I try to focus on the conversation.

"President Fisk? Um…it was kind of surreal talking to him," I say.

Elias nods, his mouth turning down into a bit of a frown. "The way he talked to you bothered me. I don't like how he knew so much about you. How he just assumed you'd want to work here."

"What do you mean? The summer internship, Elias? That's amazing! That's…"

Elias's face drops. "Everything you dreamed of, I know. But this place… I don't think it's what it seems." His eyebrows bunch up, and his face has that look again, like he's trying to decide if I can handle something.

"What do you mean?"

He shakes his head and looks off into the distance. He thinks I don't know all his faces, but I do. This is the one he uses when he's angry but not at me and doesn't want me to think he's angry at me, so he just glares at nothing.

"Okay, seriously, Elias." I stop really dancing and kind of sway in place. "What are you talking about?"

His mouth twists down on one side, and he looks down and to the side, at nothing for a second before he says, "You know how Fisk's son died."

"Cancer."

"Yes…kind of. But that's not the whole story. He was

a One."

My heart lurches. "Okay...?"

"And they tried to cure him."

"Cure him of the cancer?"

"No. Of the Oneness."

I have trouble finding my breath.

"He was doing really well for awhile. Displaying some signs he was going to go Super, even. He was a kid, then — they figured his genes were still malleable."

"Real-time mutations aren't possible. I mean, you're either born with a Super or you're not."

Elias nods, once, slowly. "Right. That's what we've always thought. But...it's epigenetics."

"Epigenetics only influence development on organisms with short life spans. Plants, fungi. The things whose survival depends on the short term."

"That's what they thought."

"That's what's in my grad-level bio book."

"You're taking grad-level bio?"

I nod. "Med school level. With, uh... It's a private tutor."

Elias looks at me with drawn eyebrows. "You should have... Mer, I had no idea." He shakes his head. "Anyway, for the last 30 years or so, the Hub has known differently. With us mutants..."

"Supers," I say firmly.

"Okay. Yeah. Or Gifteds. Whatever. Our adaptations happen much more quickly. A layer of code extraneous to DNA."

I roll my eyes. "I know about epigenetics, Elias."

"So this'll make sense to you," he says, sounding exasperated. "For Ones...they think it might be even more accelerated. We were born with only one Super, so..."

"Our genes are looking to adapt."

He just looks at me for a few moments.

"How do you know?" I ask.

"My dad... We have a lot of...resources lying around our house. Classified ones."

My eyebrows go up.

"I can't understand most of the scientific reports about Charlie Fisk, but this much I do understand. Something about attempted Super gene replication, the mutated DNA causing a cell growth explosion. But only the genes displaying the One replicated. Massive tumors invaded his body everywhere within weeks, out of control. The One took over."

I gasp. I can only imagine what a nightmare it must have been.

"Of course, the Hub continued 'treatment,' except now it was actually...treatment."

"But he died." I'd read all about the difference between mutations that caused cancer and mutations that cause Supers back in seventh grade. I remember being terrified even then at how similar they were. "Must have been so fast."

Elias nods again. "Something like a month. Six weeks, maybe."

"Why didn't they wait? Test it on rats or something?"

"They did. And they thought they had the human formulas all set. Even tailored it to his specific mutation. And it kind of…exploded. Like his One genes got excited or over-stimulated or something."

"And he was a kid."

"I know. Sucks, right?"

"No, I mean…that's why. Everything I've been able to figure about malleability… Well, there's not much, but it's only going to work on rapidly growing bodies."

Elias nods. "Little kids. Teens, at the latest. That makes sense."

"What do you mean?"

He does that thing where he looks off into the distance again and kind of blows out a breath. "The Hub has been kind of hyper-interested in me since I was a kid. Because I'm a One, you know? Testing my power, trying to strengthen it… I'm a mystery because my sisters are so awesome."

If Elias is a mystery, so am I. And the two of us together are freaking Grand Unification Theory.

"Anyway, I don't know if you want to become kind of a resident freak around here like I was, you know? You can make your own way. We can make our own way. We don't need the Hub." Suddenly, Elias seems more distant than ever. There's something behind his eyes, like he's holding something back from me.

"I don't know." I shrug, try to look nonchalant. "I always thought maybe I'd figure out a way…"

"To become a Super?" Elias shakes his head again. "If they could have figured it out, they would have. The existence of Ones… It bothers Fisk. Always has. You read the news feed, right? You sat in that lecture? He's been trying to solve us forever when no one else really seems to care."

No one cares except me.

I've never *really* wanted to tell anyone else about the flying, not even Leni and Daniel. I haven't minded that it's just ours. Especially since I've known I couldn't duplicate the dual power I feel with Elias on my own, not the full extent of it. No matter how hard I try. But now that we're here and there's so much interest in Ones, maybe we can help. Maybe our bodies have the answers.

"Should we... Do you think we should say something? About what we can do?"

Elias shakes his head, fast. "No. No, Mer."

"Seriously, Elias. They're researching it, and maybe we could even – "

"Merrin, I said no."

Suddenly, this dance feels a whole lot less romantic. I barely put up with my parents talking to me like that. My eyes flare at his sudden change of tone, and Elias sees it.

"Hey," he says, "Hey, Mer. Let's get out of here for a sec, okay?" From the tone of his voice, I know he wants to talk to me for real, not on a dance floor and not to find somewhere dark to kiss. So I nod and follow him, trying to keep the tears behind my eyes instead of spilling out from them.

SEVENTEEN

We get within about 15 feet of the ballroom exit, and Elias drops my hand and says, "Follow me in a couple minutes, okay? I'll wait around the corner two hallways down."

What are we about to do that we don't want the cameras to catch?

I nod and do as he asked. I wait a few minutes and then walk down the hallway, trying to keep my heels from making too loud of a noise in the empty, cavernous space. The lights have been dimmed so that the stark white seems much softer, probably trying to achieve the sense of evening in a space without natural light. I pass the first hallway to the right, and it stares back at me, a tunnel of more unknown emptiness, the turned-out lights leaving it pitch black.

The second hallway is just as dark, and as I approach it, Elias's hand shoots out and grabs mine. I squeak, surprised even though I knew he'd be waiting there for me. He pulls me to him and kisses me, his palm pressing against the small of my back. In the dark of the hallway, it's exhilarating, and for a second, I forget that that's not why we're here. At least I didn't think it was.

Elias pulls back and touches my face, running his thumb along my lips, and the outline of his face, dark-on-dark in the slight shadows, smiles at me. He speaks in a low whisper. "I could get used to this 'Merrin-in-heels' thing," he murmurs. "Much easier to just grab you and kiss you."

My head swims. He's right. And if they weren't so damn painful, I'd wear them all the time.

I would be pretty thrilled with this whole standing-in-a-dark-hallway scenario if we weren't right in the middle of the Hub. Or if Elias hadn't just shut me down for no freaking reason. But there's too much of everything that makes me happy or excited everywhere around me to focus on just one thing. Even Elias.

I step back and push his shoulders playfully. "What are we doing down here?"

"I want to show you something." He tugs at my arm and pulls me behind him down the hallway. As he steps, the lights flare up to the blinding levels I'm sure they're set on during the day.

"Low lights," he commands, and they dim to nighttime levels. My eyebrows go up. How does he know to do this? I look at him, and he gets it. He gets the question.

"Um, my cuff gives me clearance. I'm actually here kind of a lot," he says quietly, nodding toward his cuff.

"The security system senses its presence whenever we walk through a checkpoint. That's why no holodoors have flown up in our face yet."

We come to a solid door, probably the eighth on the right, even though the hallway stretches much farther down.

"No retina scans?"

He shrugs. "No, the process to get into the Hub in the first place is intense enough. Once you're in, the cuff is good enough. And besides, no retina scan at every door frees up funding for...other things. Like this."

He opens the door, grinning, and pulls me in behind him. I stare into a black abyss. When Elias asks, "Ready for this?" his voice echoes off the walls, and I know whatever lays waiting in the dark is huge. I nod, and his voice booms, "Lights bright."

A white light fills the room, blinding me momentarily once again, and half a second later when I can see, I gasp.

I stare at the gigantic room before me, the size of four football fields at least. Two tracks circle one end of it, one long and one shorter, running concentric with one another. Simulation stations holding giant gyro-chairs with controls staring at the largest holoscreens I've ever seen; huge clear cubes; and two swimming pools, triple Olympic length, stretch out to my right. The vaulted ceiling curves high in the air, at least five stories up, much higher than I've ever flown with Elias.

"The testing arena," Elias says, chest puffing with pride. "This is where my sisters are training — this is where the gap year does their stuff. I haven't seen them yet, but I will tomorrow." He pulls me along. "Come on. It's like the ultimate Super testing ground."

We walk through the arena for a few minutes, him pointing out 10 different kinds of the highest-tech equipment I've ever seen, until we come to an empty stretch of floor over which the roof domes slightly. Only the barest light reaches up into it, but when I squint, I see that it's actually made up of a formation of blades, their wide ends around the circumference, all coming to a point in the middle. Elias, still holding my hand, stretches behind him and hits a huge red button on the wall. The blades slowly retract into the edge of the circle, opening up to a dark purple sky that sparkles with the brightest stars.

I know my mouth hangs open, and I don't even care. This room could be my future. This room could be where I learn to fly. On my own.

He motions up. "The ceiling's like that…you know…"

"For the fliers," I finish.

He nods. "I knew you'd think this was incredible.

Knew it. So. Do you want…you know…the aerial tour?"

"No." I shake my head. "No, I want to see all of it close up, from down here. Show me everything."

Elias intertwines his fingers with mine, and suddenly, I'm jerked back to reality — the question of how he even knows this exists. My head swims.

"So," I say and clear my throat, "You've been, uh…coming here."

"Yeah," he says, smiling. "Awesome, huh?" He looks down at me, and my smile fades.

No, I think, it's not awesome. It's not okay that you were keeping something from me. It's not okay that I trusted you with everything about my One, and it wasn't enough.

Well, everything except meeting with Mr. Hoffman. And letting him test my blood.

"Mer, what's up?"

I shake my head because I don't know what to say. Two months ago, something vicious would have come flying out of my mouth, words meant to slice into him, but I don't want to hurt him, not at all. Especially when I know that my secret could hurt him just as badly.

Suddenly, I want to take him up on his offer to fly because I want the noise and the distraction of it to block out all these thoughts, to help me figure out how to deal with them. I wrap my arms around him, press my cheek into his chest again, and then tilt my head up to kiss his neck.

I so badly want to fly in this dress. I so badly want to be beautiful, flying with him. Maybe that will fix everything. But he gently nudges me back down.

"No, you were right," he says. "No flying."

There's a small eating area inside the arena, with picnic-like tables, a long top with benches attached. He hoists me up to sit on the table part of one of them, my feet resting on the bench. He straddles them, sitting down to face me. Now his face is only a little lower than mine. This is how I love to look at him, and he knows it. He's humoring me. He cups his hands over my knees and looks into my eyes, and warmth floods me.

Like he can tell what I'm thinking, he murmurs, "I need you just as much as you need me. Probably more." He grins. "At least floaters can spy on people."

"Then why have you been coming here? And why didn't you tell me?" I can hear the whine in my voice, and I hate it, but my heart twists so much that it grabs my throat and makes the words come out all funny. Needy. I don't know why that bothers me, especially with Elias sitting here and looking into my eyes and telling me how much *he* needs *me*.

He shrugs his shoulders. "I don't know. Hoping I'd see my sisters. Still haven't. Hoping I'd make my dad happy. But the truth is, they've been doing testing on me on and off for years. They're, uh…stubborn." He laughs a little and smiles at me, but I can't smile back. I must be staring at him like I don't understand because he starts talking again.

"Let me start again. I've been going for…tests, I guess. I've known the theories about how they could make us better. Make us Supers, I mean. Real ones. I wasn't going to show you the arena until they found something conclusive. You know, about me. Us."

"So it wasn't really basketball," I say, staring at the floor. There are a lot of more important things to say, things I want to find out more about. But thinking of him with needles stuck in his arm or hooked up to medical machinery makes my stomach drop. My Elias, a test subject.

"But, Mer," he says, his hands running up the outsides of my legs and reaching up to grab my waist, "Mer. They can't make me fly. I've never flown any way but with you. You make me better. You make me fly. I need you. Not some stupid tests, not the stupid Hub." His voice sounds kind of angry, and I can't tell if it's because of me or something else.

"How are you okay with that?" And now I can feel it, my real question coming out, because I always assumed Elias was okay with needing me, but of course, it doesn't make sense, not at all, with how gorgeous and sweet and popular and, apparently, powerful he is. How well-connected. How involved in what they're doing at the Hub.

"Okay with what? Needing you?" he asks.

I nod, looking at the floor next to him.

"I'm better with you than I was without. I mean, in a couple ways. I guess…even if we weren't Ones. I'd still tell you any day of the week that I need you. That I…I need you, Mer."

I sit opposite him, silent, gazing out at the arena over his shoulder, imagining what it would be like to be a part of it, for real, not just tagged onto a limited guest pass at the Symposium or sneaking into a hallway with Elias. Testing or participating or developing enhancements — I could rock it. I could be here, fit right in here. And if I could work on the research, really get my hands dirty — I know it, know it in my gut — I could fly.

"Is that why you're doing this, Merrin? Is that why you want to do the intern thing? Because you're…you're not okay with it?"

I hear the part he didn't ask. *Because you're not okay with needing me?* My words catch in my throat, but I have to say them. "Don't you ever dream of flying on your own?"

"No. Not really. Not until you brought it up. That's always been my dad's thing."

His eyes look sad, so sad they make my heart sink into my stomach. So sad they make his feelings more important, for the moment, than my frustration that he kept something from me. More important than my frustration with myself, that having Elias in my life somehow still doesn't make me quite happy enough.

I don't feel the same way about my Oneness as Elias does about his, but I'm pretty sure I feel the same way about him as he does about me. I don't want him to hurt. I definitely don't want to be the one who makes him hurt.

I reach down, lace my fingers through his hair, and kiss him on the forehead, then the lips, a gentle kiss becoming deeper.

"I don't mind being stuck with you," I murmur between kisses because I don't, I really don't.

Most of life isn't flying, I remind myself. Most of life is about the people you love. I know that. Flying hasn't made me forget.

I swing my legs out from between his and hop down off the table, standing so I look curviest in my dress. I'm not going to be dressed up like this again for awhile, so I need to milk it. I stretch my hand out, smiling an apology.

"Show me everything," I say. And we spend the next hour looking at supersonic accelerators and fireproof cubes and electron-neutralizing gel.

And I am happy.

The next day, Elias seems like himself again. I try to hide my sigh of relief that my boyfriend is back and that we can enjoy the rest of the Symposium together, even if he is mostly humoring me.

I have no idea what Michael and Max are doing — Dad's keeping track of them today since his ultra-boring presentation is over. It was something about home safety for families with early-displaying Supers — how to keep your electricity-emitting baby from blowing the house up, for example.

The biggest problem my parents ever had with the twins was that it was hard to bathe them. That's how Dad got into this field in the first place, actually — my brothers were born, and what with my being a One and all, Mom and Dad had never really faced the challenges of having Super kids to take care of.

I'm all excited to go to Mom's demonstration today, but I see it's marked "Authorized Personnel Only" when I read the listing closely on my schedule. I blow it up on my cuff's screen and shove it in Elias's face.

"What the hell?" I grouse.

He looks at the listing, too. "Yeah. And it's the only thing in the training arena at that point. What does your mom do?"

I shrug. I've never asked Mom exactly what she does — never cared enough. I mean, I know that she combusts and that she's indestructible — never had a match in the house. But she's never bothered to talk to me about it. Dad's always clued me in on what he's doing at the Hub, but Mom? Never. If I think about it, I never thought it was because her work was too awesome or important. I just thought it was because she thought I wasn't awesome or important enough to hear about it.

"What's the matter?" Elias nudges me. I would tell him, but I know he's excited because he finally gets to see his sisters today. I'm not about to ruin anything for him, especially after all I said last night.

"Nothing." I shake my head and give a closed-lipped smile. "I just... I'm really glad you showed me the arena last night. Otherwise I would never have seen it."

"Never say never, Mer." He reaches an arm around me and squeezes my shoulder, pulling me close to him.

We go to a couple presentations, including one for a pressure-enhancing suit to make some flier kid — the air-blowing kind, like Elias should be — push the air so hard and fast that she's nearly supersonic. "While we had hoped to break the sound barrier this time," the announcer intones, "this gap year student strengthens her abilities daily, and we have every confidence that by the next symposium she'll be far past supersonic status."

"Supersonic," I whisper. Elias gives me a sad smile. The girl, her skin the color of coffee glowing almost golden from the exhilaration and the sheen of sweat, runs a hand over her head, which has hair cropped so close it's nearly shaven. For speed, I think.

Elias looks at me, and I swear it's another instance where he knows what I'm thinking. "Don't get any ideas," he says, and he rolls the end of some of my hair between his fingers lightly.

Yep. He knew.

"It wouldn't be the same," he leans in to whisper, and whether he's talking about flying or kissing or something else, I don't know and I don't care. But I silently vow to keep my hair just like it is.

There's a big lunch with more milling around and networking. I sit at a table with Elias and Leni and Daniel, and for a few minutes, this feels like some surreal, awesome, alternate-dimension high school. I can tell that Daniel's just as thrilled as I am by this whole thing —

Daniel's a lot like me, now that I think about it — but Leni looks pretty much the same as always. Slightly less on edge, but then, she's looked like that since the two of them figured out the whole "flame on" thing.

Then Mom walks into the room. It's like the freaking Sea of Reeds parts for her because the people standing in front of the door where she's walked in kind of stop what they're doing and all turn toward her, and then the clapping starts. Within seconds, it's thunderous, echoing off the high ceiling and every wall.

Even my heart swells with pride for her. She must have done something really, really incredible. I'll have to talk to her about that.

She holds up her hands, trying to quell the applause, which has now blocked out everyone else's conversation, but it keeps going, and she's clearly embarrassed. Suddenly, Dad is there, with his arm around her, saying "thank yous" on her behalf and walking her away. Right after my initial rush of jealousy for her, I look at her and Dad again, and I see it.

Elias and me.

There we are, twenty-five years from now. They fit together perfectly. Just like Elias and me.

I love Elias.

I love Elias. I beam at him and tear up a little, I'm so

damn happy about it. He smiles back at me, his eyes kind. He doesn't get it, somehow doesn't see it in my face.

Great. He can read my freaking thoughts about my hairstyle and its aerodynamics, but now, with my feelings so strong, he thinks I'm randomly grinning at him like an idiot. The applause for Mom dies down after a few seconds. I squeeze his hand.

"How soon can we get out of here?" I ask, only realizing after I say it what it must sound like.

His smile in return seems distracted and a little confused. He knows how excited I am about the Symposium. "They're doing the gap year presentation after this."

Right. I feel bad that I was so stupid. Elias's sisters, the presentation, the reception afterward. He's not thinking about me at all, and I shouldn't expect him to.

It's actually not that bad that I get to keep this to myself for a while longer. I love Elias. I love him. He's almost told me he loves me, a few times. Last night. A month ago, when we sat on the rooftop, even though things were different then.

I can't wait to tell him. Can't wait to be the first to finally say it, can't wait to see the relief written across his face. Can't understand how or why it took me this long to realize it.

I look at Elias again, and some of my elation melts away, filled in by more worry. He's still so distracted, so anxious to see them.

"Have you heard from them?" I ask. "Letters or anything?"

He shakes his head. "Not for a couple weeks," he says, not looking right at me, his disturbed look.

I squeeze his hand again, put my head on his shoulder. "Okay," I say. "I'm sure they're okay."

He kisses the top of my head, and from the way he does it, lightly and kind of sideways, I know. He's still staring off, still upset.

Suddenly, all I want is to get to that presentation. Because I know that, in this moment, that's all he wants, too.

EIGHTEEN

The entire room clears after lunch for a tour through the Hub. I'm actually pretty bored as we near the Symposium's end. Elias gave me a tour of the Hub, between the testing arena last night and some more awesome lab and testing areas this morning. The tour doesn't extend nearly that far. I wonder how many people have really seen the depth of this place. I try to remind myself that Elias is lucky.

Suddenly, I feel butterflies in my stomach. This is the gap year presentation, so Mr. Hoffman will probably be here. My skin crawls again. For the first time, I wish I could tell Elias about him. About everything. But I promised, and I can't break that promise, not even for Elias.

Fisk strides onto the stage, and I shiver. I focus on Elias, look over at him and squeeze his hand, and for the first time this Symposium, he's lit up — his smile, his eyes, everything. There's something incredible about a guy who loves his sisters this much.

"Welcome to the crowning presentation of the Superior Hub's Biotech Symposium." Applause thunders through the room, and I wonder if I should have been even more excited about this.

"I know this is the show you all have been waiting for, so I won't keep you waiting any longer. It is my pleasure to introduce you to our inaugural class of Gap Year Gifteds."

The applause gets even louder, if that's possible.

The kids file out on the stage, ten total — two very muscular guys; the girl with the cropped hair from earlier; a blond girl almost as short as I am; one very lanky boy; and then, finally, Nora and Lia.

Nora and Lia smile and wave at the crowd with the rest of them. Their forearms are stiff and barely move, like they've been on a parade float for three hours and any minute they'll collapse from the exhaustion. Their eyes gaze out, empty, and their skin is so, so pale. Lia reaches down and squeezes Nora's hand, and they both look straight at Elias, widen their eyes — which look bloodshot even from this distance — and a second later, look back at the crowd again. Elias shifts and fidgets in his chair and stares at them with his chin resting in his hand.

Fisk runs through the achievements of the gap year. We know about the near-supersonic flier already, and we hear about the buff guys lifting 20 tons; the tall kid, who I'm calling "Stretch" in my head, doing some incredible body-bending stuff; and another guy running a marathon in one and a half minutes.

Nora and Lia are up next. Some Hub workers roll a thick concrete wall, set on casters, onto the stage. The girls step up to it, hold hands, and practically melt through it. Then, almost without pause, they zap to the back of the room.

"Teleportation of this type is common for Gifteds after a period of hard work, as these young ladies have been through. But you're not here to see something common." He nods toward Nora and Lia. "Ladies, let's show them something phenomenal."

A pair of coordinates — longitude and latitude — flashes on the screen behind the announcer. The girls turn back, stare at it for a second, then look up — empty-eyed — and disappear. The camera changes to a scene of Times Square, and the girls appear there in a flash. Everyone leaps to their feet in a standing ovation. Elias stands and claps politely, but he looks the opposite of thrilled. He sucks in a deep breath when the girls appear back on the stage.

"Oftentimes, twins show increased, more powerful or, in some cases, additional abilities when close to one another."

"It's the genetics," Elias murmurs, reciting some information it sounds like he's memorized. "I've read theories that the twin genes duplicate the power or something."

"Your sisters?" I lean in and ask. I'm really asking, *Your sisters and my brothers?* Michael and Max are identical — the only way I could tell them apart for the longest time is a scar on Michael's chin from where he crashed into a coffee table as a baby. And a couple years ago, they did figure out that when they hold hands, they're faster speeding across the water. But we just thought it was a confidence thing because they were only eight or so.

Elias shakes his head. "It wasn't...I mean...no. They're talking about identical twins. Identical. Nora and Lia are fraternal. They're... It doesn't make sense. That's what I don't get." He sits on the edge of his seat, his legs bouncing.

When the girls finally walk down with the rest of the Gap Year Gifteds to greet the audience members, it's obvious. I can almost see their feet drag on their way off the stage. They head in our direction.

Elias leans down to me and says, "Watch it. They're both going to jump on me. Love pile. Weird family tradition." He beams, but they still have the same plastic smiles and dragging walk.

They don't speed up as they get closer. That's when I really know something's off. Elias doesn't seem to, yet, because he slings his arms around each of their necks and pulls them to him tight. They draw in toward him, but their movements are almost wooden. He whispers something in each of their ears, then draws back and turns to me, motioning me over.

"Nora, Lia. This is my girlfriend, Merrin. Uh, the one I wrote you about."

I blush, maybe because I so seldom hear him refer to me that way. Maybe because he's been telling his sisters about me, and I know how important they are to him. But I smile, too. A lot.

"It's great to meet you," I say, extending a hand. They both nod at once. Nora shakes my hand first, and her fingers are like ice. Lia's are the same.

"Well," Lia says, "we need to be back. See you soon, right, Elias?"

"Um, yeah." Elias swallows hard, and his eyebrows tent up. He hugs them to him tight again. "Love you girls," I hear him whisper. They glance back at Elias and smile a little on the way out, not looking at us, but somehow beyond us.

"Well," I say, smiling. "That was good. You got to see them. They look tired, but…"

"They would have teased me," Elias interrupts. "They would have teased me, and they would have hugged you. They would have been so happy that I have a girlfriend, that I… And I would have made a joke about how someone's playing their damn expensive drum set that they never used, you know?"

Elias clenches his jaw, squeezes my hand hard. He doesn't yell — he can't, not here — but still. I've never seen him this angry. Never.

"Elias. Elias," I say, plaintively. He looks down at me, blinking hard. "They're just tired. They're working really hard here, right? You heard the presentation."

Elias shakes his head and clutches me to him, like I'm a substitute for both of them right now. I wrap my arms around his waist and squeeze him back, as hard as I can.

Elias strides out of the presentation hall, and I trot to keep up. He wants to get out of here, but I want to talk. I can't keep what he said about the genes off my mind.

"You said you were never powerful. Your One, I mean."

Elias nods. "Never could really do more than blow out candles on my birthday cake."

"Then how are we flying so fast? I mean, we're *fast*, Elias. We've gotta be going over a hundred miles an hour now. The only reason we're not going faster is…"

"Our skin. I know. I already got windburned." But he's not really behind the words he's saying. He looks at me, hard in the eye. Burning. Wanting to know something. "Can you float higher now?"

My heart beats a mile a minute, and I actually feel like I'm going to do it now. Float. I haven't felt this shaky around Elias since the first week I met him.

My voice is barely above a whisper. "I could only go up like four feet before...you know."

Elias's eyes widen. "Mer, we're clearing 30, 40 feet..."

"I know," I say. I nod rapidly and swallow. "I know."

If I'm going to tell him about practicing on my own and about Mr. Hoffman, this is the time. This is when I need to do it. I can't decide. I can't. The two choices thrash around in my head. Tell him and keep this whole thing honest. Get closer to solving it together. Use Elias's connection to figure out how we can fix the Oneness...but how can I do that to the boy I love? How can I admit that I've been keeping things from him, trying to break away from him?

There's plenty of time to tell him that. Plenty of time.

Except we won't be having this conversation again, I can feel it. He's closing up more by the minute, since Nora and Lia walked out on the stage, not themselves.

"I've been practicing," I murmur, almost hoping he doesn't hear me. He stops dead in his tracks, and my words rush out in a flood. "I've been practicing on my own, trying to go higher, and ever since we flew, I can, Elias."

"And?" he asks, his eyes boring holes in me.

"And what?"

"What else aren't you telling me?"

Shit. Shit, he knows. He knows me too well for me to keep a single thing from him. I lower my eyes, stare down at my shoes. Then I think, no, I have to do this for real. I owe it to him.

"I've been studying with someone. The grad-level chem."

"Who?"

"One of my teachers from Superior, he's — "

"What's his name?" Each word that leaves his mouth punches me in the gut.

I can't look away from him, but I can't say anything either.

"It's Hoffman, isn't it?" Elias's eyes burn.

"Uh...yeah." I stand up straighter. "Yes. So?"

"Did he take your blood?"

"It was mostly o-chem work, theories, tests."

"Did he take your blood, Merrin?" There is an edge of urgency to his voice that makes my heart stop.

My eyes flare wide, and I nod.

Elias breathes in sharply and mutters, "We have to get

out of here." He squeezes my hand and practically drags me down the hall with him.

Our entire walk out is fast and silent. The doorway chirps its goodbye to us as it registers our cuffs leaving the building, and I don't even get a chance to look back at the Hub before we've made it through the garage and into Elias's car. I don't know if I'll ever see it again, and just the thought of that makes a lump rise in my throat.

"Mer." Elias grabs my hand, squeezes it till my fingers scrunch together and it almost hurts.

I don't want to look at him, suddenly. I know he's upset. I know, even though I never met his sisters before this, that there's something wrong, something off with them. Something big. That's because I know Elias. He's about to lose his mind.

"Let's get out of here. You and me."

"Okay, yeah," I say, smiling at him a little, rubbing his back. "We can hang out at my house, watch a movie, raid the junk food cabinet…"

"No," he says, and there's a determined sort of glare in his eyes. "Let's get out of town. You pack a bag, we'll stuff everything in my car, we'll leave tonight. No. In the next hour."

I laugh a little, but when I look at him, I know — he's

not joking. And he's terrified. And looking at him, like this, knowing what I do, I'm starting to feel the same way.

The car zooms through the unchanging Nebraska landscape, frost glittering against the deep blue-gray night where the fields meet the horizon. I move my hand to grab Elias's, like I normally would do while we drive, but his both hands grip the steering wheel, knuckles white.

"Elias," I say, but it's so soft I'm not even sure he can hear me.

He speeds up. I don't know what to say, so I wait till he pulls up in my driveway. He parks and sits there, still gripping the wheel, staring out through the windshield.

Then he starts to cry.

I've cried in front of Elias, but he's never cried in front of me. Come to think of it, I've never seen any guy cry. I don't really know what to do. I sort of reach my arm out and put it around his shoulders, and with him hunched over the steering wheel like that, he looks so huge and my arm looks so slight and insignificant across his back.

He sits up, kind of slams the steering wheel with both hands, and looks over at me. He sniffles once.

"I'm sorry," he says, staring back out the windshield.

"Hey," I say. "No, Elias. It's...it's your sisters, I know."

"I have a really bad feeling about this. About the

Symposium, about the Hub, and yeah, Nora and Lia. I just want you to trust me, Mer. Okay? I need you to. You trusted Hoffman. Trust me."

I wince. "What do you know about him?"

Elias clenches and relaxes his jaw over and over for a couple long seconds. "I'm worried."

I rub his back, plant a light kiss on his temple, and lean my forehead there. "Elias. I've known Mr. Hoffman for a long time. He was only trying to help me get that internship. That's all." I try to keep my voice steady even as my stomach twists.

A defeated look crosses his face, and I wonder what he knows. Wonder if he wants to leave because he's worried about me or because he's worried about himself and doesn't want to be alone. Wonder if he's remembering that all I've ever wanted to do is work at the Hub, and now I have the chance, and…

"I'm not trying to freak you out, okay?" His voice shakes. "Look. I'm back at the Symposium for the wrap-up the rest of tonight. Probably they want to look at me some more, too. Meet me back here tomorrow morning, okay? We'll eat some breakfast, go for a walk, we'll figure this out. But, Mer." He leans forward, takes my face in his huge hands. "I'm worried. About you, about me… I can't say why. I don't even really know myself. You just have to trust me right now, okay? Yes, it's about my sisters, but...it's about us, too. Okay? Promise me we can talk about this again tomorrow. Promise me you'll think about it."

He puts his forehead to mine, whispers, "Please." And his hands start to shake. "I...I care about you."

"Me too, Elias. Me too." I want to invite him in, want to let him curl up into a ball next to me and hold him until he stops hurting, until the knot in my stomach eases. I think I understand. Think I do. I don't know what I would do if I saw Max and Michael and they weren't...well...Max and Michael. But my parents will be home soon, and they wouldn't understand. He might not understand if I asked him, and I'm sure he still has his curfew, especially on a Symposium night.

"Elias, I..." I want to tell him, but right before I do, right before I say the words, I understand — no matter how much I love him, it's not going to fix this because it doesn't have anything to do with this. "I will. I will."

I lean in to kiss him, closing my eyes, lingering there for a moment. For the first time between us, it feels less like a promise and more like a goodbye.

NINETEEN

I expect to see the boys hanging out in the living room, and I think how much good ruffing their hair and hassling them a little would do me. Maybe drag them outside to kick their butts in basketball, put my float into action. But they're not out there.

I walk in through the garage and Mom and Dad's car still emits warmth from the hood, the engine ticking a little. They just got home. Weird that they left as early as we did almost.

The TV sits silent, and only the kitchen light is on. I bound upstairs, dumping my bag outside my room and crossing to the other side of the hall. I crane my neck to look into the boys' room.

It looks like it's been robbed.

Their dresser drawers are all pulled out, the clothes strewn everywhere. I glance in the bathroom, and their toothbrushes aren't tossed in the sink as usual.

I head downstairs, bravely skipping every second step, and find Mom and Dad sitting at the island, eyebrows drawn, holding steaming mugs of tea. Silent. They haven't said a word since I walked in the door. I would have heard them. How long have they been sitting there?

"Guys?" I say, staring at them, hoping my eyes don't betray that I'm totally freaking out. "Where are the boys? Did they go for a sleepover or something? I wanted to beat their asses at basketball."

Mom raises her eyebrows at me, her face drawn and stern. "Language, Merrin."

"They got called to the program at the Hub." Dad looks distant. Mom smiles a little, but it's an exhausted sort of smile. "I know they wanted to say goodbye, but you didn't answer when they called. Everything okay?"

Duh. I had the cuff's ringer on silent because of the Symposium dinner. Tears prick at my eyes. I can't believe I missed them.

"Oh, God, I'm so sorry, you guys."

"They promised us it would only be a week or so. Probably not longer." Dad covers my hand with his. "They...they said the boys could help them with a breakthrough. Even got them tutors for the week."

"And with the success of the other gap year students..." Mom starts.

My gaze snaps to her face. "Success? Did you see them, Mom? Did you see how they looked?"

"Are you talking about the VanDyne girls?" Dad asks, squeezing my hand, eyes sympathetic.

"Yes!" I cry, jerking my hand away. "How could I *not*

be talking about them?"

"They're working those girls hard," Mom acknowledges. "I saw some early experimentation with them. They're…impressive."

"Yeah. Well, Elias is worried. And you guys are stupid if you're not, too."

"Merrin!" Dad snaps.

Elias was right to be freaked out. And now I know his panic. Because now we're more the same than ever before.

It's past Elias's curfew, so I try to sleep, tossing and turning, my usual flying dreams interrupted by flashes of white and the expressionless faces of Michael and Max.

Our house is dead quiet, and by eight in the morning, I'm so antsy that I give up waiting. I throw on some jeans, hop into the car, and speed through Superior toward Elias's.

I'm so on edge that even my arms feel fidgety. Something I blew off as Elias's uptightness about his sisters has now combined with Michael and Max being gone from our house just like that, without warning.

Elias's mom looks classy and put-together even in her pajama pants and slippers. For the first time, though, there are bags under her eyes.

"You're here early, Merrin. Rosie made pancakes.

Can I make you a plate?"

For once, a plate full of simple carbs drenched in sugar does not appeal to me. "I'll wait for Elias," I say, managing a small smile.

"He's in the shower, sweetheart. Just leave his door open so he knows you're here."

She doesn't say anything about the Symposium.

"Thanks," I call over my shoulder as I head down the hall to my right toward his bedroom. As much as I'd like to, it's not the best day or time to surprise Elias while he's wearing only a towel.

I notice a door Elias has never pointed out to me, at the end of the hall where I've never really gone. Elias's mom is stationed in the kitchen and his dad's not around, as usual, so I duck into the room. It's about the size of my bedroom at home — small — and it's wall-to-wall lined with computer screens, giant tablets, even a few shelves of old paper-paged books. There are actually a lot of them — a couple dozen, maybe, more than I've seen in one place in my entire life.

One of the books lies open on the desk. I tilt my head to read the title: *GENETIC ADAPTABILITY IN THE 22nd CENTURY*. I flip to the front cover to check the printing date, and it's just over 40 years old. Why would they have even printed a book so few decades ago when the vast majority was already digital? I shake my head and start to read.

As soon as I see the words on the page, I'm hooked. This book takes everything Mom, Mr. Hoffman, and Elias ever told me about Ones and elaborates on it times a hundred. I run my finger down the table of contents page and stop at a section called, "The Curiosity of the Single-Powered Individual."

The chapter that really catches my eye is: "Malleability of the Gene Structure." I've seen that phrase before — in the title of the lecture at the symposium. The one that made my heart jump and made me feel hope.

Three layers of marginalia frame the text on this page. I peer closer, examining the handwriting of some of the notes. I've seen it somewhere before. In Elias's room, in the note he sent to his sisters. This is Elias's handwriting. He's seen this book, studied it. All the "theories" he spouted to me in the cotton field that second time we flew — this is where he read them all.

I flip to the last page of the chapter, and my stomach turns at what I see written there. There's a column of names written in the long white space below the last paragraph: Monroe, Murdock, Wayne, Bavarsky, Grimm, Radd. And then I gasp as I read the last three: Summers, Suresh, and Grey.

Leni, Daniel, and me.

Shit. And the last three names, the three of us, are starred. He knew the whole time — knew we were Ones, knew the theories. He grew up with Leni and Daniel, but he must have known about my One way before he met me.

What do the stars mean? Are we the only ones still in control of our Ones?

Did he seek me out that first day?

I stuff the book into my bag even though I know I shouldn't, even though it's not mine to read, especially not the notes. I stalk to Elias's room, plunk myself down on the edge of the bed, and wait.

Five minutes later, Elias walks in, wearing sweats, his hair still damp.

I spin around. "I found the office. Thought it was another bathroom."

He smiles, clearly not getting it. Purple half-circles droop under his eyes. "Can't believe I didn't show that to you before. Stupid. I should have known you would love some of those books."

"Yeah, it was stupid, Elias." I sit there with my arms crossed, my heart burning and twisting in my chest. He sits in his desk chair and rolls himself toward the bed, so he's close. He looks sad and distant and a little worried.

Seeing him like this was totally not in my plans. I can't stand it when he looks like that. It breaks my heart as much as it did the first day I met him. That makes me even more pissed off at him. How dare he make me sympathize with him after what he's done? After all the things he's hidden from me?

"Is there something you'd like to tell me?" I ask, with a hard edge on my voice.

"Um…you're beautiful? And you're gonna skip town with me?" Elias says, smiling a slight, confused smile and flashing that stupid dimple again. He leans in for a kiss.

I roll my eyes and scoot back a little. "Try again."

He leans in further to kiss me at my jaw because he knows I'm a sucker for that. "You're smart?"

"Dammit, Elias!" I yell, and I push him away from me with both hands. I can't stand for him to be this close to me, not right now. "Let me ask it another way. What were you not telling me?"

I yank the book out of my bag, praying I didn't damage any of the pages. I hold it by its spine, and its pages threaten to flap open against the inadequacy of my tiny hand. He stares at it, eyes flashing dumbly between my face and the book. He knows exactly what I'm talking about. I know he does. He has to.

I'm suddenly furious at the damn empty look on his

face, the opposite of the ones I love, the smiling one and the determined one. This empty one is worse, way worse, than the I'm-okay-but-really-I'm-not one that he always wore when I first met him.

So now I growl at him. "I found that chapter. I found where you wrote my name. What are you not telling me, Elias VanDyne?"

And then his face looks sad, so sad, that tears prickle at the corners of my own. I look down at the book because I don't want him to see I'm so angry that I'm actually freaking crying.

"Look, Mer."

"You can call me *Merrin* till I'm done being pissed off at you." I launch myself off the bed, stand in the middle of his bedroom, arms crossed over my chest.

He clenches his jaw, shakes his head, and looks out the windows.

"Merrin." He looks back at me. "I didn't mean to hide anything from you, okay?"

"Oh, yeah?" I say. "Because you're doing a pretty shitty job of it if that's what you were going for."

Then I think of what we've been doing together and what the Hub has been trying to get at by testing Elias. My eyes narrow.

"How much does the Hub know about what we can

do?" I ask, my gaze so intense I imagine my eyeballs on fire. Maybe I should get Leni and Daniel over here and see if I can make it happen.

"I didn't tell them anything."

I look at him, dubious.

"Nothing, Mer, I swear. I was…"

"What? You were *what?*" Asshole didn't listen to me when I told him to call me Merrin. I'm kind of glad. This just fuels the rage.

"I was waiting to tell Dad until I had worked out a theory as to why exactly it was working with us."

"So I was going to be your little prize experiment at the end of this whole thing? Is that it? You found me on my first freaking day at Nelson just to try to make this happen?"

Every moment of our relationship flashes before my eyes. Was any of it real?

"Oh, Mer. We were going to be awesome. Be stars together."

"You mean, test subjects together."

He nods, his lips set in a hard line. "Yeah. After the Symposium…yeah." His voice gets softer, and he leans toward me. "Yeah. Now, I'm really worried. That's why I want us to get out of here." He stands up, just a foot away from me. The buzz clouds my thoughts. "Seriously. Screw everyone else." He reaches out and lifts up my hand, holding it gently in both of his. "You're the only thing that matters to me now."

My mind seizes. All I ever wanted was to have an in at the Hub. But since Elias came along, even though I wasn't exactly imagining a future with him, it just hadn't seemed so bad to not be a normal Super anymore. Being a One, and an awesome One together with him, had felt okay. Enough for me to ditch Mr. Hoffman in the library at least.

Now I have no idea what feels okay because nothing does. My skin crawls again. *Back to freaking square one.* I yank my hand from his and stalk out.

I'm so mad I almost don't even realize he's followed me out to my car. I whirl around and glare at him.

"Do you have memories?" he asks. "Memories of the Hub? Of being there when you were little? Of being...examined?"

"Elias. No. I mean...our parents would have had to..."

He nods, slowly, and I don't want to believe it. "I remember, Merrin. This has been a reality since we were little. It has nothing to do with me, with my decisions. Nothing at all. Me...knowing about you... Well, yeah, at first I wanted to find you. But then I fell in love with you. And now I just want to protect you, okay? Protect you like

I can't protect my sisters."

"I don't need protection. I need honesty, Elias. I need someone who actually cares about me and not my One. Not what I can make them do. And I guess I'm not getting that from you."

I get into my car, slam the door so hard I think it'll break off, and drive through the narrow country roads for a long time, until the shaking in my body transfers to the rumble of the tires along the road.

It isn't until I pull in the garage and rest my forehead on the steering wheel that I really hear what Elias said.

He loves me.

And now it doesn't even matter anymore.

TWENTY

A few hours later, my fury has dissipated —thanks in large part to my rickety drums and the abuse I gave them. Now it's just solid, brooding anger.

I call Leni, and she comes over within a few minutes. She lets me put my head on her lap and runs her fingers through my hair. That soothes me enough that I just feel mortified and empty.

When I think of Elias, that look in his eyes when I yelled at him, I totally lose it.

We sit there in my room on the floor together for what seems like a long time, me sobbing and gasping and snotting on her jeans and her not saying anything because she knows it wouldn't help. Nothing would help. I can't even eat ice cream — ice cream! — because my stomach turns and flops and twists so much.

Even though there's no way I'd tell Leni everything, I do tell her about how we got in a fight, then Elias told me he loved me, and I screamed at him and drove away.

Finally, I flop over on the floor next to her and just stare at the ceiling.

"You don't even know that anything's wrong, you know. I mean, it's not like you broke up. You barely even talked to him."

That just makes me start crying again. She squeezes my shoulders and says, "It'll be okay. This is Elias. I know Elias, remember?"

I sniffle. "Yeah. Yeah." I sit up to blow my nose and look at her. I'm so embarrassed that I laugh a little.

"You guys will figure this out," she says, rubbing my arm. "I've never seen him like this with anyone, Merrin. This is the first year I've seen him happy since he was a little kid, you know? He loves you."

I shake my head and sniffle again. "Not anymore, probably."

She rolls her eyes smiles. "Merrin. He does. Since he met you, he's...peaceful. It's been a while since I could say that about him."

Leni's cuff beeps. She answers it, then says, "Yeah. Okay." She hangs up, leans in, and gives me a hug.

"Dinnertime?" I just realized it had gotten dark outside.

"Yeah. I'll text later. You okay?" she says into my hair.

"Mmm hmmm."

I head downstairs after smearing some concealer under my eyes, hoping to find some brownies or a candy bar or something. Mom and Dad sit at the kitchen island, talking quietly.

Mom looks up at me watchfully. I never know whether she is suspicious or worried or disappointed. All I know is that the look is always there, and it's the reason we've never been close. I've never been able to figure out what she thinks of me, and there's no way I can ask her. Especially not now.

"How are you doing, Merry Berry?" Dad asks, smiling. I know he's trying to lighten the mood. His eyes crinkle upward, like it's secret code for "Just play along." But I don't want to be in a good mood. I want to cry in frustration that they seem to know what is happening with the boys and I have no clue.

The part that causes the biggest ache in my gut is that they don't seem to think I'm important enough to know.

"Merrin? Merrin." Mom puts her hand on my arm, and I break out of my daze.

"Yeah, Mom?"

"Merrin, I'm going away for a few days, too. For an intensive study at the Hub." Her eyes are a little empty, with huge circles underneath them. She's not happy, not glowing at all like she was after her demonstration at the Symposium.

"Mom, you okay?" I still can't summon that much affection for her, but I am worried. And what the hell is going on with half my family at the Hub? Half of Superior, it seems like?

"Yes. Yes, I'm okay. I've left some dinners frozen for you two."

I look at Dad. Maybe he knows. Does he know?

Dad picks at his cuticles. "Dear, I don't think this is the way to…"

Her eyes dart over to Dad, full of some weird look I've never seen in them before.

I can't stand to look at either of them anymore. There's only one person in the universe who will understand me right now, who knows me and my Oneness inside and out. So, almost without thinking, I head back to my room, pull on one of Elias's sweatshirts, and call Elias.

"Elias, I have to tell you something." After agonizing and pacing and burying my face in my Elias-sweatshirt-covered hands, I finally called him.

"I have to tell you something, too."

I blow out a breath.

He continues. "First, I'm sorry. But you know that. I mean, I hope you do. But there's something else. Dad freaked out at me about that whole backpack thing again."

I suck in a breath. "Why?"

He's silent on the other end, which I can't stand.

"What did you tell him?"

There's a pause. "Elias?" I say after a minute.

"Nothing about you. So don't worry about it."

"What did you tell him?"

"I told him I flew. Um, finally."

"You what?" This makes me sit up straight. "Elias, what happens…what happens when he wants you to do it again?" My heart races with panic for Elias, how he'll perpetuate this lie that he told on my behalf.

"I'll tell him… I don't know." He sighs, so loud I can practically feel it puffing through the speaker. "I'll tell him it fizzled or something."

I have no idea what to say. I can think of a million reasons why that's a bad idea, but I feel like it's none of my business right now. Not after how we fought this morning.

"We could tell him. Together."

"No. We're not doing that. I don't want you involved in… I just don't."

It sounds like he's saying, "I don't want you." And I can see that, I really can, because of the way I reacted, screamed at him, accused him of not caring about me. Worst, didn't trust him.

"Merrin."

I don't know if he wants me to answer or if he just likes to say my name. I'm hoping for the latter, but since I acted like such a freak earlier, I'm betting on the former.

"Yeah?" I say, after a long pause.

"I used to dream about flying."

Tears well in my eyes, and a lump blocks sound from leaving my throat. I can hear Elias breathing on the other end. Waiting for me, as he always has. After a long minute, I finally say, "Me too."

"I was dreaming about you, Merrin. I was missing you. Before I even knew you. Before…"

"Before you knew my name?"

"Yeah."

"But you still knew that before you met me. Didn't you?"

There's a pause, and I can hear the rustle of sheets or blankets or something. He must be lying in bed. I guess that would make most girls hot and bothered, but I'll never be able to truly separate my vision of what I'd like to do with Elias from a cornfield with the scent of autumn fires in the air.

"Yeah," he says finally. "Just a few years. I've been waiting for you to transfer to Nelson. Couldn't believe it took you so long. And remember…you wouldn't tell me your name for days. So, really, it could have been any random transfer I had a crush on before you finally broke down and told me." He laughs shakily. "Besides, the dreams… They were even before then. I wish I could prove it to you, Mer. After that first time we flew together, I wouldn't have cared if it was our last. After that, all I wanted was you. I wish you could know that. Wish you could know how much I…"

I can't stand this anymore, can't stand being angry with him but loving him so much that it hurts. I can't stand not having anything to say. I can't stand not telling him about the boys and not knowing why I can't bring myself to get the words out.

I sigh. "Goodnight, Elias."

"Goodnight, Supergirl."

I dream of white rooms and cold air. My body doesn't rest on anything, and I feel like I'm floating, even though my body feels heavy as usual. I can't see the sky and I can't feel the air moving at all. Something pinches my arm, and then I feel dizzy, and the dream turns to dark coldness. I can't get warm under my covers.

I want Elias more than anything in the world, and I'm terrified, because even if I looked for him now, I know I'd never find him.

TWENTY-ONE

I wake with a start, my legs tangled in the sheets. My breaths seize my chest, quick in-and-outs, and I scan the room for something, though I have no idea what.

Not something. Someone. Elias. I want to be near him so badly it hurts. I fall back on my pillow, staring at the ceiling.

Then my cuff on the nightstand buzzes its notification that I have a message. I strap it to my wrist, squint away from it when its light glares at me the darkness. I blink hard, straining to see. Five missed calls. One message. I punch in the code and listen.

It's Elias. His voice chokes out short sentences. "I'm not gonna be around for a while, Mer." He takes in a sharp breath, and my heart wrenches. "I'm sorry." And then he hangs up.

I feel like the entire world stops around me, like I have to work hard against its frozenness to blink or breathe or think.

What the hell? Where is he going? Are his parents transferring him to Super? That wouldn't be such a big deal; I could still see him. Are they moving out of town?

I'm sorry, too. I'm so, so sorry. I'm sorry for a lot of

things, and I'm a little ashamed. That clouds my thoughts so much that I can't imagine what I'd say to him, especially over the phone like this, not in person. I'm not mad at him; now I just wish I could see him.

I'm still wearing one of his sweatshirts from bedtime — threw it on over the camisole, t-shirt, and long-sleeved shirt I was already wearing — because the smell of him is one of the only things that can calm me, even when I'm angry at him.

I toss on some jeans, socks, and my Chucks, and then push out the door in the dark, heading to my car even though it's only 4:15. All the better — the next shift is probably just getting into the station or maybe grabbing their morning donuts.

I race the whole way to the VanDyne house. Elias's car reflects blue from my headlights, and I sigh with relief.

I want to wiggle into bed next to him, wrap my arms around his waist, bury my head in his chest and forget the rest of the world exists. Whisper to him in the dark that I'm sorry, tell him we're in this together, that we'll figure out this whole stupid backpack thing and the Hub thing, and if we can't, we'll run away together, anywhere, anytime, just like he wanted, as long as we're together.

I knock on the door right after I realize how freaking early it is, how normal people aren't even awake at this hour. No one answers, of course. I run down the side of the house and start chucking gravel pebbles at Elias's window. After a few minutes of that, there's still no movement from inside. I know I'm definitely not supposed to be here, with his weird curfew and all, but still. Elias would know it was me, would open his window.

I hook my fingers onto the window sill and float up just a tad to peer inside. It's still dark in there, but the blue glow of his alarm clock illuminates the room enough for me to see that his bed is empty.

My arms shake, so violently that I almost can't hold on to the sill anymore. My stomach twists painfully. I dash all the way to the other side of the house, right outside the music room door.

I raise my palm up to the smooth black panel and whisper, "Hey, Rosie." Just as I'm about to press my hand to it, I spot something sticking out of the narrow gap where the panel meets the house's outer wall — a scrap of paper. I tug it out and unfold it with trembling hands. When I read what's written there, my stomach twists even more.

M —

Knock knock.

— E

My heart stops, and I can't fill my lungs. He's at the

Hub. Oh my God, they've taken him to the Hub, and they're going to try to get him to fly.

I push my sleeve up to look at my cuff, but it loosened in my scramble to get dressed, and it flops off into the garden. I scrabble around among the plants, leaves scraping my arms, soil caking under my fingernails, trying to find it. But it's dark, and under the shadows of the plants, I can't see anything. Hot tears stream down my face. Finally, kneeling in the dirt, I find it and search for his call in the log. He called me at 3:30 AM.

"Dammit!" I scream at the house, at all the shit that Elias has gone through, at all the more he'll go through on account of me. I slam my palm against the scanner, open the music room door, and streak past the drum set that two months ago I thought was the most awesome thing in the world.

I'm already in the hallway by the time Rosie has finished saying, "Welcome, Merrin Grey," and my heart nearly stops. Why does the damn house have to announce every person who walks through the door?

"Rosie, go silent," I hiss, hoping that command works.

I tear into the main area of the house. All the lights are off, except in the kitchen, like always. Frantically, I run my hands along the counters, looking for a note, a key, anything that will help me think of how to get to Elias, tell me what to do. Anything.

A sudden, loud, rasping noise startles the hell out of me, and I whip around, waiting to see Elias's dad — or worse, some Hub official — waiting there in the for me. Then a pungent, familiar scent hits the air, and I calm down the tiniest bit. It's the damn coffee maker, automatically starting to brew first thing in the morning. Like this is a normal freaking day.

 Of course it's not a normal day. The tears start up again.

Then it hits me. I have my cuff. I'm such an idiot. I'll just call him, see where he is, at least let him know I'm trying to get to him. At least text him. I call first, jittery as I listen to the ringer once, twice.

Another sound makes me jump, a harsh trill from three doors down. Elias's room. His freaking cuff is still here.

I run back outside to my car, barely able to see through the black after my eyes have adjusted to the house's low light.

Just last night, Elias told me the very reason he's gone now. The fear in his voice was of something real. His dad's been waiting for him to fly, pushing for this.

Whatever he'd been letting them do to Elias there at the Hub, they think it's working. They took him because they think they've finally made him fly.

They wouldn't think that if he hadn't lied to protect me. And we wouldn't be in this situation if I'd really believed he was trying to keep me from harm instead of keeping me down.

Tears slip freely from my eyes now, as if they're part of my face, a normal part of my being. My body doesn't even react to them anymore, doesn't heave with sobs. My determination keeps it from doing that because if there's anything I'm going to do, it's going to be the one thing Elias tried to do for me — save me. And I can't do that if I'm doubled over my freaking steering wheel and weeping.

I swipe at my cheeks with a sleeve. I have to pull myself together — it's all up to me now. I'm the only one who cares enough to try to do anything to stop what's happening to Elias and to my brothers, whatever it is.

If I don't find him, step up, and tell the truth, what are they going to do to him? What are they going to do to all the Ones? Will Daniel disappear in the middle of the night? Will Leni?

Just as I think her name, my cuff beeps, and I jump in my seat, swerving. I look down at the glowing screen and see Leni's name there.

I hit the speaker button. "Hello?" I'm sure my voice sounds as panicked as I feel.

"Merrin?" Leni's voice is a little gravelly. "Is everything okay? Daniel got this weird text from Elias this morning..."

"Wait. He texted Daniel?"

"Yeah, at like quarter to four. But it was weird. *M will need you.* Or something. Hold on." Her voice muffles a bit. "Is that right?"

"Is he there?" I ask.

"Yeah, he, um...yeah, he's here. Anyway. What's going on? It had better be important for before dawn on a Sunday."

"Where are your parents?" I ask, my mind racing. If I have the two of them, we might have a chance of getting somewhere with the Hub.

"Soccer tournament with the kids. I had to stay back for the cheerleading meet tomorrow."

"Len?" I ask, my heart aching when I use the nickname only Elias uses for her. "How big of a deal is it if you miss that meet?"

"Merrin, you are freaking me out."

"Just...get ready to go. Both of you. Okay? Drive by my house in half an hour, and I'll explain everything."

My thoughts run through my head in a loop — what I have to do, where I have to go, how I'm going to get there. I know Elias is at the Hub and that I have to get in and get him. My parents aren't going to be any help. They're all rallying around the Hub and its experiments, even Dad. Maybe they're even pulling my brothers in with them.

Then a whole new panic strikes me. How am I going to even get in? I know if I can break into the Hub's main entrance and if I have Leni and Daniel, somehow we'll figure out how to find Elias, get him out of there. Maybe use their firepower or my One somehow. At this point, I don't care how we do it — I only care that I see Elias again, in one piece. Hopefully get him out of there.

The only thing I have to my name besides my cuff is a few thousand dollars' worth of rolled-up bills from summer jobs. If we're going to run, we're going to need some cash.

I kill the headlights a couple houses from mine and roll to a stop in front of it. Through our front window, I see a yellowish glow from deep inside. Mom must be up making coffee already. She likes to go for a run on Sunday mornings and needs a cup as soon as she gets out of bed.

I sneak around to the side door and duck beneath the windowsill, peeking up so I can watch Mom. I want to sneak in the minute she leaves.

She moves so slowly I can barely stand it. A slight whine escapes from my throat, and I realize that, while the tears have stopped streaming down my cheeks, I've started to bounce my knees, crouched like that, so that my whole body vibrates. I hold myself back from springing for the door handle the second Mom walks out of the kitchen and wait till I hear the front door slam.

I burst in, rushing to the mudroom bench in our front hallway where we're supposed to hang our jackets and put our bags up every night. My chest squeezes when I see only three of the five hooks filled. Everything's pristine without Michael and Max here to throw their stuff everywhere — not even a stray soccer ball in the corner. My heart flips a little when I realize I never told Elias the boys had gone to the Hub. Would that information have told him something? Would it have been a warning to him?

I shake my head. I can't think of that stuff right now.

I grab my bag from its hook and step over to the hall closet where I hid my cash. I would have stuffed it in my sock drawer, like a normal kid, but Michael and Max would have found it there in five seconds — they'd never think to look in the family closet. As soon as I open the door, Dad's work bag falls out, and his gigantic key chain clinks against the ground. I suck in a breath, waiting to hear him stir upstairs. After a few seconds, he doesn't.

I stand on a folding chair, almost collapsing it when I step too close to the back of the seat. I curse, then regain my balance and stick my arm to the back of the high closet shelf, letting loose a sigh of relief when my fingers brush my old beat-up wallet.

When I pull my arm back out, my fingers brush a box. I curse at Mom for shoving boxes of junk all over the place in the name of keeping a clean living room. The folding chair creaks, and as I reach down to steady myself, I knock the box off the shelf, spilling its contents everywhere.

TWENTY-TWO

I scramble down from the chair and start to put everything back. There's a bunch of random stuff — a faded movie ticket, a worn out twist-tie, a hospital bracelet so tiny it can only be from one of our births.

Then I spot the crinkled edge of a photograph — an old-fashioned print. It's of me as a little kid, sitting on the grass in a cotton summer dress, fine hair still faintly curly, my fingers bearing a hint of baby pudge.

In the photo, preschooler-me tosses an apple in the air. On the back of the picture, Mom's handwriting says, "Apple picking, Merrin, 4 years old."

Mom has every picture ever taken of the three of us printed, catalogued, and filed in albums that line the bookshelf in our living room. It's something my grandfather, who was in the internment camps, made her promise to do, she told me once. The government seized all the Supers' computers when they shoved them into the camps, and most of them never recovered the files.

When we were little, we loved to leaf through the albums. I could narrate my infancy and toddlerhood just from having seen the snapshots. But I have never seen this picture. I look like I'm two instead of four, so miniature next to Dad's shoe planted on the ground beside me.

The grass pokes up around my bare legs, and the path behind me stretches on and on, out of frame, lined by thin-trunked trees. It's the apple orchard, I realize, the one we've gone to every year, except this one, when I made excuse after excuse why I couldn't go. Why I had to hang out with Elias instead.

Mom must have taken this photo. She's the photographer in the family, or at least, she was until we all pushed our indignant palms into the lens — me first, and then, more quickly, the boys. The oval leaves of the apple trees, browned at the edges, flutter down diagonally in the background. Even that young, I must have been so happy to feel that wind on my face.

In the photo, I'm tossing an apple in the air. Mom's gotten such a clear shot that it looks like the apple's not even moving. I lean in to take one last look and realize — there's no movement to that apple. None. No blur at all. Which would mean that Mom had a really fast shutter speed. Except for how blurred the wind has made the leaves in the background.

My thumb senses a little bump in the back corner of the picture where I'm holding it. I lift it and see a tiny rectangular sticker: "Hub submission 497870c."

What would the Hub have wanted with this? And why

would Mom have given it to them? I shove it in my bag.

I pick up the box, which lays overturned and empty on the floor, and start tossing the stuff back in. My nails hit the inside base in my rush to stuff everything back in there, and the solid surface shifts down, ever so slightly.

There's a false bottom to this box.

I wedge my nails into the sliver of an opening, breaking one of them. It still doesn't pull up. I swear and suck at my fingertip, then try again to wedge it into the gap and pry up the false bottom. The space underneath is so shallow that it would be impossible for the casual looker to realize that any of the box's space was missing. Inside is a single file folder, about an eighth of an inch thick. The top tab is labeled, "Grey, M — 497870."

It's a damn paper file.

My hands shake so hard now. I will them to steady so the papers inside won't fall out onto the floor. Every paper reads in stark black-and-white.

Mom must have made a copy of this folder and smuggled it out.

The cover page reads: **"Testing Group (in order of age): Merrin Grey, Britton Murdock, Matthew Grimm, Helen Summers, Addison Parker, Daniel Suresh, Erik Prince, Sarah Danvers, Rebecca Banner, Elias VanDyne."**

My name was highlighted — I can tell from the light gray sweep over it — but all I can see is the names that surround it: Sarah Danvers, a One who I heard, when she was young, could stretch her body but not control it or bring it back into shape once she did; Britton Murdock, whose amplified hearing went so out of control, drove her so crazy, they say she drowned herself when she was eight. Daniel. Leni. Elias.

I flip to the next page, and my heart races. I can't tear my eyes away from the chart headed, "Subject: Merrin Grey — 5 years old — Spontaneous lightness of body." The words "transfer of powers" are underlined three times. There is a subparagraph that says, "Testing will attempt to enable transfer of powers to independently animate subjects."

Humans. They wanted me to try to make people go light as well as apples.

The top of the sheet right below mine reads, "Subject: Elias VanDyne." There's a picture of a tall, scrawny little boy, tufts of hair poking up every which way, thick-rimmed glasses, mouth half-curved up in a grin. Dimples. My Elias, eleven years ago. Happy.

I flip the page again. A lump forms in my throat when I read the classification behind the name: "Subject — Helen Summers — 6 years old — Regeneration." I shake my head — this has to be a mistake. Indestructible is what Leni is not.

Then, from all the way in the back of the file, out falls a contact sheet of photographs. It's marked: "Testing Overseer: Katherine Grey." I gasp at what I see next.

A time-lapse photo of a limp, sleeping, kindergarten-aged Leni going from sliced on the forearm to completely healed in — I add up the seconds — a minute and a half. And that's just for a little kid.

Maybe this isn't the same Helen Summers — this can't be our Leni — although the flaming hair and pale skin splashed with freckles is too much of a coincidence. But something about this must be wrong. Leni's not indestructable. At least, not without Daniel. On her own, she's only combustible. Pretty rare power, actually. The only other person I know that can do that is...

Mom. Mom's combustible. But she never burns. Another picture drops out. Mom with Leni sitting on her lap, Leni's fragile arms slung around her neck, her face nuzzling into Mom's. Happy. Relaxed. Mom smiles, too, if a bit more distantly. I wonder, with an ache, if there are any pictures of Mom and me at that age doing something like this.

My heart pains when I remember — Leni lost her mom around this age. Probably right before this, from the way she clings to Mom in the photo.

I can't decide whether to be most horrified that Mom was the one who tested Leni; that the Hub sedated a six-year-old girl and sliced up her arms to see how fast they could get her to heal; or — possibly the craziest part of this whole thing — Leni used to be indestructible. No mention of the combustibility. Now, she's combustible with no sign of the indestructibility.

What did they do to her? And how much did Mom have to do with it? Is it possible — even theoretically — that she could have swapped powers with Mom?

My stomach turns, realizing I'm about to see Leni again. Can I ever look at her the same way again, knowing what I know? Does she remember any of it? Does she know the woman who comforted her is my mother?

I slam the lid of the box down and haul myself off the floor. I balance myself on the seat of the folding chair again and shove the box back to the spot where I found it. With one last look at the house, which two days ago felt so full and now couldn't be more empty, I duck out the front door, closing it softly behind me.

I jog down the street toward the intersection I know Leni and Daniel will pass on the way to the house.

Over the decades-old suburban rooftops, the sun finally begins to rise over Nebraska. The pink clouds sprawling out against a deep purple expanse reflect in a neighborhood's worth of solar panels, giving the illusion that they're just within my reach.

Daniel's car turns the corner. "Where are we going?" His voice slices through the air, sharp and fast, as the driver's side window rolls down.

"The Hub," I say, scooting into the back seat and clicking my seatbelt into place.

"How do you know that's where he is?" Leni asks.

I shake my head and swipe more tears off my cheek. I can't form words.

"What did he say, Merrin?" Leni's voice wavers.

"He... There was a letter and..." The more I try to talk about it, the more I feel myself losing control. I swallow, shake my head fast. "I just know. Okay?"

Daniel's hand hovers over the shift, hesitating to put it into drive. "Merrin, I don't know if we really should be..."

"Okay," Leni says. She presses her lips into a hard line, looks at Daniel, and then stares out the front windshield as we drive off.

TWENTY-THREE

Some cross between panic and hope tightens my throat as the minutes tick by and we finally reach the plains over the Hub. I haven't even thought about how we're going to get in.

But when we get to the ramp that will take us underground to the garage, the gate swings open.

"How did you...?"

"It's my parent's car," says Daniel. "Scans right in. Now. How is us breaking into the Hub going to help Elias? How do you even know for sure that they brought him here?"

Just as I'm about to say, *I don't,* every hair on my body stands on end. My skin prickles and pinches. I haven't felt anything this intense since that day in art class.

"I... I can feel him."

Daniel snorts a little, but Leni speaks up. "The buzz, Daniel. You know what that feels like." She turns to me. "We still get it. When we're, um...close." She blushes.

I look down at their hands. Leni grasps Daniel's so tightly her knuckles almost glow white against the rest of her skin in the dim parking garage light.

"So what are they doing with him?" Leni's eyes pool

with tears.

My heart surges with love for her. Because of how much she loves Elias and because of what I know she's been through. Because I know how she got that scar on her back. What no one was ever supposed to know. How will I tell her?

I do know when I will tell her. Not now.

"I...I don't know. I just know it's bad. He left a message on my cuff and one at the house. He was scared."

They both stare at me, waiting.

"I don't know, you guys, okay? But that's why we're here — to figure out why. There's something they want him for, and I'm not going to let them have him."

"I don't get it." Leni looks genuinely confused. "You're obsessed with the Hub. All you want is to get in here."

"Did you see Lia and Nora at the Symposium?"

"Yeah." Daniel snorts. "Smiling like good VanDynes."

I whip my head around to look at him. "Did you even see them? Did you talk to Elias afterward? Because they were not okay. He knew it, and he knows them better than anyone."

Daniel and Leni both kind of look down at their hands. I don't know if they're convinced or doubtful, so I keep going.

"My brothers are here now too, doing God knows what. The Hub took them almost without any notice."

"Okay, so? They want the phenoms. Big deal."

"Yeah, but Elias is not a phenom. They *think* he is. But he's just a One."

"Why would they think he's a Super now?"

"Well...it's...it's my fault, actually. I can't go into it now because I'm afraid we don't have time." My voice cracks. "All I know is that, whatever they're doing to him, his body can't take it. They think we — Ones — can do stuff we can't. Or that he can. Maybe. I don't know. But I don't want to risk waiting to find out."

Leni's gaze darts between me and Daniel, and I can tell she's going to be the deciding factor here. There are a couple seconds of silence, and then she turns to Daniel.

"You know how to get in, don't you?"

"I have an idea. But I have no clue where to go from there. No one really knows the layout except high clearance."

"I do." I sit up straighter, encouraged. "I know the layout. I've seen it — Elias has clearance. He showed me around at the Symposium."

Daniel's eyes go wide. "Elias has — what? Well, okay," he says, shaking his head, "but *you* don't have clearance."

"No. But she does have you," Leni says, staring at him. "Hack her cuff."

"You can hack my ID file that fast?" I gasp. "But most people — "

"Yeah. Would take days. But he's a genius."

"Do you have any idea how much trouble I — " Daniel stammers.

"Daniel. Seriously? She'd do it for you." Leni motions for my cuff, and I whip it off and hand it to her. Daniel takes it when she shoves it in his face and pulls a tiny screwdriver out of his pocket, going to work on the cuff and muttering about how he's only doing this because he loves Leni. I can't help but smile.

In just a few minutes, he's got the cuff put back together, and I strap it back onto my wrist, praying that his clearance hack is good enough to get me where I need to go.

A soft "thank you" is all I can get out, and then Leni reaches to pop open her door. We stride silently, shoulder to shoulder, toward the elevator that will take us into the Hub.

The elevator opens into a long hallway, the white shining surface barely reflecting back the dull grayish light. It's on low lights status and doesn't automatically change when we walk through, to my surprise and relief.

"We're before the checkpoint, so the building doesn't care what we do. Not yet," Daniel explains. "But right at the end of this hallway…" he gestures to a box on the wall right before the doorway to the entrance. I remember it from the Symposium.

"Facial recognition and serum," Daniel whispers. "You have to let it scan you, then give it a drop of your blood."

My thumb rubs against my middle finger, which is the one I used to get the blood sample for Mr. Hoffman.

"Shit," I say. "Dammit." No way can we pass this scanner. The way the two of them look at each other, I can tell they're thinking the same thing.

"Okay, Merrin. That's enough." Daniel's eyebrows squeeze together, and he puts a hand on my upper arm, trying to turn me back toward the way we came. I shrug away from him, my face screwing up with the tears and anger I'm trying to keep from flooding out of it. "We'll figure this out back home," he says, his voice dropping even more. He turns toward the door, back from where we came.

I plant my feet firmly on the floor. "I know he's here, you guys. I know it. He told me he needed me." I dig the white slip of paper out of my pocket and wave it in front of me. "Daniel, he texted you. Trusted you. What else could

M will need you mean besides 'Help Merrin get into the Hub?'"

"A lot of things," Daniel says, clenching his jaw, although he stops, facing the wall, not ready to go back or to continue.

Leni's eyes turn sad again, and she grabs Daniel's upper arm.

"Helen," his voice is soft. "My parents…"

"Merrin is serious. Elias needs us. Elias, who we've known since we were little. Okay? If he's really in trouble…your parents won't care."

I want to ask them what the hell they even think they can do, but I'm so grateful for Leni, that she's even making Daniel hesitate at all, that I bite my lip.

He looks up, his eyes burning a hole in me. "Do you know where to go?"

I close my eyes for a moment, and I can imagine where the hallway curves around, can visualize where it leads into the main lobby and the demonstration rooms. Can remember the hallways I sped past with Elias and the one he pulled me into that night at the Symposium.

"I have an idea."

"Okay," Leni says. "After we do this, you just…go. We can take care of ourselves."

"What are you going to do?" I hiss in a whisper. I'm

almost as worried about them as I am about Elias. Almost.

Daniel closes his eyes and shakes his head. Leni snakes her arm around his waist and puts her forehead up to his while she extends her palm out toward the retina scanner. "This is Elias. He would do it for us." I can't tell whether she's speaking to me or Daniel or both of us. "He would do it without thinking."

I nod, watching her, knowing what she's going to do and half-wanting to stop her because I know that nothing that comes from it will be good. Not for them, anyway. Not for any of us, but at this point, I don't really care what happens to me.

A low *whoosh* emits from Leni's hand, followed half a second later by the most intense column of blue-fading-to-white fire I've ever seen, three times denser and brighter than a blow torch. She targets the column behind the retina screen where all the computers are.

The metal glows hot and red, and Leni winces. Something bubbles out from the joints of the box and melts down the sides. She's completely destroyed the insides, and the plastic has melted and is oozing out of the scanner.

It's surreal how quiet the whole thing is except for the low, steady whisper of the flame. Like I'm moving in slow motion, I step past the scanner, and nothing happens. It works. No alarm.

"It should take the mainframe a few seconds to catch on. Go!" Leni whispers, her eyes wide.

I reach back, squeeze Leni's hand, and start down the hallway toward the main section of the Hub.

And then, the alarms sound. Huge whoops that start down the hallway and creep toward us, running through the building section by section. A robotic voice echoes through the speakers: "Facial recognition checkpoint compromised. Please check and reset."

Yeah. Resetting that thing's never going to happen.

The sound of footsteps echoes down the hallway. When I imagined the hallways, I forgot to visualize the security checkpoint with real, live guards just around the corner.

Leni and Daniel press up against each other and fold themselves into a small, tight closet a few feet behind me. But there's no going back now. I squeeze my eyes shut. If there's any time for going light to work perfectly on demand, now is it.

Leni hisses, "Go! I know you can!" She gives me an apologetic look, then swings the door shut, pulling it the rest of the way closed with a soft snick.

I tell my body to float, and when I fly upward, I can almost feel it sigh with relief. When did it start to feel more normal for me to be up in the air than down on the ground?

The air must be blowing through the ventilation system at a pretty good pace — even though in this high-tech building it makes almost no noise — because I drift, little by little, around to the corner.

At six o'clock on a Sunday, there won't be many backups. They'll have to run to get someone else out here quicker than the few minutes it will take them to find the location of the sirens.

Two rows of security guards, each six deep, patrol down the hallway, checking inside every alcove and unlocked door. When they reach Leni and Daniel's, and it won't open, one of the guards in the back reaches for something in her pocket and pulls out a key. My heart beats a mile a minute.

I plunge my hand into my pocket, searching for something — anything — I can throw. I find a balled-up foil wrapper from some junk food I ate God knows when and roll it in my palm for a second. I hurl it down the hallway, and it clatters to the floor, startling the guards and moving them all forward.

I hover an inch below the ceiling, keeping my body rigid as a board, holding my breath inside me, hoping it doesn't push me down like it always used to back when my biggest concern in life was trying my hardest not to float.

TWENTY-FOUR

O nce the guards leave, I reluctantly sink down to floor level. As relieved as my body felt at going light, as much as it needed it after all that pain, I can't move that fast — not nearly fast enough — when I'm light.

Plus, the system will register my cuff, and if it doesn't sense my weight on the floor, I'm pretty sure more alarms will go off.

I speed down the hallways, the alarms from the entrance echoing down and sounding almost as loud as they did back there. The noise makes everything seem chaotic, a grotesque contrast to the spotless gleaming surfaces of the floors and walls.

Next to each door hangs an identical etched placard, all bearing equally boring names like "Meeting Room" and "Conference Hall." I stop at some that say "Lab," but peering in the windows, see nothing but empty space and tall lab benches holding only trays of empty test tubes.

I whip around, not knowing what to look at, where to go. How to find Elias. My eyes catch the words on one of the placards: "Medical Wing."

There's an entire medical wing here? My heart sinks

just as a familiar warm buzz takes over my whole body. Elias is in here. Are the boys in here, too? Or Elias's sisters?

I burst through the door, and the system gives off a pleasant *ping* instead of a screaming alarm. Nice work, Daniel.

A short hallway leads to one other door, labeled simply, "Lab." I peer in through the narrow wire-crossed window, just like the ones on all the doors at school, and see empty lab benches, long tables at standing height. A few microscopes, countless incubators, a mass spectrometer. No big deal, nothing out of the ordinary.

My hand hovers over the door handle, and I'm about to turn away, look for a room with people in it maybe, when something glints off the wall. I look harder and realize — these walls are lined with glass cabinets. Worth a look.

I walk into the room, and the lights flare up. Startled, I say, "Lights low." They go down again, and I try to blink the shock of the sudden brightness out of my eyes.

It's dead quiet in here, except for the faintest hum of electricity. With my palm out, I step up to the door of one of the glass cabinets, and I feel the chill of it from inches away. These are all refrigerated. Now that I'm closer, I can clearly see that behind each door are rows and rows of solution-filled vials.

The liquid in the vials glows bright pink, orange, green, yellow. Labels clearly identify their type according to color: Generative. Opener. Terminative. Developer. I have no idea what exactly they're supposed to generate, open, terminate or develop. Some look like they were typed on an old computer program, others with punched labels, others with wax crayon. Some of them have stickers with sloppy handwriting. The only other thing on them is a rectangular sticker showing the formula for whatever's inside.

My brain works a mile a minute, piecing each chemical together in my mind. Hydrogen, nitrogen, oxygen, joining into hexagons, linking together. I've seen this pattern before, the one listed on this pink vial. It's a deaminator. It will break down the guanine in someone's DNA. It is a mutagen, designed to mutate someone's DNA on the spot. Reversible, maybe. Barely. If conditions are perfect.

I read the formulas on the orange tubes in the same way. This combination of chemicals, in theory, would stop someone's DNA from mutating further. Ever. The Terminative formula. In theory, this is what Charlie Fisk would have needed to stop his One from taking over his body.

My hands shake, but I wrench open one of the fridge doors and grab the green vial. I have to know. One more time, I stretch my brain, structuring the formula in my head. *Just pretend this is an organic chem assignment, Mer.*

I gasp a little at this next one. This one will deaminate cytosine into uracil — hydrolysis. This is a mutagen. Most of the time, your own body would know how to address the breakdown. Most of the time, a chain reaction would start. Enzymes would sense it and repair the damage in the DNA. Make it better.

This solution would force a mutation. And it depends on the body's instincts to make it work. But only after it's fundamentally changed what already exists there.

If the Hub is giving this to people — to Ones — it would take away even their One. Could the Hub really be trying to kick-start bodies into making their own powers?

If I hurt my One — if I made it so I could no longer float — would my body know how to correct it? Fill in the gap? Make it better — make me fly? Would my DNA know what to do? Could it be true that all I have to do is inject myself with this green stuff?

I do know one thing for sure: It could just as likely kill me as give me a Super. Or take everything away completely.

The yellow one is unlabeled. Somehow, that scares me

even more than the others.

Then I see, on the label, in the tiniest print — names. Each one of these is personalized. My heart sinks. Each one is designed for a specific person. Allen, Baker, Cole, Dunham — a categorized, alphabetical lineup.

Now, I can't stop myself. I really can't. I move from cabinet to cabinet until I reach the Fs. I run my index finger along the vials, squinting at the tiny print. The Fs move to Gs. One, two, three names precede the one I'm looking for. And then I find it, and the world stops around me.

There are three, maybe four times as many tubes labeled "Grey" as there are most others. I force my lungs to take a breath and grab every vial labeled "Grey" I can find, slide it into one of the test tube racks on a cart nearby.

I move three doors down, guessing, and breathe out with mixed sadness and relief when I'm right. Two rows full of vials marked "Summers" and, right next to them, a row marked "Suresh."

I shove all those in my bag too, pulling a few "Grey"s out to make room for them in the stand. They clink in the bottom of my bag, whispering, *What if we're the ones?* in the back of my head.

There's only one other door in the room, and I whip around to it, ready to get the hell out of there and finally find Elias. But something tugs me farther down the wall, to the last cabinet. My hands shake even harder, and I take a deep breath, telling myself this is the right thing to do. He would want me to take these.

There are three times as many vials marked "VanDyne" as there were for the Grey. I take all of them, too. I probably have 40 altogether in my bag now, and some of the "VanDyne" vials won't fit either. I yank my arms out of Elias's sweatshirt, shimmy out of my long-sleeved shirt, pull it off, and roll the whole stand up in it so the light clicking of the plastic vials is muffled, tucking the ends of the shirt in around them. I stuff the whole thing into my messenger bag.

Whoever thought that Fisk's plan to quit any kind of dangerous experimentation after his son died either didn't know about this or was hiding something. Even in Supers, whose genes have already taken so much mutation and still left them human, these mutagens could kill.

Or they could make a One a Super.

I glance back at all the cabinets. Who are all those people? Are they kids, walking around Nelson, Nebraska, or moved somewhere away from here? Were they all in a Hub study like we were? If they were, did they know? If they knew, did they survive it? If they survived...what happened to them? Where are they? Can they do what we can do? Can they combine to make a Super?

There is no placard on the only other door to the room. My skin buzzes, drawing me toward it, telling me that I have to go through. I crack it open and, hearing no alarm, swing it open the rest of the way.

The testing arena spreads out before me, high domed ceiling directly above. And in front of me, there's a hospital bed. And Elias is on it.

TWENTY-FIVE

He lays there, in white cotton pants, chest bare, some kind of sensors strapped all over it. The knot in my stomach starts to loosen when I realize his skin is too pink for him to be dead.

Unconscious and without his glasses, he looks so young, so peaceful. Worst of all, he looks weak. His whole body jerks once. I look at the machine attached to the electrodes, and it shows a steady heart rate. So what the hell have they done to him to make his body jerk like that?

Then I lift my eyes and see something even worse.

Oh, shit. Oh, no. Not them.

Michael and Max lay just yards away. Immobile on exam tables, turned on their sides, IVs in their arms. A figure in a white coat leans over them, checking their heart rates, first one, then the other. Strange because they're hooked to monitors. No one should have to check on them. No one cares about how Elias is doing enough to bend over him.

White drapes leave a square open on each of the boys' backs, and my stomach turns. They're prepped for spinal taps. Someone's going to draw their bone marrow. The sob that started inside me at seeing Elias finally reaches my throat, and I choke it back, trying to stay silent, trying to tamp down the gasping and sniffling I know dances at the edge of my restraint.

I understand all the pieces of this individually. The testing arena. Elias, hooked up to machines, for experiments. Because they think he can fly. Michael and Max. Bone marrow taps to see why the Wonder Twins are faster when they're together. But if I try to assemble them all into one coherent picture, none of this makes any sense.

Just as I take one step closer to Elias, someone grabs my arm, jerking me backward almost off my feet. I gasp, but another hand claps over my mouth. My eyes flare wide as I'm dragged, my protests muffled to near-silence, back into the room where I collected all the vials, then spun around to face my captor.

Brooding blue eyes as familiar to me as my own stare back at me, wide and terrified.

It's Dad.

A memory, fuzzy and distant, hits me out of nowhere. Dad looked at me with those eyes once, in a room like this, so long ago I've almost forgotten it ever happened.

I'm sitting on a table with a thin padded cover and a length of white paper running down it. I stare down at the red sparkling shoes I got for my fifth birthday, swinging above a floor feet below. A shining metal rolling table waits against the wall, and it's covered in paper, too. It holds some disinfectant wipes, cotton balls, and band-aids.

A man walks in, but I don't remember his face. I do remember the bulb of his stethoscope swinging back and forth as he walks and a flash of the suit underneath his white coat. Pinstriped. Dad grasps my hand, and I don't understand why at first. Then the man in the coat rubs my arm with one of the wipes, and the alcohol leaves a patch of cold there. The chill spreads up my arm and across my shoulders, running down my spine. Dad says some words to the man, words I don't understand like "enhancement" and "additive capabilities" and "no indication of emergent risk."

But his voice is deep and soothing and almost the same as when he reads me a bedtime story, so I know it's okay, everything will be okay. The man draws his arm back, and I see that the pink liquid is on one end of a syringe and a long, shining needle is on the other. It can't be meant for my arm that was just swabbed with alcohol. I won't believe it.

When the tip of the needle pushes into my skin of my upper arm, it stings, burns, and then a dull, thudding sensation reverberates over my whole body. The needle has bumped my bone, and I cry out, even though I want so badly to be brave.

Dad brushes his fingers through my brown waves and tells me how brave I am anyway, how proud he is, how soon this will all be over. How, soon, I'll fly like an airplane.

Then everything goes black.

"Your mother has been part of this initiative from the beginning. As have you. I gather you've discovered that." Dad glances around the room at the disturbed cabinets. So he knows what's in them. That same sick feeling punches me in the gut.

"I'm an *initiative?*"

"Well, an experiment. Part of one. A short one, unfortunately."

My voice rises. "I'm an *experiment?*" I knew this. I knew it an hour ago when I found that box, knew it in my gut longer than that, but the confirmation from him starts the disbelief all over again.

"Let me start over. You know your mother is Gifted."

"Yeah. She's a Super. So?"

"You're old enough to use the proper terminology, Merrin." Dad narrows his eyes at me, and though part of me wants to shrink a way, a bigger part pushes me to stand taller. He said "old enough." I'm old enough for him to tell me something. I'm old enough to keep someone else's secrets.

Still, I roll my eyes because he has the gall to scold me here and now. Like this. With formulas and chemicals and serums based on my body clinking around in my freaking messenger bag.

"Yes. Since your mother was a child, she had the spontaneous combustibility, combined with indestructibility. Never very powerful, but…"

"Right. A fire girl."

"When you were five, she received an injection. We knew it had enhancement properties, and we thought it would give her greater heat or range. But it added a new ability instead. We actually don't know if it might have been latent, but…"

"But what? What else can she do?"

Dad takes a long breath and looks at me, giving me that same damn look Elias used to give me when he thought I couldn't handle hearing something. I challenge him, stand up as tall as my frame can stretch, and growl, "What. Can. She. Do?"

"She can fly."

"Are you kidding me?"

Dad shakes his head.

"Are you telling me that Mom is the *freaking Human*

Torch?"

"Merrin. Calm down. Let's be serious now."

I look back at him, cross my arms, wait for him to say anything reasonable.

"The Human Torch is a story. A comic book character. Your mother...your mother...can actually go quite a bit faster than that," he says meekly. "But yes, it's a lot like the Human Torch."

My mouth hangs open. I don't know what to say to that. I'm sure I look like I'm about to lose my lunch because he shakes me a little, jolting me back to reality. I fill my lungs and look Dad in the eye.

"There's something else," I say. "Isn't there?"

Dad swallows and looks down. "The amazing part about all this — about you and the reason you were involved in the experiment in the first place — is that she couldn't do that until you were born. The day we brought you home from the hospital, she started floating in her sleep."

"Floating in her sleep," I repeat, my lips feeling numb.

"Yes, it was incredible, actually. There had been theories about transference of powers, but we never proved... Anyway, she went through intense studies. It was painful — excruciating, actually — but the enhancers turned the floating ability into a flying one, and for the longest time, we thought it was she who had absorbed the power from you. But we realized pretty quickly…" His voice trails off.

"That I was *transferring* the power to her," I say, like he's simple, forgetting that I've been hiding it all from him.

"Yes. But when we tested you, we couldn't get your body to pick up a second. We gave you the enhancers, but for whatever reason…"

"It didn't work," I say, and Dad nods. *Until now,* I think, but I can't bring myself to say it, can't get the words out of my mouth.

He nods. "Didn't even make your float stronger. But, then, none of the Ones responded. Not in the way we'd hoped. We thought the youngest would be…"

"The most malleable," I finish.

He stares at me for a second and then takes a deep breath. "But you *were* the youngest, and you didn't respond. And since then, we haven't seen you transfer, either."

I stare at him, my eyebrows raised. I probably didn't transfer after having a needle shoved into my arm because I was so damn terrified that I didn't think about my One for a long time. Couldn't engage it. But later, when I really tried, I floated higher and higher. I wait, listening to see if

Dad really hasn't thought about chemicals not being the only factor in this.

"Some stayed the same, like you," he continues. "Some…became very ill. One girl lost her power entirely."

"Leni," I say, under my breath, so low I'm not sure he hears it. She didn't lose a power, she switched. She used to be indestructible. She got Mom's power in place of her original. Mom, her tester. She transferred then, but never did again. Until Daniel. Same story with Elias and me.

"And Elias," Dad says, "transferred like you. To his sisters. Their ability became even more powerful, accelerating their teleportation speed significantly."

My brain bounces from piece to piece, my attention span some crazy warp-speeded pinball inside it. "So, transferring means we give our power away and absorb another at the same time?"

"Yes. Well, no. You were unique in that regard."

Elias does it, too. I know that, but I won't say anything. Can't reveal anything to Dad now.

"So we transferred — okay. And then we didn't. It's over. Why is Elias back here? And what the hell are they doing with Michael and Max?" I know my voice rises, I know it, but I can't stop it.

"Merrin! Get a handle on yourself," he says and steps

toward me, looking like he's going to clap his hand over my mouth again. Something rumbles deep inside of me.

I can't stand feeling this way about Dad, absolutely can't stand it, and now that it's happened — him keeping secrets and shushing me — I'll never be able to forget it.

"You have to keep quiet," he says, more gently, and glances out the door's narrow window. He pulls me toward it, turns me so I'm looking out.

The petite figure in a white coat hovers between Michael and Max's beds and then looks anxiously toward our door, right at Dad. It's Mom.

"See? Your mother's got everything covered. They're letting her oversee the bone marrow tap, but she's not going to do it, okay? When she takes them back for the procedure, she's going to give them something to wake them up, and we're all going to get out of here. I'm going to take you to the back room, and we'll all leave together."

"After all you've kept from me, you expect me to believe you? How do I know they're not going to just come and drag us back to the Hub?"

Dad reaches out to try to take my hand, but I pull away. "We very much regret everything we put you through all those years ago. How much you've suffered. We wanted to give you a better chance. And it didn't work, and we're sorry. But we have a plan. Plans work.

Storming the Hub with your friends from high school to save your boyfriend without a plan? Stealing valuable formulas that you have no idea how to implement? Without a plan, Merrin? That doesn't work."

I just glare at him for a second.

"And giving your blood to Stephen Hoffman in the Nelson High School library doesn't help much either."

"You knew about that," I say, pushing my shoulders back, trying to breathe deeply.

"There's a reason he didn't want you to tell us, Merrin. We would never have... Well, let's just say that them having current genetic material from you complicated things quite a bit."

Bile burns at the bottom of my esophagus, and it takes everything in me to keep my voice steady. "That's why the boys are here, isn't it? So they can take some of their genetic material to figure me out?"

Dad looks at the door. "They wanted to see how close the match was..." He shakes his head. "The whole family is leaving town. Today."

"Leaving?" My eyes narrow. I can't leave Nebraska, not when the other half of me — of my Super — lies strapped to a table with electrodes dotting his chest. "I'm not going anywhere." I look pointedly out the window at Elias.

"There's nothing we can do for him, honey. He told us he displayed a second, after all this time. Vice President VanDyne brought him in, saying he finally flew. But when they tested him, nothing showed up beyond his One. They're doing some more intensive testing with the girls now — to see if they can transfer between the siblings. But I'm afraid... Well, I don't even know what substances they've got in him, to be honest. It's best to leave him."

At that, it's all I can do to keep from snarling at Dad, from lunging at his throat and beating him senseless. If there was ever a time I could bring myself to do it, now would be it.

"Dad, I *love* him. I am not leaving him."

Dad takes a step toward me, reaches an arm out, looks at me with sad eyes. "Oh, honey..."

"Don't you dare call me that after all you put me through, after all you've kept from me. And when you want me to just leave Elias here like...like a failed experiment."

I jerk my arm from his grasp, surprised at my own strength.

Dad's face twists, and his lips set in a hard line. "You're not thinking clearly. Your mother and I have planned this. Just stay here while I make sure the coast is clear. Your being here... Well, it's a complication,

Merrin." I bristle at the way his voice raises at the end, the way he uses my full name. "But we are going to get you out. We're not going to let them test you like they've tested…others."

I cross my arms and stare at the wall. I have nothing to say to him, can't look him in the eye.

He closes the door carefully behind him, and I watch him cross the testing arena floor, check Elias's chart, and grimace. He looks back at the window, meets my eyes, and shakes his head, slightly, once. I don't exactly what that means, but tears prick my eyes. I know enough from the look on his face to know that something's wrong.

Dad crosses to stand next to Mom, who seems to be the only one besides the nurses in the arena. Must be too early for anything to have really gotten going yet.

He leans in to her, puts his lips to her ear. Her eyes jerk over to me, then close for a few good, long seconds like they do when she's upset about something and needs to take a deep breath.

She reaches out and runs a hand over one of the twins' heads — Michael's, I think. Then Mom and Dad walk out together, through a door on the other side of the arena, not looking back.

I peer through the window, my stomach twisting

more and more and more as I look from the boys to Elias, then back to the boys again. All three, so terrifyingly still.

Making the leap. Filling the gap. That's what we did. Or I did, at least, with the transferring, with the damn floating apple. Made them think they could close the gap from One to Super. Tie one Super's powers to another. And after all, isn't that what we did? Aren't I the one whose birth got this whole thing started? Who made Leni burn herself and countless other horrible things happen to Ones?

Then a sick sensation freezes me where I stand. I understand now. Why the boys are here, and why there are three times as many vials for "Grey" as there are for "Suresh." It's for me. For all the Ones they tested 11 years ago. They're testing our siblings, the ones who actually have powers, to figure me out, to figure us out. Figure out why we didn't respond to that study. Why I can't make other stuff go light.

To figure out how Fisk could have saved his son.

Unless we did respond. Unless I can still transfer. And then it hits me like a ton of bricks right in the chest.

That's what we've been doing. We've been transferring every time we flew. Every time Leni and Daniel flame on.

If they knew that, it would save Michael and Max. The

Hub wouldn't ever leave us — Elias and me, and probably Leni and Daniel — alone, but they might leave the twins alone. Might leave Nora and Lia.

I have to get Elias out of here. Because together, we're the only ones who can do the same for the twins. And for Elias's sisters, wherever they are.

I have to get to them. Because I might be the only one who can stop this.

TWENTY-SIX

When I push the door open and step into the arena, the buzz runs over my whole body — suddenly, powerfully, but not painful or unpleasant at all. This is warm, thrilling, bonding me to him.

I sneak along the wall and up to his bed, and his eyelids flutter. Relief washes over me so hard and fast I think I might collapse and lay beside him, there on the bed, where his long legs stretch a little too far, his heels hanging off the end.

When his brow starts to furrow, his eyes still closed, I can't wait any more. I can't. I press my lips to his, gently, then firmer. He doesn't respond. *Please let my Elias be somewhere in there.*

The buzz intensifies even more, running through my veins, charging my muscles. Here, with my lips to Elias's in the most dangerous place for us I can think of, I feel safe. More important than that, I feel — no, I *know* that I am — strong. I can literally do anything.

He twitches again, and my heart breaks. How much have they done to him in the short time that he's been here? Has he been through pain? I have to know.

Behind me, a door snicks shut.

Instead of trying to find a place to hide, I go light. I did it so fast in the hallway, and it happens much faster this time. The air gusts against my body as I go up. I flatten my body against the vaulted ceiling, 25 feet above Elias. He lies so still it's terrifying.

Two women in white coats stride into the arena with syringes in hand. From this angle, I can barely see an IV port poking out from the sinewy muscles at the inside of Elias's left elbow. It's not hooked up to a bag of fluids or anything, so I know it must be there so that they can inject him — quickly and maybe even often. One of the women chatters about her weekend, and the other babbles about her nephew's wife's food allergies.

I want to spit on them.

The one on the right pauses beside Elias, injects the entire syringe into his port, and walks away. As they're moving toward Michael and Max, Mom walks over and intercepts them. She doesn't even let them touch the boys.

"I've got these two, ladies, thank you," she murmurs. My body heat rises with pure anger. Even though Dad explained to me what she's doing here, I still can't get my head around it. I wonder how much Michael and Max have already been through, how much she and Dad have known about, and my stomach turns.

But I do believe Dad. Still trust that he loves Michael

and Max enough that they're going to get them out, to run away.

And I'm too in love with Elias and feeling too guilty about letting him get this far — all the way into the Hub — to leave here without him. There's no way in hell I'm doing that.

The nurses walk out, and I go heavy again. Mom hovers over Michael and Max, but her head whips around when I land.

"Merrin!" she whisper-shouts, her eyes wild. She gathers herself and says with a hiss and a jerk of her head. "Your father's through that door. Get in there."

I lock my knees, standing my ground. "Look," I say, setting my jaw to match my legs, "I know you have to get the boys out of here. I want you to. But I am not leaving here without him." I reach back and grab Elias's hand, which lays limp on the bed. I swear I feel a twitch from the tendons on top of it, but when I glance back at him, he's still as death.

Mom draws in a sharp breath. "Merrin Grey. You listen to me. You are in great danger. So much more than the boys. If you understood..."

"I understand, Mom. I found the files in the closet. I understand that I can transfer. And I understand that you brought me here when I was little. I could have understood a hell of a lot sooner if you ever freaking talked to me. If you were ever honest at all."

She sucks in a breath. "It was either keep you here in Superior or have them chasing after you. After all of us."

The giant white room is silent but for the rhythmic beeping of the machines attached to the boys and Elias, documenting heart rates and blood pressure. The tick of Elias's heartbeat on the monitor steadies me, strengthens me. I squeeze his hand hard, only stopping when my fingernails dig into it.

"Elias is lucky, honey. They've decided to stop testing him. Decided he's useless. Eventually they'll let him go. He'll be back to normal."

I clench my jaw, and tears burn at the corner of my eyes. "They might leave him. But I'm not going to."

"But you are so young. You have so much time. You'll find each other again someday."

"You don't get it. This isn't just that I love him. Something…happens when we're together."

Mom's eyes flare wide, a mix of shock and interest and fascination and the fulfillment of expectation, when the door on the opposite end of the room swings open.

President Fisk walks in.

TWENTY-SEVEN

He's impeccably groomed, a Cheshire-cat smile spreading across his face. The swish of his expensive suit fabric echoes annoyingly off the pristine walls.

But seeing Fisk grinning at Elias, connected to tubes and helpless, isn't the worst thing. Not by far. Because right next to him, Mr. Hoffman stands gazing at me. He pushes his glasses up and says, "You made it, Merrin." He doesn't smile. Not even a little.

"Welcome back to the Hub, Miss Grey," Fisk says, his voice steady and quiet. My skin crawls — again.

"I don't want to interrupt you," Fisk says. "Please. Continue. What, exactly, can you and Mr. VanDyne do?"

"I didn't say we could do anything." I raise myself up to my full height and summon every bit of resolve in my body to keep my voice from shaking.

He takes a step toward where the boys lay, and my skin bristles. "Your brothers are quite remarkable."

I keep my mouth shut. I don't know whether cursing or vomit would come out, but neither would be good right now.

"You must know just how fascinating they are. When

they are together, their speed and agility across water nearly doubles."

"Doubles?" I didn't realize it was that dramatic, and interest about how and why worms its way through my brain.

"Quite. We think they may have actually inherited the same quality that allowed your mother to attain an additional ability at such an advanced age. One that, if I'm guessing right about you and Mr. VanDyne here, you exhibit most strongly of all."

"The boys can only do that because they're so close…"

"That doesn't make any sense, Miss Grey. None at all. If closeness was the answer to our genetic problems, no one we love would have any."

"Weaker powers are not a problem. *Oneness* is not a problem."

Fisk tilts his chin up a little and laughs, three staccato beats. Like a robot.

"Merrin," he says, approaching me. "You yourself know what a problem you are. You've done the research, snooped in your mother's files, I'm sure. You know that half-Gifteds are a sign that something's gone wrong. There are so few of us Supers, Merrin, and we're just starting to gain a stronghold in this society that thought it was necessary to put us in camps 90 years ago. We have to make you better, strengthen you. Or we all weaken. And Supers haven't come this far to weaken, slowly fade away, become useless. Ones could ruin us. It's the Biotech Hub's job to keep that from happening."

"And, Merrin," Mr. Hoffman says, stepping up next to them. "No has ever wanted to change her Oneness as much as you."

"The VanDyne twins are similar to your brothers," Fisk says. "When they are together, they are able to transfer at a near-constant rate. It's like pressing a gas pedal. You can move in 'drive,' but if you press down, you go quickly. We think they can control it. We can *get* them to control it, here in the arena. Only in a sedated state, at this point, of course, but one day, we should be able to push their powers to such a level that they could move at light speed. Be invisible. Be endlessly useful."

"Useful for *what*?" I glance back at Elias. I could swear he's breathing faster than he was a minute ago.

Has he woken? Has he heard?

"At any rate," Fisk says, "with the help of some formulas we've been carefully developing over the years — since you were born, in fact, Merrin — we're hoping to research a little…deeper. Your mother's blood," he says as he crosses over to a locked cooler on the wall, "has helped us develop this formula. Along with our most recent addition — your sample, which Mr. Hoffman so kindly collected for us."

Mom's wild eyes flash to me. Like I've betrayed her.

I fight to keep my voice even. "If you already know how to fix me, what do you need Michael and Max for?" I know he doesn't need them for a goddamned thing.

"Their bone marrow will tell us something, something we have never been able to figure out about you because, well…you've never proven you can do anything. Won't admit to it. Even to Mr. Hoffman. So, you see…" He moves over and puts his hand on Michael's head. "…we simply have no choice."

That's when I totally lose it.

"They are babies!" I scream. Mom's small hands clamp around my upper arms, and her nails dig into my skin. "They're just *kids*. You keep your goddamned hands off of them."

He clicks his tongue and shakes his head, and the combination makes me want to hurl myself across the 15 feet between us and claw his eyes out.

Instead, I move back toward Elias's bed, hoping getting nearer to him, to the buzz, will steady me. Maybe help me figure out what the hell to do in a room with passive parents, an evil Super mastermind, and an unconscious boyfriend. And my poor baby brothers, who should never have had anything to do with this, prepped for spinal taps.

Mr. Hoffman chuckles. "You, who wouldn't be caught dead with a boy your first year at Superior High, suddenly now have a boyfriend? What makes him so important to you that you would risk everything, break into the Hub, just to make sure he's okay?"

My stomach twists, churning out resolve to get out of this, and then make Fisk pay.

Fisk lowers his voice to barely above a whisper. The only ones who can hear him now, I'm sure, are Elias and me. Or at least he would be able to if he was conscious.

"He makes you feel beautiful, makes you believe in yourself, all that. Yes, yes, fine. But that is boring. So I'll ask you one more time, Merrin: What can the two of you do?"

Something inside me snaps at his use of my first name.

"Without each other, you are useless, pathetic Ones. Without us, you will always be nothing. We can make sure you're without Elias for a very long time, Merrin, if it's true that he's no use to you as he is. We could use his body in...other ways."

I stare at him, half to challenge him and half because terror seizes me so strongly that I have nothing else to say.

He shrugs. "Fine. So Elias VanDyne is...a nothing. In

two days of testing, we're very sure of that. He is powerless — weakly pushing air will never make him a Super. He was nothing but a false alarm. His sisters, on the other hand…"

Fisk pushes a button on his remote control thing, and I glance at Mom, hoping that she can prepare me for what I'm about to see or hear by how she looks at me. A tear runs down her cheek, and her jaw is clenched. I've never seen Mom cry.

She looks down, her face twisted.

One of the walls of the arena spins around to reveal the girls, wearing nothing but black swimsuits that cling to their frames — thin and almost skeletal — suspended in a tank of green goop. Breathing tubes snake down their throats, and nodes dot their heads, which are shaved bald. Their eyes are closed, and if I could ignore all the tubes and wires, they would look like they were sleeping. Every once in awhile, one of them twitches, her eyebrows draw together, then after a few seconds, she relaxes again.

"It's a sensory deprivation substance," Fisk explains, his voice measured. I look over at Elias, and I swear he grimaces. The hint of pride I hear in Fisk's voice — the one that causes the vial of solution to practically dance between his fingers — makes me want to sprint over to Fisk and tear his throat out with my bare hands, just to stop his voice from ever existing again.

"We've been trying to utilize them and what they can do to make Elias more…effective. Now that you've confirmed that nothing — and no *one* — can do that, we're going to try it the other way around. The stasis will kill him, eventually, but, from what you're saying, that's the most good he'll ever do here at the Hub."

Fisk stands there, perfectly calm. "Show us what you can do, Merrin Grey. Show us why you've always been obsessed with biochemistry. Show us why you have a premed student's library of genetics and organic chemistry notes on your tablet. Show us why you're better than any high school student we've ever known at these things. Why do you care?"

I clench my jaw and stare back at him. I will not cry. I will not scream. I won't.

"I can fix you, Merrin. I know you want me to." He motions toward the small lab behind me, the one whose walls are lined with the neon-liquid-filled vials bearing my name. Or were before I stole them.

"There are amazing things here. Discoveries that can push you to your full potential. That can make Elias's sisters' sacrifice — and your brothers' — not be in vain. That can make you soar." He leans in, lowers his voice again. "On your own."

My lower lip trembles. Mom pulls me in for a hug, and my whole body stiffens. Mom never hugs me.

She presses me to her, her wiry arms so much stronger than I ever would have expected, and I can't pull away. She pushes her face into the hair hanging by my ear and whispers, "The two of you can fly?"

I nod the slightest bit.

"Fast?" she whispers.

I nod again. I hope, with Elias under, it's true.

She loosens her grip. Steps away. "President Fisk. We want to get this over with. I'll put him under myself."

I let forth something between a whimper and a yell and fall on Elias. Mom bends over me, digging her fingernails into my upper arms so hard it sends streaks of pain down my back.

"It'll happen quickly," she says, her voice so low only I can hear it. "When he wakes, you two get out of here."

I summon all I have in me — my love for the boys and Elias, my desire to protect my friends and get us all the hell out of here — to trust her.

Mom moves to a small stainless steel tray on a table nearby and stabs a needle into one vial of clear liquid after another, lifting, peering at it in the light, tapping the air bubbles out.

Dad walks in and sees me holding Elias's hand, crosses over to me, and wraps his arm around my shoulders. He tries to pull me away, but he couldn't get me away from Elias with a crowbar. Especially not right now.

Mom looks right at Dad, back to me for a second, and then back at him again with determined eyes. She holds up the needle-tipped syringe and quickly nods, the movement so slight that no one else would notice it. Mom injects it into the port. Dad draws back from me, his eyes slightly wet, his mouth set in a hard line. I've seen that face before. He's steeling himself. Saying goodbye.

A row of ten, a dozen, no, fifteen people in scrubs and white coats, just like my parents, has lined up along the wall. But they don't stand like nurses. They stand rigid, shoulders squared, muscles tensed. Like soldiers. That and the way they react to Fisk's every move as he paces the room — checking the girls' monitors, watching Mom mix the stuff in the needle, walking too close to Michael and Max — says it all. They're security, ready to jump on me the second I — *we* — try to run.

Besides that, there's nowhere to run. The testing arena crawls with security, dotted with obstacles we could never really sprint around, and every section of the building locks down if we try to go somewhere we don't belong. Which, I imagine, is everywhere by this point.

We're stuck.

But Mom didn't tell me to run. She asked me if I could fly.

That roof. All the doors have been locked down, but maybe that roof hasn't. Besides, that thing opens directly to the sky. What kind of security could really be on it — bomber jets?

I feel a shortness of breath, high in my chest, paralyzing my shoulders.

We don't get out unless we fly. If we fly, they won't get what they want — hooking us up to monitors and injecting solutions to watch the transference — but they will want us even more. Enough to hunt us down. And between Nora and Lia in sensory deprivation fluid and the boys getting prepped for spinal taps, I know there's nothing Fisk won't do to figure us out.

Which means if we fly out of here, we can't stop flying. Ever.

I glance over at my brothers one more time. Mom leans over and brushes Michael's dark curls from his forehead, kissing him there.

Like Fisk is reading my mind, he croons, "Show us that we've done something useful here, Merrin. Show us we're on the right track. Let us send your brothers home."

He reaches a hand out to me, touching my arm, trying

to draw me away from Elias. I fling my arm out and he steps away, still smiling that same stupid smile. I want to kill him.

"You're not touching me ever again."

"Oh, we'll have to if you want us to stop testing them. And you'll have to do it willingly. But if you won't... The secret to why you displayed transference all those years ago could lie in their genes. We think it does. We've gotten so close. The only thing we can't do is make Ones into Supers. But we will. When you show us exactly how that works."

There's no way he's going to grab Elias and me and just let the boys go. Not when he can keep them for whatever freaky side experiments he has going on.

"Prove to me that figuring out Elias and me is the only thing you really want," I say. "Let my mom and dad take my brothers."

"Excuse me?" Fisk scoffs.

"I don't like to repeat myself."

"You mean, let them go? Oh, my dear, you can't be serious."

"They get to leave. You won't need them anyway, when you have us. Then — only then — I show you what we can do."

Fisk nods to the guards-dressed-as-nurses, and they

step to the side so Mom can wheel Max out. Dad watches me, and I see anger, pride, and sadness in his face all at once. Each one of them kills me.

"I'll get the car ready," he says, nodding at me. "She'll be back for Michael." Then he follows Mom out.

"And the girls." I nod toward Nora and Lia, still floating, unconscious in that goop. I swallow hard. I don't even know them, but I know what they mean to Elias, and I can't stand to see them this way. "They go, too."

This is the first time Fisk lets his face fall, and it fills me with a small amount of glee. He swallows and then nods his assent to the nurses. They head toward the tank.

Fisk stays there another minute, standing too close, breathing so close to me that I'm afraid to open my mouth for fear we'd use the same air. He stares me down, looks at my hands again. He's seen that photo of me levitating that apple. He knows I can go light, that I can make Elias do it, too. He knows we can fly. He just wants his damn machines and serums to pick up every second of it.

Now that I've gotten the boys out of here, I have no idea how to stop that from happening.

The weird sucking-and-whooshing sound of the huge door to the testing arena opening, the one that made me jump and giggle during the night of the Symposium, startles me now.

One of the guards says, "We found more of 'em."

My heart races. I hear the sounds of struggle first and then see a swoop of bright strawberry blond hair.

My heart sinks, then soars again when I see that Leni isn't freaking out, shaking and crying like I would have expected, and Daniel stands tall. Half as second later, I see why. The guards have made one big mistake, one they wouldn't have known not to make because Leni and Daniel burned out the lines to the security feeds.

They've bound their hands together.

TWENTY-EIGHT

"**F**ound these two trying to sneak out the way they came in. They won't tell us a thing," the guard reports.

Fisk chuckles. "Yes. Thank you," he says to the guard and then turns. "Helen. Daniel. Welcome to the Hub's state-of-the-art testing arena. I'm giving more tours than I anticipated today, but no matter. The more the merrier."

Daniel's jaw clenches, and he stands up even straighter.

Fisk turns to Mr. Hoffman and says, "Pity the son of the famous Doctors Suresh couldn't make more of himself, isn't it? It's no wonder his parents never had any more children since he was such a disappointment."

Fisk grabs each of their hands and walks them over to where we stand. Leni moves with jerking steps, like she wants to stand her ground, to fight him touching her, but she knows it's futile. Daniel hangs his head.

He pushes them so they're standing right next to me, shoulder to shoulder, like we're dolls or pawns on a chess board. Like he's posing us for a picture.

He steps back, clasps his hands together, fingers interlocked, and brings them to his mouth, smiling a little behind them.

"Yes. Yes, lovely."

Behind me, the paper on Elias's bed rustles, and my heart thuds to a stop. I whip around and watch his chest inflate fully and quickly. His head moves to either side, and his eyes flutter open. I squeeze his hand for dear life, but I don't bend over him. I won't make myself look weak either. Not now.

Next to me, Leni gasps. Her eyes focus on something behind Fisk and become pools of tears. She sees Nora and Lia in the sensory tank, now only a quarter filled with green goop, behind me.

"What...what are they doing to them?" Leni chokes, staring at Nora and Lia. But I want to maintain eye contact with her. Need to.

"Getting them ready to go home," I say, keeping my voice steady, squeezing Elias's hand to tell him that it's true because I know he can hear me now. Elias's head moves one way, then the other, making the paper under his pillow crackle.

Fisk's voice floats between us like noxious gas. "Trust me, Merrin. You'll be glad you agreed to this."

If he keeps saying my name like that, I swear to God I will kill him. I will rip his throat out through his eyes.

I didn't agree to a goddamn thing, but I know what he

means. Staying. Testing. What Elias has been doing since he was a little kid. Poking, prodding, sensory deprivation goop. I look up to where Nora and Lia's tank is being drained, where nurses pull tubes out of their throats and wrap waffle-weave bathrobes just like the one I have at home around their atrophied bodies. I choke, try my best to keep the vomit down. Something that reminds me of home has no place here.

"Mrs. Grey," Leni wails when she sees Mom coming back into the room for Michael, "You said they were making me stronger."

I look from Leni to Mom and back again. Leni's remembered. After all this, she remembered what Mom was to her and what Mom did to her all in the same breath.

"We... Honey, we thought we were. Thought we could enhance your indestructibility."

"Indestructibility," Leni says. "I'm not indestructible. Only when I'm with... But if I ever was... I could have..." She looks quickly at Daniel, then stares at the ground, her face contorting between pained and composed.

I think of that snapshot of Mom and Leni I found. Of course she needed a mom-substitute. Sucks that it was just for research purposes. A flash of hate for Mom burns through me.

Yeah, Leni trusted her. Not only that. Leni loved her.

That's why it worked.

I was just a kid, too. I should have trusted Mom. It should have worked for me, too. But my instincts have always been pretty damn good, apparently, because I've never really trusted anyone — never transferred a thing — until I met Elias.

Mom stares at the ground, too, then clenches her fists around the side of Michael's bed and walks him out without another word. My heart twists for Leni, but there's no way to comfort her now.

Suddenly, the electric prickle of the buzz overwhelms me. I turn around to see Elias sitting up.

I whimper and bury my face in his shoulder. I can't possibly do anything else. "You're awake."

"You made it," Elias says. "You actually broke in to the Hub." His voice is filled with awe. "But, Mer," he says, his breath hot against my neck. "Michael and Max. They're…"

"I know. And the girls, too."

He swallows, blinks hard, and I motion behind me. Nora coughs and sputters from the tube removal. Lia's still. A look I've never seen on Elias before roils in his eyes. Pure, unadulterated rage.

"I heard them talking about me. They said I was going under…indefinitely. What did you do? How did you get them to wake me up?"

"I told them if the twins all go home, we show them what we can do."

Tears fill Elias's eyes. "Thank you."

I nod, resting my forehead against his. Then something catches his eye to the side, and he takes in a shuddering breath.

Leni murmurs, "Elias..." and puts her head on Daniel's shoulder.

Elias's head jerks up and then falls back to my shoulder. "They got Len and Dan, too."

I don't say anything. I can't.

"They helped you. They helped you get in."

I nod. "I never wanted them to get involved in this."

"They always were. You knew that."

"How are we going to get out of here?" My voice breaks.

"Hey," Elias says, his arms shaking, fighting to stay around me. He's still so weak from being sedated. "It's going to be okay."

Fisk clears his throat, causing me to whip around and glare at him. I feel Elias's shoulders tremble above my arm, which I've wrapped around his chest. Elias may know what he's going to do to get us out of here, but he's not going to do it when he's so weak.

I've got to buy us some time.

Behind me, where my hands join with Elias's, my messenger bag bobs against my back. I swing it around front and fumble through, my hands shaking as I hold out a vial. "I know what you're doing here. Know what you have been doing, ever since we were little kids."

Leni's face screws up.

"This is your whole life's work, isn't it?" I continue, glaring at Fisk. "Trying to fix all the Ones? Using us as a key to the whole problem?"

"Not a problem, Merrin. Not anymore. Not now that we know about you and Elias. Helen and Daniel. You are the next step in the evolutionary chain. To lift the Ones up from their pathetic situation and make them better. If you'll only show me what you can do... Merrin, you could change the world. Be the biggest biotech advance the Hub has ever seen."

I only ever wanted to help formulate an advance that could help kids like me, something that could give us options. Not something that could manipulate us into experiments or weapons.

I don't want to be something that the Hub could use against others.

Behind me, Elias clears his throat, and I notice how hard he's squeezing my hand. His shoulder steadies.

"Where are the rest of the vials?" he whispers to me, so light that I swear only I can hear it. I motion toward the lab door with my head.

Fisk strides over to the door to the lab and flings it open. Inside, behind all the lit glass cases, the vials of creepy neon liquid wink and gleam.

"All my life's work, since Charlie died — it's all in here. The highest security, the deepest part of the Hub. I've been keeping it safe, you see, for exactly this moment. And now, with so many of you here…"

I swear his eyes glisten with tears. I wonder if there is remorse behind the smirk, if there was ever a time he felt guilty when testing or injecting a little kid. I like to think there was. I'd like to think he never meant to use weird green sensory deprivation goop or throat tubes or electric sensors or sedatives or spinal taps. I'd like to think he never meant to put pieces of the poor little transferring five-year-old Ones in vials and collect them, hoping that one day all the pieces together would add up to more than the loss of his son.

I'd like to believe all that, but looking at him now, I can't.

Daniel speaks up. "How come I never knew about this? I would have…" He clears his throat when Leni looks at him, her eyebrows bunched together. "My parents would have brought me in for testing…"

"Ever since Charlie died… Well, of course we were supposed to stop all this activity. The trustees sanctioned us. But he so badly wanted to be more than a One. And for all the times he came home with a black eye, for all the opportunities he was denied while he was alive, I couldn't bear to give up on him. Besides, there is always some way, some other channel, to get what you want." Fisk steps even closer. "I'm sure you can understand that, can't you, Merrin? Can understand the desire to be something more than a sad, mediocre outcast who will never fit in anywhere? Something more? Something your family always wanted you to be?"

"I'm fine with being a One," I say, my voice low and snarling.

"Then why are you here?"

"For my brothers. For Elias."

And for the first time ever, I mean it. Now that I thought I could lose Elias, lose the boys, I'm fine with being a One. As long as it means we never have to come back here again.

Fisk pulls a vial out of his pocket again, and a solution sloshes inside of it, so thick it coats the glass. "And for this. The solution based on your blood. It could be the key to making you a Super, Merrin, but only if you let us test it on you."

My heart shudders to a stop. He knows that the promise of flying on my own can convince me to do anything.

Almost anything.

I open my mouth, about to sling another retort his way, and then a strange ripping sound steals through the air.

Elias gasps and sits upright. "They're back," he chokes.

TWENTY-NINE

Before I can blink again, a robe-wrapped emaciated figure appears in front of Fisk. Her hands are cuffed behind her, and her head still has red marks where the nodes were attached. She whips around to assess Elias, looks him up and down, and her eyes flash blue. It's Nora.

"It's nice to see you awake, Miss VanDyne. I hope the titanium cuffs aren't uncomfortable. Security measure, you understand," Fisk says, smirking.

In one swift motion, Nora pulls her wrists apart, breaking the chain and shattering the cuffs, and lifts Fisk off the ground by the throat.

"I think we get stronger the more pissed off we are. But since you hacks didn't test for that... What do you think, Leelee?" she calls over her shoulder.

Fisk's eyes practically bulge out of his head.

"Holy shit," Daniel breathes. He looks back at Elias, who stares back at him with wide eyes. I gather that this super strength is new.

Another ripping sound follows, and one of the guards cries out. Lia has teleported between two of them and busted out of her cuffs as well. She elbows one of them between the legs while wrenching the guns, one at a time,

~ 322 ~

out of the holster of another. She cocks one and tosses the other to Nora.

Nora fixes her eyes on Fisk, who struggles and gasps. She wedges the gun against the inside of his jaw and takes another hard look back at Elias. "This won't buy you much time."

"But —" Elias sputters.

Nora shakes her head hard and steps back to brandish her gun at the rest of security as Lia rips through the air again to take down the guard calling for reinforcements at the main door.

In an instant, the room fills with 30 Fisks, all grinning maniacally, all dangling vials of the serum he knows I want.

"What the…"

"He can make duplicates," gasps Daniel. "With kinetic energy?"

"Yeah, but they're not that strong. They can barely think for themselves," says Lia. "And he forgets that girls who see through matter can tell which of these ugly assholes is the real Fisk. I mean, he's practically a One himself."

"You can tell?" the Fisks all sputter at once, and panic runs wild in their eyes.

Nora laughs. "Yes. Half-assed duplicated matter looks different than the real thing. Idiot. Couldn't one of these fancy electrodes show you that?"

She looks at me as she steps back from of a crowd of 10 Fisks, then trains her gun on one, nodding her head upward once.

"This one, Merrin," she says.

Fisk gives an anguished shout and yells, "Take them all down!"

His duplicates swarm toward Leni and Daniel, who squeeze hands and send streams of flame in their faces. Mr. Hoffman dashes in, yelling, and grabs for one of the vials of serum a dupe is holding. A strangled sob escapes my throat as the white-hot fire devours his clothing and blackens his skin before my eyes.

Nora and Lia each pick a crowd of dupes and start firing. I grab Elias around the waist and yank him off his hospital bed with all my strength, ducking for cover. I pull off his sweatshirt that I wore over here and tug it down over his head. He still shivers beneath it.

As the duplicates' bodies hit the ground, they dissolve into shimmering nothingness, and Fisk screams and drops to his knees.

Nora presses her gun to his temple. "Just try to muster up some more kinetic now, you sorry excuse for a human being. I dare you." She looks at Elias. "We can take care of ourselves," she says, her voice stronger than I would expect for having been in disuse. "You just take care of the lab."

"There's no way you two can — " Elias says, just as Lia draws back and delivers a roundhouse kick to one hulking security guard, sending him skidding halfway across the arena and leaving him unconscious on the floor.

"We. Can take care. Of ourselves."

Still holding the gun to Fisk's temple, Nora inclines her head to read the label on the vial he still clutches in his hand. "Merrin," she says without looking away. "I think that President Son of a Bitch here was about to hand this over to you."

Without even thinking, I drop Elias's hand and stride over, grab it, and tuck it greedily into my bag, inside the sleeve of the shirt I stuffed in there, then hurry back to him.

Nora speaks to Fisk again, her voice getting louder and steadier each time. "Now. You're going to let my baby brother and his friends out of here. And you know how they're going to leave. So you might as well call all your goddamned security off the roof."

Fisk groans.

"Fisk," she growls. "don't make this harder on yourself than it has to be."

"Guards," he croaks. "Call off the missile surveillance."

Lia shouts a warning from where she stands, 20 feet away. "You can quit playing these games, you asshole."

"I don't know what you're — "

Nora delivers a swift elbow to the side of his head, knocking him flat on the ground. She digs her heel into his collarbone, edging it against his esophagus, and trains the gun between his eyes.

"You know damn well what I'm talking about! The lasers! The lasers, too!" Lia shrieks, her eyes growing fiercer by the second. "I'll be damned if my baby brother's getting sliced to ribbons after all this!"

"Lia," Nora says, much more quietly, shaking her head once.

"And the lasers," Fisk moans.

Nora looks back at us one more time, her eyes darting between Elias and me, who nods curtly, his eyes glistening.

Elias swings his legs down from the bed. "Get ready, you guys," he chokes to me, Leni and Daniel. Leni whimpers. The smell of melting plastic and smoldering cloth fills the air. They've got to be exhausted after torching half the place.

Fisk's voice, weak and wheezing, comes slithering through the air. "You'll never be anyone, Merrin Grey. Not without us. And you'll never be able to come back after this. You'll regret it the moment you leave the arena.

You know the life of a One is… Well, it doesn't have much of a point."

No, it doesn't.

No, it doesn't, I want to scream, but life without Elias doesn't either. And gaining a Super for myself while others pay the price certainly doesn't.

Elias cocks his head toward the wall about 10 feet away at one edge of the testing arena, toward the huge red button that will open the ceiling. He looks up at the hatch that unfolds to the sky.

"Get ready," he mouths. Leni and Daniel step closer to us.

Fisk's left the door to the lab with all our formulas — all the ones except those I'm smuggling out — gaping open. Elias hasn't missed it. His gaze burns past me right at the door.

Elias drops his hand from mine, holding his palm out flat. He sends a blast of air against the ground, swooping one of the medical-grade oxygen tanks up from the floor and sending it careening through the air. I have no idea what he's trying to do — create a distraction? — until it hits the doorjamb and cracks open, hissing.

Elias says, "Flame on, Len."

Leni clamps her eyes shut, reaches out, squeezes Daniel's hand tight, and stretches her other one out toward the door. A powerful column of flame shoots out and torches the inside of the lab, together with all its vials, in less than 10 seconds.

Elias sends a stream of air straight at the button. The blades of the ceiling split open, petals of a flower gliding out toward the edges like they're welcoming the sunlight, which now streams down into the area in ash-filled beams.

Some of the guards, coming out from cover now, try to tackle Nora and Lia, but Nora rips over to Lia in a flash. They join hands and teleport out so quickly and violently that the whole room trembles.

Elias wraps his arms around me, and I almost sigh with relief at the sensation of takeoff. Together, we zoom across the floor, picking up Leni and Daniel, grunting against their weight.

Now we really lift off to go back up through the ceiling. I put everything I have into helping Elias push us out of that roof — this is our only chance.

From 20 feet above the arena, I see my parents roll the boys out a side door to a waiting car hands placed protectively on their bodies. I have to trust Mom and Dad now, with Michael and Max at least. I'll go crazy if I don't.

Fisk limps into the lab, making a strange noise like moaning and screaming combined, and another stray oxygen tank rolls into the room after him. I wonder if Elias did that, too.

A great boom sounds, and a plume of flame shoots up after us. The fire must have reached the second oxygen tank. We just destroyed the years of research about how to make Ones into Supers, how to transfer powers, and who knows what else?

We did our job.

So why is my heart sinking into my stomach even as we climb up into the sky and out of the arena?

The ceiling closes, probably automatically, before any of the security can jump on a hovercraft or summon a flier to chase after us. I know they won't die unless they're stupid enough not to close the door to that lab. One good thing about an underground compound is that it's very hard to blow up — the lack of renewable oxygen will quench any explosion. The arena will still be there.

The rest of the Hub's research won't suffer — that, at least, is something.

We thud down, and the frozen grass field crackles beneath our feet. Leni and Daniel gasp and place their hands on their knees to try to catch their breath — they're not used to the sensation or quick ascent of flying like we are.

Elias snags my wrist and whips me into him for a tight hug. I can't tell if he's gripping my waist this hard on purpose or depending on me to keep him upright. He breathes hard against the biting cold air.

"Thank you," he chokes as he presses his face into my hair.

I squeeze him even tighter. Having him here in my arms after all that is almost too good to be true.

"Can you run?" I ask him.

"I think so. Better than I can fly right now, at least." He lowers his voice. "And we can't leave them."

I turn out from Elias's grasp, as much as I hate to. "You guys," I say to Leni and Daniel, "can you handle a sprint?"

They both nod, still trying to catch their breath.

"Let's put a good mile behind us."

We run for a very long time, until the sun is well into the sky. Our lungs huff hot air into the cold, pushing clouds out against the perfectly clear white-blue expanse ahead. It's a new day.

The tracks of Leni's tears have left bright, freckled lines through the soot on her face. Daniel stares down at the dirt like there's a weight on the back of his neck.

No matter how cool Daniel acts, I know how much he loves his parents, how much he doesn't want to disappoint them. He gestures toward my messenger bag. "Did you get any of ours out?"

"Let me…" I look down into my bag. I know for a fact I got one of his and one of Leni's, at least. I debate for a split second. Do I send them with this stuff, with no knowledge of how to inject it or exactly what will happen if they do?

All I know is that if I were them, I would kill me for keeping it from them.

I fish out a couple of their vials, hold them out between my fingers. He glances at me quickly, takes them, murmurs a "thanks."

Leni looks at him with tears in her eyes, then squeezes his hand and shifts her stance.

"We're going West," Leni says. Maybe finding work, maybe hiding out. Definitely not going back to school. Just until we know things are settled. Until we know we're not in danger. We don't want to lose you."

"Okay," Elias says. "Here's what you do. When you settle anywhere, put an ad in the local paper's classifieds. Look for a biochem tutor with eleven years' experience. And, uh…a personal interest in the topic."

Daniel finally smiles. "You going all badass spy on me, man?"

Elias punches him on the shoulder. There are some things I'll never understand about boys.

Then Daniel pulls Elias into a fierce hug. Leni and I grin at each other, and for the first time since we broke into the Hub, I cry. Giant tears roll down my cheeks, and I can't even move.

She crosses over to me. "Hey, it's gonna be okay."

"I'm just..." I snot and sniffle into her shoulder. "I'm so, so sorry."

Her whole body shakes, and I can't tell if she's laughing or crying or shivering.

"For what?" she asks, and I hear the smile in her voice.

"I don't know. For dragging you here. For my mom. I don't know. For everything."

"Listen." She lowers her voice, glances at the guys, who talk in quiet voices. Daniel grips the back of his neck and scuffs the ground with his foot. "I would have ended up at the Hub again anyway, okay? Except maybe...it would have been in some green goop. With no Daniel, and no one to save me. And Fisk wouldn't have... Well, everyone wouldn't have heard that. Heard what happened to us. To me."

I nod a little. Her eyes flash over to Elias. "Take care of him, okay? We... He's like my brother, and he can't see his real sisters for a long time, so..."

"I know." I nod again, and a lump rises in my throat.

"I remember now." Leni says, looking at nothing in

the distance. "I remember… It was right at the beginning. I remember your mom. But she was kind. And then…I remember him. Fisk. He was like this even then. Now maybe he's a little worse than he was."

"Yeah. Guess we don't know, do we?"

"No. And we won't."

I don't tell Leni about the duplicates I glimpsed lining up along the wall on our way out. No point in mentioning the possibility that Fisk, in some form, will be back. Not now.

I hug her one more time.

"You guys be careful. We'll see you again. Maybe take this whole shabby operation over," she says.

"How are you traveling?" I ask.

She shrugs. "There's a car rental place half a mile south if my GPS is right. Daniel has a debit account and plenty in it to get us overseas if we need to go."

"Oh. I didn't realize…"

"I don't think anyone really did. But, yeah. Trust fund kid, and he just turned eighteen, so…" She huffs out one laugh. "Okay. Now let's laugh a little. So they'll think we're alright."

I do my best to do that. It feels like an eternity since I last laughed, a memory stuck in my old, beautiful life that I used to think was so ugly. Leni goes off with Daniel, and without another word, they duck into the woods and they're gone.

I look over at Elias again, and I see him tremble just before he stumbles and falls to the ground.

"Hey! Hey." I run over and wedge my shoulder under his armpit. "What's up?"

"Just the medication from my drip, I think. I'm still a little weak. Plus..." He winces. "...I think Nora and Lia gave me something."

"What do you mean?"

He reaches over, grabs the Swiss army knife from the pocket inside my bag where I always keep it, and slices it across the palm of his hand. I gasp, but he heals within seconds.

"My skin feels like a suit of pain right now," he says, shrugging and smiling a little. "I figured it was a pretty good guess."

"Okay," I say, my head spinning at the thought that Elias is no longer a One, wondering if it's permanent and whether he can give it to me, too. But I won't let myself obsess over that right now. "Okay. Let's keep walking."

We trudge along in the direction of old Route 136. After a few minutes, when Elias seems to regain some of his strength, he says, "They figured it out."

"The Hub? I know."

"They paired me with another One who goes weightless — a kid. A couple years older than Michael and Max, maybe. Dragged him in from New York or something. Old enough for his parents to be frustrated he hadn't changed yet."

"What happened?" Panic grips my heart. I wanted to be the only one who could do this to him. I need to be the only one.

"Strapped our arms together. Gave us some enhancing serum. We scooted around the arena."

"Scooted?" My relief comes out in a weak giggle.

Elias presses the heel of his hand against his eye. "Um. Yeah. I didn't get it. Still don't get it. Kid cried the whole time. The serum... It burns. But we didn't fly. Could never race with cars or anything. Not like you and me."

I put my head on his shoulder, turn it to the side, and kiss wherever my lips land. His collarbone, I think. He doesn't turn into me.

"No one's like you and me," I say.

I hug Elias as close to me as possible, my skinny arm like a thick rope around his waist, cutting into his sweatshirt, praying my slight frame can support him. I feel his torso's shakiness — his entire body still trembles. When will this weakness resolve? It has to — soon.

"How much does your Dad know? About what they

were doing with the girls?"

Elias stiffens. "I don't know. But if I find out it's anything other than 'nothing,' I'll kill him."

I'm so angry at my own parents, knowing what they hid from me. I can't imagine what thoughts run through Elias's head right now. He doesn't have any answers, and he has no way of knowing when he'll get some.

After sitting there, on the side of the freezing, pocked road for 10 minutes, then 20, Elias starts to fidget.

"Sorry about that," he says.

"Are you okay?"

"I will be."

He turns to the side, smells my hair. I hate it when he does that. But when he does, it stops him shaking so much, and that makes me smile. I would do anything to have strong Elias back. I would do anything to have strong Merrin back. Now I'm left hoping with everything I have that we can find a way to be strong together.

Finally, after many breaths in and out, Elias says, "It's all our fault, you know. If we hadn't kept the secrets…if we hadn't hidden what we can do…"

"I know." And suddenly, in his presence, the rage turns to a weight that I'm desperate to shake off. That my lightness can never fix. My fingers play at the back of his neck.

"What are we going to do?" He raises his eyebrows, and his mouth turns down at the corners.

For a split second, all I can think of is his mouth, and how we haven't really kissed since we've seen each other again. But there's only thing I want to do more than kiss him: Get the hell out of here.

"How do you feel?" I whisper.

"This was what I needed," he responds. "You. You're like a battery charger."

This makes perfect sense to me. I never realized the power of the buzz until Elias left and I didn't feel it anymore.

"Yeah. Yeah, me, too." I look him straight in the eye. "Time to go?"

"Time to go."

I crane my neck from the direction we came, toward the flat field covering the Hub, looking for signs of smoke or flame. Nothing. No shouts, not a smell. The Hub is as quiet and dignified as ever, even when its very center has just exploded. Only the occasional chirp of a songbird pierces the silence.

The whole world has changed, and not even the sparrows have noticed.

THIRTY

The cold has injected a shock of vibrancy into the broad, brush-stroked colors that paint the horizon. Indigo layered with gold highlighted by burning ochre, playing against the deep brooding gray-blue of snow clouds rolling in.

The spindly skeleton of a windmill traces a hard framework against the masterpiece, jolting me back to reality.

My heart jumps. We have to get far away. Find someone who can help us figure out what these formulas all do. The Social Justice Hub to the West? Warfare to the South? Neither seems good. Seeking help at one feels inevitable. I shudder.

Elias must think it's because I'm cold because he rubs my arms, trying to warm them.

"That's how they used to get electricity from the wind, before the turbines," Elias says, his voice having taken on a soothing cadence. It's comforting that I can't hear the anger there even though I know it's just beneath the surface. For now, I need that.

"I didn't know," I whisper, and a choke strangles my throat. Still, this is the one thing I need him to know —

need him to be absolutely certain of, without a second thought. "I didn't know, Elias, or I would have... We could have... I would have listened to you. I'm..." The tears come, slow, creeping down my cheek one at a time. "I'm sorry."

"I know," he says simply.

"You should have told me," I say, my voice a bit stronger.

I feel more solid in myself, my whole self, my One self, than I ever have in my whole life, even though I just apologized — something that used to feel like losing myself. For the first time, I know for sure that I will not float away. I am in control of this moment. I am in control of myself. I push my shoulders back.

"I know," he says, looking down at me, straight into my eyes. "I'm sorry."

I can't say anything. Can't make any words come out of my mouth. I'm sorry, and he's sorry, but neither of us is. Not that the whole thing happened. Not really. This has cemented what we always thought. We don't belong at the Hub, and we don't belong at Nelson. The only place we really belong is with each other.

Our breaths are quiet, shallow and waiting. The white cloud of steam coming from my lips brushes Elias's arm.

We are standing too close to be comfortable not saying anything, not doing anything.

"I heard what you said to your Mom about me," he murmurs. "At the Hub. When I was waking up."

"How I wasn't leaving without you?"

"Yeah. That, too." A smirk spreads across his face, growing bigger with each breath he catches.

I half-turn and snake my arms around his waist, falling into him, burying my face in his chest. I savor the feel of my heart swelling with it. Love. His and mine.

"It...uh...it makes sense, doesn't it?"

"Hmmm?" Elias hums into my hair, breathing deeply. He's smelling it again, and for the first time, I don't care. I'm amazed he can still find the shampoo's perfume — whatever it is — with all the smokiness, dirt, woods and cold that must be laced through it now.

"Well. The only reason it worked with Michael and Max, and Nora and Lia — the transference, I mean — is because of how close they were. Are."

"It's not true transference for them." He rubs the tops of my arms protectively. "They're not Ones. They already have those Supers. They just get stronger when they're together."

"Right. Yes. We're different. But the only reason we can actually transfer our powers to each other is because of how close we are. Because I — I mean, we — I mean I — feel this way. I've never trusted anyone like I trust you. Never felt this way about anyone, Elias."

He draws back, still holding on to the tops of my arms, and beams. "Well, you might as well just say it now."

"Yeah. Might as well." I smile at him with my lips still closed and try to make my eyes tell him everything I'm thinking. He smiles back the same way and draws me to him again.

After our teeth have stopped chattering, he stops holding me so tightly, and the telltale vibration takes the place of the shiver. The warmth. The buzz. So intense now, I can barely stand it. Suddenly, faith surges through me so hard and fast that it almost knocks me off my feet. I let one of my arms drop, and we stand there, side-to-side, fingers interlaced, gazing into the crisp, gray-white Nebraska sky.

"Ready?" Elias asks.

I squeeze his hand, hard. I nod, and my heart jumps. With all the things I've had to say in the last couple of hours, somehow, this is the hardest.

"That's not why I love you, you know. I don't love you because you make me fly. You make me fly because I love you."

"Wait a minute," Elias teases. "I didn't hear that last part."

My heart pounds as hard as it did that first night we walked beside a cornfield together. "I said," I murmur, my eyes still trained on the horizon. "I love you."

"You talking to me or the sky?"

"Both." A grin cracks across my face. I still don't look at him. He laughs once, the sound of release. My heart calms a little.

Then he swallows hard, bends down, cups his hand around my jaw, and kisses me, moving his lips hungrily against mine. I draw back and kiss him once more, light as a whisper of wind.

I take a deep breath, then stand tall at his side again. He bends down and kisses the top of my head.

"I love you," he says into my hair, then pushes a shuddering breath outward. I nod, close my eyes, surprised by how happy it makes me to hear him say it, no matter how long I've known it. Since Homecoming. Since the first time we flew, maybe.

Something warm and heavy and exhilarating floods my whole body. I look up at him. He nods, then we both look up at the sky again. I drop his hand.

I take off first. The buzz from those three words propels me forward faster than ever before.

It takes me two seconds to memorize the feeling of flying on my own, its power and strength, the wind biting at every surface of my body.

It takes Elias a good 10 seconds more to catch up with me. I am the lighter one, after all.

It takes me no time at all to decide that even though I can fly without Elias, I don't think I'll ever want him to leave my side.

We join hands again, grinning like we did after the first time we kissed. When I remember that, my smile grows even wider. For a moment, we both forget what we're leaving behind, what we must face ahead, because at least, at the very least, we have each other.

A shooting pain bursts through my body, under my skin. I don't mind, though, because I know what it means we can now do. We grip hands tighter. Then we go so fast that a great ripple of air shakes the ground beneath us, and the world is nothing but a blur of color and light. I close my eyes, savoring it.

I think we just went supersonic.

ACKNOWLEDGEMENTS

Publishing a book is a labor of love for so many more people than just the author.

Jamie Grey, thank you for being the greatest editor, best friend, plan-hatcher, and constant support I could ever dream of. From publishing decision day to the release, you kept my chin up and my head in the game. I love you.

Thanks forever and ever to Trisha Leigh, my mentor and hand-holder. You and your books were the single greatest thing that made me believe that *One* could be a real, beautiful book. I love them and I love you.

Becca Weston, my incredible copyeditor, thank you so much for your eagle-eye, unparalleled patience, and willingness to work with me again despite my crazy. Jaclyn Hirsch, you were the most exacting proofreader I could have asked for – thanks for that, and for accepting payment in the form of Jeni's ice cream.

Nathalia Suellen is the genius behind the cover of *One* and its sequel, *Two*. Nathalia, I can't thank you enough for giving my debut a more beautiful face than I ever thought possible. You make dreams come true.

KP Simmon, my publicist – thank you so much for believing in *One* so fiercely, and for working tirelessly to get the word out. You, my friend, are a force of nature and a miracle worker.

Andrea Hannah and Megan Whitmer, you were my "Who cares how it's published?" cheerleaders without fail. You two made my heart lighter when it was heavy. Thank you.

Thanks for reading the first page of *One* before I gave you permission, Chessie Zappia, and being its first fan. You don't like that many books, so either you're lying to me or this one is really good. I appreciate it, either way.

Alexa Hirsch, you are my number one fangirl and very first reader for everything I write. To have both those things in one person is quite a rarity. Thank you.

John Hansen, thank you for volunteering to be my assistant and throwing all your enthusiasm into this little project even before you knew whether you liked it. It was a brave thing, and I didn't take it for granted.

Cat Scully, how did you know exactly the sort of book trailer *One* needed? It was brilliant and perfect, and I won't forget your kindness and enthusiasm while creating it. Thank you.

To my first readers, Gina Ciocca, Maggie Hall, Jenny Kaczorowski, Marieke Nijkamp, Jessica Silva, A.K. Fontinos-Hoyer, Elizabeth Light, Amber Tuscan-Clites, and later readers Erica Chapman, Kat Ellis, Jani Grey, Abby Robertson, Cait Peterson, Darci Cole, Sarah Blair, Angi Black, Naseoul Lee, Amanda Olivieri, Rachael Harrie, Deanna Romito, Emma Pass, and Valerie Cole, thank you for your incredible powers of critique, brainstorming, and encouragement. You all are rock stars.

Brittany Howard, you gave *One* a chance when no one else in publishing was willing to. I'll never forget it. Thank you.

My street team is the best on the planet. All fifty-four of you came ready and willing to work, and work you did! From blog interviews to carting ARCs of *One* to local book shops to hijacking storefronts on Madison Avenue to tweeting and reviewing your butts off – you all were the groundswell that made *One* impossible to ignore. So, Rachel Simon, Stephanie Diaz, Michelle Smith, Olivia, Elyse G, Alex Brown, Nikki Diehm, Madison Louise, Rachel Solomon, Elizabeth Briggs, Tara Allen, Clare Davidson, Mark O'Brien, Jamie Krakover, Aimee Arnold, Morgan Hyde, Suzanne van Rooyen, Jolene Haley, Louise Gornall, Heidi Schulz, Leigh Caroline, Amber Mauldin, Samantha Sessoms, Raven, Ellie, Liz Lincoln, KK Hendin, Cassidy Monger, Sam Hager, Rachel O'Laughlin, Kaye M., J.C. Lillis, Caitlin O'Connell, Virginia Boecker, Tawney Bland, Helen Boswell, Jessica Ward, Paul Adams, Veronica Bartles, Louisse Ang, Catherine, Sarah Hudson, Carla Cullen, Becky Mahoney, Jessi Shakarian, Ashley Hufford, Hero London, Brianna Shrum, Lindsay Leggett, Sarah Wedgbrow, Dianne, Christine, Kelsey Macke, Chyna Ngie, Katalina Lee, Sarah Guillory, Joy Hensley, and Amy Zhang, thank you, thank you, thank you.

To my husband, David – Thank you for never treating my writing like a silly little hobby. From day one, you've supported me, and it's just one reason I love you.

I love and appreciate you all so much more than the end pages of a book can express. So, one last time for good measure – thank you, thank you, thank you.

ABOUT THE AUTHOR

Raised on comic books and classic novels, Leigh Ann developed an early love of science fiction and literature. As an adult, she rediscovered her love for not only reading, but also writing the types of fiction that enchanted her as a teen.

Leigh Ann, her husband, and four children live in Columbus, Ohio. When she's not immersed in the world of fiction, you can find her obsessing over the latest superhero movie or using her kids as an excuse to go out for ice cream (again.)

Turn the page for a sneak peek at two incredible upcoming Young Adult novels – *Ultraviolet Catastrophe* by Jamie Grey, and *Wavecrossed* by Andrea Lynn Colt.

Ultraviolet Catastrophe
By Jamie Grey

CHAPTER ONE

You know your life is never going to be the same when your mom pulls a gun at the shopping mall. It started out as just another boring Saturday in August. Mom was tired of me moping around the house, so she dragged me out to spend the day shopping in the air-conditioned mall. About half of Columbus, Ohio, had the same idea.

We pushed through the crowds gathered around the Cinnabon and I paused to inhale, but Mom tugged me away from the sweet, cinnamony goodness. "Let's get some school shopping done," she suggested, pointing at one of the anchor stores. "I know we have a few more weeks, but you need some new clothes."

I smoothed the front of my faded t-shirt and frowned. "What's wrong with my clothes?"

Mom shook her head, grabbed my sleeve. "Lexie, you look like you're homeless. Look at the fraying at the hem. I'm going to get picked up for neglect."

"Moooom." I brushed my bangs out of my eyes and gave her my puppy dog expression. Not a typical girl thing to admit, but I hated shopping with a fiery passion.

She slung an arm around my shoulder. "Fine," she said, raising an eyebrow. "But when they haul me away, it's on your head."

"Ha ha. You're so funny." I let her lead me to the store anyway. If I was going to have to shop, at least Mom had pretty good taste. Even better, she usually paid for everything.

She headed for a table full of pastel-colored polo shirts and I wrinkled my nose. "Nothing yellow. I hate yellow."

"I know. How about this purple one? It would look so pretty with your dark hair."

I sighed and let her hold it against my chest. She chewed her lip and studied me for a moment before her gaze slid past me deeper into the store.

She stiffened, her hands turning to claws and digging into my shoulders.

"What?" I whipped around to look behind me.

Mom dropped the shirt on the table and shook her head. She'd gone pale, but pasted a smile to her face. "Nothing. I just don't think purple is your color." She peered past me again and clutched her purse closer to her side. "You know what? I'm not feeling so well. I think we should head home."

I frowned at her. "Home? Seriously? You dragged me all the way to the mall just to turn around and go home? I should at least get a smoothie out of it or something."

Her right hand slid into her purse and stayed there, like she was searching for something, but she kept her eyes trained on the back of the store. "I'm not dealing with your smart mouth right now, Lexie. Let's go."

She moved to grab my hand, but I jerked out of her grasp. "What is going on? Why are you being so weird?"

Her eyes darted around the store one last time before she turned to me. "Nothing. We just need to move." Slowly she slid her hand out of her purse.

And I froze in place, gasping at the shiny black gun in her grip. Blood roared in my ears. "What the hell is that? Is that real?"

"I'm sure you've seen a gun before. It's for protection." Mom grabbed my hand and pulled me from the store.

"Protection from what?" My voice threatened to erupt in a shriek and I swallowed back my fear. Oh my god. Had she gone crazy?

Something that felt like an electric shock zapped inside my brain, and the world spun. I clutched Mom's arm as my mind lurched and sputtered. It felt like a computer had switched on inside my head, whirring and buzzing until it was all I could hear. My gaze focused in on the small details of the gun she tried to hide behind her purse - the curve of the handle, the faint etching on the barrel. Thoughts reeled through my head until they clicked in place. Instantly I recognized the gun was a .38 caliber, snub nose revolver by Smith and Wesson.

Even though I knew absolutely nothing about guns. Even though I'd only ever seen a gun on TV.

"What's wrong, Lexie? Are you all right?" Mom tucked her hand, the gun still in it, into the pocket of her sweater before inspecting me with a worried gaze.

"Do you think I'm all right? You have a gun." And my brain might be broken. It was enough to totally freak a girl out.

"Yes, I do. Now come on." She tugged my arm and I let her speed walk me through the rest of the mall. I was still in too much shock to resist.

Mom and I burst through the glass doors, and as soon as the slap of the humid Ohio summer hit me, I found my voice. "Mom. Stop. What's going on?"

She kept moving across the parking lot, despite the heat turning the pavement into a shimmering river. "Get in the car. We've got to go."

I dug my heels in until she stopped. Crossed my arms. "How long have you had that thing? Do you even know how to use it?"

She threw a worried glance back at the mall doors, tucking a strand of her honey-colored hair behind her ears before turning to me. "We're two single women living alone. It's for our protection."

I shook my head. "What exactly do you expect to happen?"

"Anything can happen," she said with a frown, her glance flicking past me again. "Now really we need to get home. Will you please get in the car?"

"Fine." I yanked open the door and slid into the sweltering interior. Mom had us in reverse before I'd even slammed the door shut.

I glanced at her from the corner of my eye as she drove. Her knuckles were white against the steering wheel, and a muscle jumped in her temple. Dread felt like a heavy hand on my chest and I stayed quiet until we pulled into the driveway. She switched the car off, but I didn't move.

"What's going on?" I asked softly. "You've never lied to me before."

Mom turned to face me, her eyes serious. "I'm not lying. The gun is for protection. I want to make sure you're safe."

"Safe from what? What did you see back at the mall?"

She shook her head. "Nothing you need to worry about. I promise. Now let's get inside before we melt in all this heat." She used her firm tone of voice, the one that told me the conversation was over, even though I still had more questions. I had no choice but to follow her into the house and ignore the fear already twisting my insides into knots.

~

"Lexie, your Dad's on the phone," Mom called from downstairs later that night.

I tugged my headphones off with a frown. The music was the only thing keeping me from freaking out about what had happened at the mall. Now Dad was on the phone? What the hell was going on?

"What does he want?" I called back.

"I don't know, just pick up the phone."

I sighed and stared at the phone beside my bed. I hadn't talked to Dad in over a month. He'd been away on some sort of top-secret research trip to Japan. And before that, he had been busy at work. Talking to his daughter had never exactly been a priority. Why would he choose now, of all days to call?

A sudden lump formed in my throat. Even worse, what exactly was I supposed to say to him? About Mom? The gun? Or that weird flash of knowledge I'd had?

Even worse, that hadn't been the first time I'd felt that strange zap in my brain and had a weird surge of knowledge. It had happened just a few months ago, while I was taking a math test. All the answers popped into my head without even having to work at them. Yeah, it had freaked me out then too. But I thought it was a fluke. Now I wasn't so sure.

I pushed aside all of that and took a deep breath. "Hey, Dad."

"Lexie, honey. How are you?"

I ignored the surge of homesickness I felt at his warm, familiar voice. "Fine. How was your trip?"

"It went really well. I think Quantum Technologies is going to be opening a new branch in Tokyo."

My stomach clenched and I clutched the phone in my suddenly sweaty fist. "Are they sending you over to open it?"

Dad let out a surprised laugh. "Oh no, that'll be someone else's job. I just went to scope out the location and talk to some of their scientists."

I forced my hand to relax. I barely saw Dad now, it wouldn't really matter if he moved to Japan. Much. "Cool. So, um, what's up?"

"I wanted to see how you were doing."

"I'm fine." Mostly. If I didn't think too hard about what had happened today.

Oh my god. Was what he was calling about? Had Mom said something? But that was unlikely, she never talked to Dad if she could help it.

"Your mom said you'd been having some headaches lately. Are you still taking your ADHD meds?"

Well evidently she'd told him something. "Yeah, of course. It's nothing, I'm sure it's just the heat."

"Just make sure to tell your mom if they get worse, okay? I worry about you."

I frowned at the mouthpiece. Mom had basically said the same thing earlier when she explained about the gun. My skin erupted in goosebumps. "Why are you guys so worried about me all of a sudden?"

Dad paused, then said softly, "We're your parents. It's what we do."

"Not like this. It's like you guys are watching for something. What, am I suddenly going to develop magical powers?"

"Of course not. There's no such thing as magic."

"It was a joke, Dad." I rolled my eyes. Sometimes I wondered if the job description for rocket scientists had a no sense of humor requirement. "Just forget it. It doesn't matter. I'm fine."

Another awkward pause stretched between us. "So how's that little project of ours going?"

I gritted my teeth. The little project wasn't so little, especially after he'd abandoned me to work on it alone. "It's just fine. No thanks to you."

"Sweetie, I'm sorry. You know how crazy it gets here at QT."

"I know that you dumped some circuit boards and project plans on my desk six months ago and expected me to take care of it. Well you know what? I did. The quantum sensor is up and running, I attached the thermometer to the heat sink, and it's ready to start reading the gamma ray spectra of nuclear materials. If I had access to any. Look at me, I'm a freaking genius for figuring it out."

Dad cleared his throat uncomfortably. "What did you do about the infrared sensitivity?"

"I re-designed the bolometer to measure the electromagnetic radiation."

"Wow. I'm impressed. That's really advanced work."

And I'd figured it all out on my own. When he suggested the project, I'd thought finally we might have something to work through together. Something in common. Obviously, I'd been wrong.

I didn't bother to respond, and Dad finally cleared his throat before saying, "So I was thinking you could come visit me before school starts, and you could try out the sensor in my lab. I'd love for us to spend some time together. I haven't seen you in months."

Whose fault was that? But I bit back my angry response. I learned a long time ago that the drama wasn't worth it. "We'll see. I have plans with some friends next weekend. And then school starts up again in a few weeks."

"Honey, I think...."

"Anyway, was there anything else? Mom's calling me for dinner."

The line between us practically throbbed with hurt feelings, but finally he said, "No, that's all I had."

"Well, glad you're home from Japan. Talk to you later."

"Love you, sweetie."

"Bye, Dad."

I clicked the phone off and threw it down on the bed. He couldn't be bothered to visit more than twice a year. How dare he try to guilt me into feeling bad about our lack of relationship?

My head throbbed even worse than usual and I rubbed at my temples. It was seriously none of Dad's business if I'd been having headaches. He'd lost the right to care when he left us ten years ago. He meant well, but Mom and I were just fine on our own.

Maybe I'd ask if she'd let me learn how to shoot her gun too.

CHAPTER TWO

Mom usually worked late on Thursdays, so I'd taken over making dinner for us that night. It had been a week since the gun incident, and I'd brought it up over and over, but Mom kept shutting me down. I'd poked in her closet, dug through her desk. Nothing. Not even a scrap of information. So I'd finally had no choice but to drop it.

Tonight we were going to have pizza and watch a movie. Our usual Thursday night date. Hopefully we could get back to normal. I hated how pale she looked lately, the dark smudges under her eyes. I hated even more that she was keeping something from me.

I pulled the ingredients out of the fridge for homemade pizza. Quick, easy, and my favorite. After a while, it had kind of turned into our thing, though Mom had made me add a salad to the menu. Parents and their vegetables.

Tonight I was going to try something a little different - a new sauce. I needed the distraction of trying something new, and maybe the change would be good for both of us. I pulled the recipe up on my tablet and scanned through it. Seemed easy enough for a white sauce. I put a couple of tablespoons of butter in the saucepan and then started to add the flour. I paused and chewed my lip. Was the milk next, or the garlic?

A zap sliced through my brain again and the kitchen spun. I threw out my hand to steady myself against the counter and a second later, the whole recipe popped into my head, almost like I was seeing it on the screen.

"Oh my god." I dropped the whisk in the pan and moved to the sink. Sweat beaded on my neck and my heart thundered like I'd been running. I flipped the faucet on and splashed my face, but the words and images still floated behind my eyes.

I sucked in a deep breath, then another, but my lungs still felt like they'd stopped working. Tears prickled behind my eyelids and I scrubbed at my face with the kitchen towel to keep them from spilling out.

This was beyond headaches. It was like my brain was possessed. Maybe I had a brain tumor. Or cancer. My stomach clenched and I forced myself to think calmly. I was going to have to say something to mom. But not right now. Not upset like this.

I folded the towel carefully and hung it back up. Then I went back to the stove to finish the sauce. Keeping busy seemed liked a good idea. If I could bring up the weirdness like it was no big deal, maybe we could talk about it rationally. The last thing I needed was for her to freak out. Because then I'd freak out too. It would be ugly.

The pizza went into the oven a few minutes later. By then, my heartbeat had almost returned to normal. I glanced at the clock, then quickly set the table

"I'm home," Mom called, as if on cue. Her keys rattled on the hall table as she dropped them and she let out a sigh as she slipped out of her shoes.

"Dinner ready yet? I'm starving," she said, coming into the kitchen and snapping on the TV. "It smells wonderful."

"New sauce. Hopefully we like it." I chewed the inside of my lip. I should say something now. Before she got distracted.

She kissed me on the cheek and grabbed a bottle of water from the fridge. "I'm sure it'll be delicious. What did you do today?"

I shrugged and pulled out the big salad bowl full of lettuce and put it down on the counter. Deep breaths. Play it cool. Get her into our normal routine, then slip in the possible brain tumor.

"Not much. Finished a book. Watched some TV. Pretty typical summer vacation stuff." I grabbed a knife out of the drawer. "Want tomatoes?"

She nodded. "Sounds like a good day. Hey, Leslie at work said that new sci-fi film is really good. Want to go to the movies this weekend?"

"The one about the robots? That would be cool." I pulled another tomato from the bowl and started chopping. "Hey, will you pour me a glass of milk?"

Mom nodded and poured two glasses. The soft murmur of voices on the TV filled the house. "Bad news from government facility Los Alamos today. Hackers broke into a classified server and downloaded a terabyte of top-secret military plans. An explosion rocked the facility, killing three…"

Crash.

One of the glasses shattered on the floor, but Mom stared at the television, her face as white as the spilled milk.

"Mom?" I set the knife down on the cutting board as my heart jumped. "Are you okay? What's wrong?"

She shook her head and held up a finger. My skin prickled as I turned to the TV and watched as smoke billowed from a squat, nondescript building in the middle of the desert. A piece of paper fluttered against the wall and the camera zoomed into show some sort of logo. A rifle and a microscope crossed like an X on a field of pale blue.

"Until the culprits are found and the records retrieved, the government is treating this as a matter of national security." The news anchor turned the next story over to his co-host and Mom stepped through the puddle of milk and turned the TV off.

Her hand trembled.

"What's going on?" I asked. She looked like she had in the mall last week. Like she was going to be sick.

Mom shook her head. "Will you take care of the mess? I need to call your father."

My jaw dropped open. "Dad? Why?" I couldn't remember a single time in the last ten years when she'd actually chosen to call him. Now she'd talked to him twice in one week.

"Lexie, please. I'll be back in a minute. Just clean up this mess." She grabbed her cell phone off the counter, rubbing the back of her neck as she left the room.

I did a few quick swipes with a handful of paper towels, dumped them in the garbage under the sink, and then tiptoed down the hall to the living room. I pressed myself against the wall so I could peek inside.

"William, I just saw the news. What did they get from Los Alamos? That really was Grant at the mall, wasn't it?" Mom paced between the couch and the window, her cell phone pressed to her ear. She moved stiffly, like all her muscles had tensed.

Almost a minute elapsed as my dad spoke. My chest tightened as I waited for her answer.

"Three days? That's it?" She let out a soft sigh. "I understand. I wish it hadn't come to this, but we've been lucky for the last few years." Another pause. "I miss you, too. We'll see you soon." She clicked the cell phone off and then dropped it on the coffee table with a clatter before burying her head in her hands.

My stomach hit the floor. Miss him? Mom could barely stand the guy. I leaned back against the wall and took a shaky breath. She needed to tell me what was going on. Now.

A moment later, Mom sighed and marched out of the living room, spotting me in the hallway. Her gaze narrowed. "What did you hear?"

I pressed my palms against the cool wall and tried not to lose it. "Enough to be completely freaked out. What is going on?"

"We're going to take a trip to visit your dad this weekend. How about you start packing?"

I shook my head. "Uh-uh. You're not getting out of it that easily." Panic twisted my stomach into one big knot. Mom and I were close. I told her everything. And I'd thought until last week she did the same with me.

Her brown eyes were full of worry, but she put on her best everything's-okay-voice. "Nothing to worry about, but your Dad needs to see you about your ADHD meds. The clinical trial is almost up and they need to finish collecting data on you."

I blinked. "Why didn't he tell me that when we talked last week? And what does that have to do with the news?"

"Nothing at all. Just jolted my memory. Besides, it's been a while since you've you're your dad. He's been talking about you coming to visit. Now's a good time before school starts."

That was the last thing I wanted. I shook my head. Anger shot through me. I was tired of the lies from both of them. "I'm not going to Tennessee. I'm not doing anything until you tell me what's going on. Now."

"Watch your tone, young lady."

I crossed my arms over my chest and glared at her. I hadn't even gotten started with the attitude. I could do this all night if I had to.

And Mom knew it. She threw her hands up. "I can't talk to you rationally when you're like this. I need to go make a few calls. And since you can't be trusted not to eavesdrop, I'm going to my room. Go ahead and eat without me." She turned and walked away down the hall.

I stared after her. Hurt and fear fought to take hold and my arms slid down to wrap around my waist. I could count on one hand the number of times Mom and I had seriously fought. But this was different. I'd never seen her like this before.

She was scared.

~

I shoved the last of my clothes into my suitcase and glanced around my bedroom to make sure I hadn't forgotten anything. My mini telescope and my Albert Einstein action figure were neatly positioned beside the T.A.R.D.I.S cookie jar I'd gotten for my last birthday, and the dust that had covered my bookshelf since I'd gotten my tablet was gone. Mom had made me clean while we were packing, so there was a distinct lack of Lexie-mess in the room. She'd even insisted I box up some of my other books and knick-knacks while I was at it. A weird, forced spring clean in the middle of August.

"Almost done?" Mom asked, leaning against the door. "Did you make sure to pack those extra clothes and books?"

"Yep. I have a full suitcase, an entire box of stuff, my diary from third grade, and the kitchen sink. Seems a little overkill for a weekend visit." I arched an eyebrow at her, but she shook her head, her eyes still shadowed and haunted. I knew I was being melodramatic, but I'd tried arguing, begging, pleading and tricking her into telling me what was going on, and Mom'd remained tight lipped.

We were on the road an hour later. Mom's Buick sedan was old but comfortable, and the passenger seat cushioned me as I watched the flat Ohio countryside slowly give way to the green hills of Kentucky. She drove with her lips pressed together, only the soft murmur of the radio to break the silence between us. The silence that had seemed to fill all the space between us since that little incident with the gun.

My fingers drummed against my knee in time to the whirr of the tires on pavement. I'd never visited Dad in Tennessee before. He'd always come to us. First in Washington when I was little, then in Ohio when we moved here three years ago. Every time it got more and more uncomfortable.

I couldn't wait to deal with the awkward silence this time as we danced around the fact that we barely knew each other.

I watched a pair of horses chase each other across a pasture. The soft hills of Kentucky grew into the Appalachian Mountains, their peaks lavender gray in the distance as we approached Oak Ridge, Tennessee.

The Secret City.

I'd done my homework, of course. As soon as Mom had let the name slip about where Dad was working, I'd dug around the internet and found Oak Ridge was one of the sites of the Manhattan Project, the World War II effort that produced the first atomic bomb. It had been a secret, government-run town until 1959. And then Quantum Technologies, the company Dad worked for, had taken over the former government buildings and science facilities, as well as added buildings of their own. Once, the whole town had worked for the US Government, now most of them worked for QT.

The car slowed as we pulled into town. Gas stations and fast food restaurants lined the wide street, giving way to a several small strip malls and a grocery store. It all looked perfectly normal.

And then we drove into the downtown area.

A large yellow sign reading "Welcome to Oak Ridge" greeted us, bearing the symbol of an atom surrounded by ellipses. A few kids on skateboards hung around the main square park, doing kick flips and ollies on the stairs. I watched one try to nail a landing, but he slipped instead. I sucked in my breath, thinking for sure he'd land on his butt. But the board flipped on its own at the last minute, a tiny jet of fire moving it to land beneath the kid's feet.

I gasped. It was a freaking hover board!

A thrill of excitement made my skin prickle with goose bumps. Maybe Quantum Technologies wasn't just a research facility. Maybe this whole trip wouldn't be completely wasted. If I could bring one of those back with me to school…

Mom stopped at the light in the middle of the downtown area and I scanned the rest of the street. A young couple picnicked under one of the large oak trees, while across the green, a kid was playing catch with her golden retriever. I smiled as the dog leaped and bounded after the ball.

And then ran right through a big blue mailbox like it wasn't there, catching the ball on the other side. The dog's plumed tail wagged frantically as it trotted back to the little girl. Through the mailbox again.

I pressed a hand to my eyes. No. Not possible. I looked again and the image of the dog flickered briefly, pixelating before it snapped back together.

Oh my god. A hologram.

"Mom?" My voice was barely a whisper.

"Yes, dear?" her eyes stayed focused on the line of slow moving traffic through town, but a muscle jumped in her jaw.

"What is this place?" my voice quivered and she looked up with a small smile. The one she used when she was trying not to freak out herself.

"Oak Ridge is a very…interesting place. Quantum Technologies develops a lot of really new inventions you won't see anywhere else."

My head had started to pound and I rubbed the back of my neck. My headache was back. But a headache was the least of my worries right now.

I still hadn't told Mom about the weird flashes of knowledge that popped into my head, or being able to solve problems I didn't even know I'd been thinking about.

What was the air-speed velocity of that swallow's flight? Ten meters per second.

It was amazing and scary at the same time. I knew things I had no idea I'd even learned. Had I read it somewhere once, and now it was popping into my brain at random? Unexpected photographic memory maybe?

But whatever it was, it was freaky enough that the metal security robots patrolling the sidewalk and talking to the people sitting at the outdoor café almost seemed normal. Like dining with freaking Cylons was perfectly ordinary.

I winced as I got another brain jolt and blurted, "Mom, why did they design the robot's ankle bolts like that? The angle's all wrong." With just one glance, a series of images and plans had popped into my head and shown me the bolts should be cut differently to optimize movement.

A whimper escaped my lips as panic reached up and tightened the muscles in my shoulders.

Mom's eyebrows rose to her hairline and she squeezed my knee. "It's okay, Lexie. Relax. Everything's going to be all right. We just need to get to your dad's and we'll explain." She followed the signs toward Quantum Technologies headquarters, but turned off the main road into a small subdivision of post-war track housing before I could get a glimpse of the facility.

She pulled up in front of a shabby ranch-style house and parked the car. I stared at the empty flower boxes and overgrown front garden and tried to breathe. The place looked abandoned.

"This is Dad's house?" My voice rose in shock. Evidently, his neglect didn't just extend to his only child.

Mom's lips thinned but she nodded. "Just remember your dad's very busy at work. He doesn't have time to focus on gardening."

"He could have gotten a Cylon to do it," I muttered.

I pushed open the car door and a wave of sticky heat instantly turned my dark hair frizzy and coated my skin with sweat. I tugged at the strap of my tank top and slowly turned in a circle to check out the rest of the neighborhood. It was full of houses just like my dad's, though most of them looked neat and tidy. Half a dozen kids played basketball in a driveway down the block, but otherwise, the hot, humid afternoon was silent. Even the trees felt like they were asleep, their leaves heavy and still.

"Grab your bag." Mom struggled up the front walk with my suitcase. She'd packed light, just an overnight bag, and I frowned at it sitting on the back seat before gathering the rest of my things.

Mom grabbed the key from under the front mat and went inside. A bead of sweat trickled down my back and I squared my shoulders to follow her. Then I paused. She knew where the key to Dad's house was? Robot security guards weren't the only freaky things going on in this town.

Inside, the house seemed nice enough, if a little bare. The front door opened directly into the living room, with a long hallway off to one side leading to what I assumed were the bedrooms.

"Your room is the last door on the left." Mom glanced around the house and shook her head before dumping my suitcase on the floor and heading back outside for the last load.

It smelled of cologne and stale air, like Dad was only here often enough to shower. Maybe he was. Yet another thing I didn't know about him. I tucked my hair behind my ears and tightened my grip on my bag. I wasn't going to find my room just standing here.

The first door was open, and a quick peek inside at the navy bedspread and sparse decorations confirmed it was my dad's bedroom. My heart did a little flip at the picture of me and Mom on his nightstand. The next room was empty, though it seemed to be a decent size. Might be nice for an office or something. I didn't pay it too much attention; I was already drawn to the last door on the left.

My hand shook as I turned the knob and pushed open the door. I don't know what I expected, but it looked just like any other room. Full sized bed, a large wooden dresser, plain vanilla walls. Empty of personality. Dad obviously hadn't gone to any trouble to make me feel welcome here. To make his daughter feel at home. I tried to ignore the disappointment clogging my throat and dumped my suitcase on the bed.

Then I heard Dad's voice floating in from the hallway. I was tempted to wait for him to come to me, but instead I squared my shoulders and headed toward the kitchen.

〰〰〰〰〰〰〰〰〰〰〰〰〰〰〰〰〰〰〰〰〰〰〰〰〰

Ultraviolet Catastrophe, Available Fall 2013

For more information on Jamie Grey and her books visit www.jamiegreybooks.com.

Wavecrossed
by Andrea Colt

Chapter 1

Midnight is the perfect time to eat a turtle.

Submerged in an icy river, I focused briefly on the thought, then let it go. My brother should be close enough to hear, and it would make him come running, so to speak. Mentally, I grinned.

My lungs craved air, so I flicked my hind flippers to propel me upwards. As my head broke the surface, I spun to scan both sides of the forested shore. No human faces peered back in the moonlight, but I pivoted in the water to check again as I sucked in a breath. Not that a nighttime fisherman would see anything odder than a seal poking her head out of a coastal Maine river—which wasn't a totally crazy sight, though most seals kept to saltwater—but it wasn't random humans I was worried about. It was the other kind, the kind who knew what I was. The lying-in-wait kind.

But if anyone lurked in the shadows, I couldn't see them. Or, I noted as I drew another breath, smell them. So I was safe. Probably.

Letting my muscles relax, I lifted my nose further into the air to let the crisp breeze ruffle my whiskers. I spun in the water again, this time for fun. Despite the danger, I loved these nights, these escapes. For a while I could lose myself in motion and instinct, forget the problems waiting for me ashore. Here, I didn't have to pretend to be a normal teenage girl, didn't have to smother my anger and growing desperation. Here, weightless in the river, the world felt *right*. For a moment, at least.

The water around me shifted as my brother surfaced two feet away. The seal version of my twin was darker than my dappled cloud coloring; he was gunmetal spotted with shadow, his eyes round wells of midnight as he huffed out a breath.

Cass, you can't eat turtles. Brennan's thought was tinged with outrage. *What would Nicky say?*

Nicky was the snapping turtle Brennan had found injured in a pond when we were in middle school. He'd taken him home and kept him in the basement bathtub for a week until his leg healed. Now whenever we met a snapping turtle, Brennan claimed it was Nicky's uncle, or grandmother, or sister-in-law.

Nicky can't talk, so he wouldn't say anything. I dove, abandoning the moonlit surface. Water pressed against my fur and skin; from below came the faint clicks and rustlings of crayfish scuttling over rocks.

The bottom of the river beckoned, a fascinating murky dark, and as always a part of me wanted to paint it. But if I tried, the result would probably look like a squid threw up on canvas—oils could never capture the life and motion of an inky midnight river.

In any case, I didn't paint anymore. Not even in human form. I'd won schoolwide awards for it freshman year, but now I wouldn't touch a brush if you paid me.

Brennan fell in beside me as I swam upstream.

*Maybe turtles **can** talk. Like we do.*

Mind-speaking reptiles? I snorted, bubbles betraying my mirth. I started to tell Brennan how ridiculous that was, then paused. Three years ago, when I thought I was just an ordinary high school freshman, I'd have called the idea of creatures like us ridiculous too.

They can't talk to **us**, I pointed out instead.

Brennan swam above me, a shadow against the pale surface, then butted my shoulder with his snout.

Well, in any case, selkies don't eat turtles. Weaving through the water, he sped on ahead.

I frowned. *Says who?* Not our parents, for sure. They found the ways of our people too painful to talk about. And in the two and a half years since Brennan and I discovered the truth about ourselves, we'd never met another selkie.

Without opposable thumbs, how would they get through the shell? Brennan's logic floated back to me as he somersaulted through the water.

They could eat them while in human form. Turtle soup is a delicacy in France, right?

Gross. Brennan paused to nose under a submerged log. I surfaced to snatch another breath, then ducked safely down before continuing upriver. My whiskers caught vibrations through the water: I sensed fish milling about below, tasty swimming morsels, but they'd get a pass tonight. It was late.

After another thirty seconds, I realized my brother had fallen behind. I paused, twisting in the water, but the moonlight only penetrated a few inches; I couldn't see him in the darkness. The river's weak current tugged at me, the flow undisturbed by another seal-sized body nearby.

I sent a thought out like a beacon: *Come on, Brennan, let's go home. Tomorrow's shift is going to suck even more if we don't get any sleep.* We were scheduled to work the Sunday brunch rush at the Golden Fish, our older brother Declan's restaurant. I'd rather roll in needles, but skipping wasn't an option.

In my mind, I heard a monumental sigh. Then, hardly more than a shudder of a thought:

What if we just left, tonight?

My stomach clenched. Whirling, I swam upstream without answering. Maybe Brennan hadn't meant me to hear, and didn't realize I had—sometimes the line between musing and directed thought was thin. Usually we laughed at apparent *non sequitors* from stray thoughts, but this one wasn't funny.

Selkies belonged at sea. I knew that. And it wasn't that I didn't want to bid Granite Harbor, Maine, a thoroughly un-fond farewell. Frankly, staying on land sucked. It meant rules and bargains and danger, and being forced not to spit upon faces that desperately begged to be spit upon.

But selkies couldn't become their true selves without their sealskins, and my parents and older brother were trapped apart from theirs, forced to stay ashore in human form. Until three years ago Brennan and I had been trapped too; we hadn't even known of our true natures then, so we'd grown up like normal kids, or near enough.

Now that we knew the truth, and had our sealskins—a gift with a price I hated to think about—we should be at sea. It was unnatural for selkies to stay on land. But though Brennan and I were free, the rest of our family wasn't. I couldn't leave them behind, not without a fight—and despite his possibly-unintentional comment, I knew Brennan wouldn't either. If I looked back, he'd be following.

He'd better be following.

When I reached the stretch of bank where we'd left

our clothes I finally turned to check, but no torpedo-shaped shadow darkened the water.

Brennan? I called mentally, but there was no response. My heart seized. **Brennan?** If thoughts could sound shrill, I'd certainly accomplished it. For an agonized second I thought he'd left us behind after all, but then I heard a faint snap, as if of teeth.

Just let me eat this catfish, will you?

At my brother's happy distracted tone, relief surged in like the tide. Brennan was my twin, and my best friend. My only friend, if you wanted to split hairs; we couldn't trust any of our classmates with the truth about ourselves. Brennan still went to parties, but I found it next to impossible to socialize with classmates when my paranoid side branded the word THREAT invisibly on their foreheads. If any of them found out what we really were ... Disaster. So if Brennan ever did leave, I'd be alone in my fight.

But he was still here, and I exhaled a bit, bubbles trickling from my nose up to the surface. I let Brennan enjoy his fish; I'd make sure the shore was safe.

Edging toward the bank, I raised my head out of the water and scanned the woods carefully. This was always the most dangerous part of our nighttime swims. What if someone had come across our haul-out spot while we were downstream? What if they'd found our clothes? What if they were waiting for Brennan and me to emerge and *change* back into human form so they could snatch our sealskins?

That's what happened to my parents long ago, before I was even born: a human stole their sealskins and hid them so my parents couldn't return to the sea. They'd had no choice but to follow him home and do as they were told. Two decades later, they and Declan were still slaves, in a country of people who thought they'd eradicated slavery.

And they'd stay that way unless I freed them.

Earlier I'd made sure we entered the river on the upwind bank, so now I inhaled deeply, my nose sorting scents: tangy pine needles, rotting fall leaves, a faint trace of fox scat. Nothing human besides our own belongings. I counted silently to thirty, but heard nothing beyond the normal rustling of small birds. As far as I could tell, we were alone. Time to trudge back to my landlubber life.

Bracing myself, I started the *change.*

Bone-deep hurt stabbed my body everywhere, stretching and cracking and reshaping my limbs and flesh. When I was ten I'd broken an arm, and it felt like that— except all my bones at once, while my skin was raked by sandpaper. I kept going, and after an agonizing seven seconds—Brennan and I had timed each other once—my form solidified into one with legs and arms and breasts and hair.

And, thank God, thumbs. Lack of such miraculous appendages was one of the main downsides to my aquatic form. I never knew how awesome thumbs were until I tried to scratch my nose as a seal.

I used my lovely thumbs and fingers to grab for my sealskin, now floating like a cape beside me. Still underwater, I wrapped it around my torso before kicking my legs to take me to shore. The shallows here were little more than a two-foot-wide submerged ledge between the deeper part of the river and the earthen bank. I pulled myself up onto the ledge, crouching, and set my feet on the slick rock. The water here was just deep enough to shelter my shoulders in my curled-up position. Steadying myself with one hand on an adjacent boulder, I stood.

Heavy. That first moment out of the water always felt like being saddled with a backpack of granite. Air wasn't interested in supporting my weight. Though the now thigh-deep water was cold enough to turn a normal human's toes blue in twenty seconds—it was October, after all, and winter showed up early on Maine's doorstep—I stayed stock still. My gaze raked the shadowed underbrush for dangers I might have missed from the water, and my ears strained for the sound of a footstep. My muscles were tensed, ready to hurl me back into the river, but after a few moments, the night was still quiet. All clear.

Bending over, I found two smooth river stones and rapped them four times against each other underwater— the signal to let Brennan know it was safe. Our mind-speech only worked in seal form.

As I clambered onto the dirt bank, Brennan surfaced mid-river, whiskers gleaming white. Waving, I slipped behind a thick, squat fir tree and found my backpack, nestled among the branches close to the trunk. I pulled out my clothes, then reluctantly unwrapped myself.

Once I was dressed, my fingers lingered on my sealskin, this strange key to my secret self. Growing up, my sealskin—and I—had been another's possession, but it was mine now. *I* was mine now.

I'd never give that up again, not for anything.

To the untutored eye my sealskin looked like a dark, misshapen towel. The skin side was rough but supple, the reverse sleek and padded with guard hairs. There were no claws or a face or anything creepy like that, just an amorphous shape roughly twice as long as it was wide.

Home, I thought. My sealskin was home to me, more so than my bedroom in my parents' house, or even the ocean. Contact with my sealskin made me feel strong. Cleared my thoughts. I'd been anxious and tightly wound this afternoon, in a mood Brennan classily termed *megabitch*, but now that I'd had a good swim I felt steadier.

I folded my sealskin, smoothing down the guard hairs gently, possessively. My whole freedom was tied up in this thing. It killed me to part from it, stow it in one of a dozen hiding places we'd found in the area, but we couldn't take our sealskins back to the house. It wasn't safe.

Slipping my sealskin into my backpack, I shouldered it and returned to the riverbank. Was Brennan getting dressed? But I heard nothing from behind the holly bush where he'd hidden his backpack of clothes, and when I glanced at the dirt beside the water, it was dry except for my damp footprints.

I peered into the depths just beyond the ledge.

"Come on, Brennan," I called. My voice would be distorted by the water, but Brennan would hear me. How long did a catfish take to devour, anyway?

I inhaled, but my nose now caught only the overwhelming scent of pine. My senses were always sharper in seal form, except perhaps for touch. My human skin, without the guard hairs that covered my other self, was definitely more sensitive. And delicate—I'd nicked myself on a thorny bramble earlier, and I stretched out my hand to inspect it. The pad of my thumb, which had sported the wound, was pristine again. *Changing* healed little injuries, though it didn't, sadly, maintain things like manicures. I hadn't bothered to paint my nails in over a year.

A shadow in the river caught my eye. Finally. Brennan was ... coming up too fast. "Wait," I yelped, but before I could move Brennan exploded out of the river, leaping into the air right beside the ledge and flopping down again. The wave of wet hit me nearly full-on.

Sputtering, I shrieked a curse as Brennan disappeared underwater. Surprise cannonballs had been my brother's signature move at the public pool when we were younger—his and every other boy's.

My twin surfaced ten feet offshore for my reaction. My jeans were drenched, my sweater half-soaked. Not that it really mattered—my long dark hair dripped down my back anyways—but getting mad was part of the fun. I stamped my foot and cupped my hands around my mouth.

"That's it—I'm making turtle soup out of Nicky's cousins!"

Brennan blew out his breath in what amounted to a seal laugh, then submerged. I hastily backed up, but when Brennan reappeared he simply pulled himself onto the ledge. I sat down on a tree stump to wring out my hair, averting my eyes while Brennan shifted forms and wrapped his sealskin around him.

"You wouldn't dare," Brennan said, a little breathless from the *change*. It had only taken him four seconds; I wasn't sure why he was faster than me. I rolled my eyes as he pushed himself upright. In human form my brother stood two inches taller than my five-foot-eight frame, his driftwood-colored hair lighter than my dark brown waves. But we shared the same blue eyes, and our mother's narrow nose. And, of course, our selkie genes.

Still grinning about his prank, Brennan jumped up

onto the bank and headed for his holly bush to swap his sealskin for his clothes.

As I finished wringing out my hair, my thoughts returned to our trapped family. They were admittedly never far from my mind, but swimming, although it cleared my head and calmed my nerves, always brought home exactly what our parents and older brother were being denied. We'd been trying for two years to get their sealskins back, but so far we'd failed. Sometimes it felt hopeless.

"What are we going to do, Brennan?" I said quietly, my humor gone.

"About what?" he called.

"About our parents." As if I could mean anything else.

"We're doing everything we can." His muffled voice was not nearly as urgent as I'd have liked.

"It's not enough."

I heard a sigh. "Give it a rest, will you?"

My mouth went flat. A rest. That's all Brennan said lately. Remembering his possibly-private thought, I wondered if he'd given up entirely, if he was just biding his time until I gave up too. Anger twined itself through my voice.

"They'll die here if we don't free them."

Brennan stepped out of the shadows and shouldered his backpack.

"Melodrama alert." Seeing my face, he hesitated. "Let's sleep on it, okay?"

I wanted to tear into him, but getting into an argument now wouldn't do any good. Taking a deep breath, I stood and twisted my hair into a bun, securing it with what looked like innocent hair sticks—knives, after all, weren't allowed in school.

"Okay." I jerked my lips into a smile and picked up my backpack. "There are sandwiches in the truck, right?" *Changing* took a boatload of energy, so we were always ravenous once we returned to land. Peanut butter was more filling than crayfish—and didn't take nearly as much effort to catch.

"Two for me, none for you," Brennan joked.

"Not if I get there first," I shot back. Falling into comforting, well-worn banter, we headed up the dark path to the truck.

We never did see the camcorder propped in the trees, watching us go.

<hr />

Wavecrossed, Available Summer 2013

For more information on Andrea Colt and her books,
visit www.andreacolt.com.

Made in the USA
Middletown, DE
14 May 2015